Upside Down And Falling Up

A novel by
Michelle Jacklyn Miller

Cover art made by Flintenvibe

Archives Of Blood And Sorrow
Book 1

Chapter One

Namrips

It was the year 2040, and the United States was at war. Namrips was only twenty years old. He was lying in a puddle of water with his rifle aimed at the enemy. He could see them, but they couldn't see him. He had an Asian looking man in his sight with the crosshair set on his head.

Namrips was wearing camouflage. He was literally wearing a bush on his back. His face was covered in mud. He was in a jungle, and it had been raining for the last two days.

He knew that he needed to be patient. He had learned that nothing worthwhile was ever achieved without perseverance. There were at least thirty-five enemy soldiers that he could count. They were moving around preparing for something. Namrips got the feeling that they were about to go on the move.

He observed them closely. He saw a young soldier quickly shoving items into a bag. He saw others taking their tents down. Another soldier was sitting on a tree stump gobbling up some food as if it might be his last meal. There weren't very many people with smiles on their faces. There were a couple of people that seemed to be joking around with each other, but they were screamed at by an officer in an Asian language, and they promptly got back to work. The majority of them were cleaning their rifles and loading their guns.

The sun was beginning to rise, but it was hidden behind the rain clouds. Namrips could hear the sounds of birds and monkeys in the distance. A spider crawled on top of his arm. The spider looked like it was a species of the genus Haplopelma called the *Black Earth Tiger*. This species can have a leg span as large as eight inches long (20cm). The particular spider on his arm had a leg span of five inches.

Namrips was trying to keep an eye on the spider to make sure it didn't bite him when a soldier's foot stepped next to him. He could see the soldier's boot in his peripheral vision. Because he was in the prone position, his rifle was hidden by the bush that he was wearing on his back; it was a fake bush that was designed to cover him and his rifle whenever he was in the prone position. However, if the soldier had kicked the bush, it would have revealed his weapon, so he set his rifle down gently into the mud.

He turned his head slightly to the left extremely slowly so that he could see the soldier more clearly. It was an enemy soldier that was looking for a place to urinate. He hadn't seen Namrips yet. Suddenly urine began to flow down on top of Namrips head. Namrips didn't move.

When the soldier finished urinating, he began to take steps back as he zipped up his pants. His eyes made contact with Namrips' eyes through the bush. Namrips immediately raised his gun and shot the man in the face.

Namrips fell back down hiding his body under the bush. He began shooting the higher ranking officers first to create chaos and a lack of leadership. The spider began crawling up his arm towards his neck, so he quickly brushed it off with a knife that he had quickly pulled out with his left hand.

The other enemy soldiers that he hadn't killed yet picked up their guns and began shooting. However, because of the chaos, they hadn't paid enough attention to know exactly where the shots were coming from. Therefore, they had begun shooting in any direction; the bullets weren't even close to Namrips.

Namrips crawled over to a tree and sat up behind it. Then he prepared a grenade. He threw it. It killed three enemy soldiers. He continued to shoot and kill enemy soldiers. Every bullet killed a man. Every bullet was expertly placed either in the chest, neck, or head.

However, he knew that he could not stay there. There were too many of them, so he tried to retreat. He was running in the opposite direction when he was suddenly spotted by another large group of soldiers. These soldiers were not part of the group that he had been scouting. They were battle ready, and they had their lieutenants with them.

Namrips hit the ground behind a tree and loaded his M203 grenade launcher. He fired. He reloaded, and he fired again. He repeated this process. He had killed some of them, but they had taken cover. They began to lay suppressive fire. There was heavy machinegun fire being directed at him. Therefore, he couldn't stick his head out to shoot at them. This gave them time to move close to Namrips.

However, they would have to lift their suppressive fire to get all the way to Namrips' position. As soon as they lifted their suppressive fire, he began to fire back at them. However, there were too many of them, and they came upon him too quickly. As Namrips was shooting one of them, another enemy soldier had come from behind and grabbed him.

He had grabbed Namrips by the neck with his gun on the front side pressing against his Adams apple. The bush that Namrips was wearing on his back was pushed over to the right as the enemy soldier had taken an angle from his left. He had been shooting on the right side of a tree with his left side slightly exposed.

There was no explanation as to why the enemy soldier had chosen to choke Namrips instead of shooting him. However, it seemed just as likely that he would end up killing him. His gun was firmly placed against his throat as he used his arms as levers against the back of Namrips' head.

Namrips pulled out his knife with his left hand and quickly shoved it inside of the soldier's genitals. He had shifted his body to the right to create just enough space to his left for it to be successful. He pulled the knife out and changed the knife's position so that the point was in the direction of his thumb. Then he shoved the blade into the soldier's throat who immediately released his grip.

With the intense struggle, Namrips was sure that many soldiers should have surrounded him by this time. However, he didn't see anyone, nor did he hear any gunshots. He walked around slowly scanning the area with his eyes looking for signs of life. Nothing was there except the jungle and its creatures. That is when he saw several gray aliens that were about four feet tall. There were three of them.

Did they save me? Namrips wondered. He was speculating about the possibility that they had influenced the enemy soldier's decision to choke him instead of shooting him. He was also wondering if they had caused everyone else to disappear. They turned around and walked away. Namrips went back to base and never told any of his comrades what he had seen that day.

Ten Years Later

The war had ended, and life had gone back to normal. Namrips had needed therapy after having so many near-death experiences. It was hard for him to get used to life outside of the army. He had tried to find love, but instead of love, he only found lovers. There was never anything as deep and profound as he had hoped for. He wanted to find someone that he could love with all his heart. He wanted it to be deeper than sexual interest. He wasn't able to find that one special person that he was willing to say that he wanted to spend the rest of his life in her arms.

Namrips had also bounced around to different jobs. One day, he had received an invitation for an interview for a sales job. He had accepted it. Because of his quick wits, he made the perfect salesman. He had found himself quickly being promoted to manager.

He was selling an abstract product. The company that he worked for was helping people start up their businesses. So he only needed to convince the potential clients to start their businesses with his company. He had learned a tactic that was called *the takeaway. The takeaway* was a strategy that used reverse psychology. Instead of trying to convince them that they should start their business with

Namrips' company, he staged it so that the new client had to convince him that they were the right kind of people to start their business with them.

On one particular day, Namrips went to work without having breakfast because he had woken up late for the third day in a row. He had grabbed a cup of coffee from the McDonald's down the street from his job. He arrived at work in a taxi. When he stepped out of the taxi, he looked up towards the sky trying to see the top of the building; he worked in the tallest building in the city, and it never ceased to amaze him just how magnificent the building looked.

Hundreds of cars were on the streets. People were walking around busily. Some were talking on their cellphones. Some people were walking quickly. Some were walking slowly. Some people were laughing, and some looked concentrated on a task.

The sun was hidden behind the dark clouds. It was a little cold outside, so most people were wearing coats. Namrips was wearing a red tie and a light blue shirt. It wasn't cold enough for Namrips to wear a coat just yet. He was six feet tall with short red hair. He walked into the building and took the elevator up; he didn't work on the top floor, but it wasn't far from the top either.

Namrips arrived at the correct floor. He got off the elevator and walked to the meeting room. Several of the salesmen that were under his authority were there. "What's up, guys!" He called out. "Are we ready to break the record for sales in a day?" They had been talking just before Namrips had entered. As soon as they heard his voice, they stopped talking. "Let's go, guys!" Namrips called out. "Remember the takeaway is your friend. You are not sure if you want to sell them our product. They need to convince you that they are right for our product."

"What if I get someone who knows about the takeaway and tries to play games with me?" Johnny, the new salesman, asked innocently.

"Send him to me. That's what I'm here for. All right, guys! Remember: you are in control of your destiny. Go grab it by the horns!" Everyone cheered and ran out to their cubicles.

He walked into his office, and that is when it happened; the world turned upside down. His desk fell upwards towards the ceiling and broke the lights. His chair hit the ceiling at roughly the same time as he did. It was as if gravity had reversed. Everything was falling up.

Namrips lost his breath at first. He lay on the ceiling facing the floor trying to catch his breath. People were screaming from every direction.

He stood up and looked towards the window. He saw people, cars, and anything that might be found in the street flying up into the sky. Everything was being ejected into the abyss of space. It was a weird sensation looking down upon the sky as if it were below and up towards the earth as if it were above. It gave him a sick sensation in his stomach.

When he looked inside, he saw people who were crushed underneath large objects like desks. Some people were bleeding. Some were dazed. Yet others were walking around on the ceiling trying to help the others who were injured.

Namrips walked over to his desk and moved it off of the computer monitor. He picked it up and threw it at the window. The window shattered, and he watched the monitor plummet towards the sky. Then he looked over at another very tall building and saw how it was beginning to crack. It gave him the sensation that it was going to be ripped in two, and the top half was going to fall into the sky.

That is when it hit him. Namrips ran to the door of his office. "Get everyone to the first floor now!" He screamed. "The top is going to fall off!"

Everyone looked at him like he was crazy. "You want us to take everyone downstairs?" Johnny asked.

"No, we need to go up!" He yelled. "Everything is upside down. The first floor is now the top floor. Go UP to the first floor."

"How do we move up the stairs if the stairs are now on the ceiling?" Johnny inquired further.

"Figure something out for God's sake! We're all going to die if we don't get to the first floor!" That is when the gravity of the situation hit them all. They were fighting for their survival. Namrips saw it

11

in their eyes. They all understood what was happening.

Chapter Two

There had been three rows of cubicles that had been lined up on the floor before gravity had reversed. Each row had had thirty desks. When gravity reversed, they had more or less maintained this order, but now, they were upside down. People that had been sitting at their desks when gravity reversed were either dead or severely injured.

Namrips had to raise his right leg almost to waist level in order to go through the door to get out of his office. If one looks at the doors that we always pass through every day, he or she will notice that if we were walking on the ceiling, we would have a hard time going through the door because of a part that connects the ceiling to the door. In buildings where the ceiling is very high, one would have an impossible time maneuvering from room to room on the ceiling. At Namrips' workplace, that part was almost waist high.

Johnny and several others had begun going around looking for survivors to help. They were trying to collect everyone into an area where they could make a plan. Namrips kept thinking about the oxygen levels. If gravity had really reversed, the oxygen levels would surely begin to get thinner and thinner. On top of that, the moon would surely spin away from the Earth, and the water would be ejected into space. Everything was going to die no matter what they did, but Namrips had always been the type of person to survive as long as possible. One could never guess what could happen in the future.

    Namrips walked slowly towards the cubicles. The cold air came in through the window that Namrips had broken and made contact with his skin causing him to shiver for a moment. His time in the army had made him indifferent to the cold. He still remembered the icy cold days that he had lined up in formation with nothing more than black shorts and a gray t-shirt that said, "ARMY" on the front. In a weird way, the cold air gave him nostalgia for his days in Fort Bragg.

    He could picture Ardennes Street full of airborne soldiers running in gray shirts and black shorts just as the sun was rising. A sergeant was calling cadence, "C-130 rollin' down the strip! Takin' off like a rocket ship!" He remembered how he had to cross Gruber Road on a daily basis to get to his car. He remembered sitting late at night on guard duty cramming wads of Copenhagen smokeless tobacco into his mouth trying to stay awake in the mid-January cold that had placed a layer of ice all over the ground.

Seeing all of the dead people on the ceiling also brought him back to the time he had spent fighting in Cambodia. There was one poor fellow who was excessively fat. When gravity had reversed, he had been standing around lazily trying to avoid going to work as long as possible. He had fallen directly on his head and snapped his neck. The force of his body weight had sent streaks of blood in all directions. The sight was ghastly and best left undescribed. However, such a scene reminded him of what the Chinese were doing to the Cambodians who resisted their regime.

Then there was the young man who was in front of the vending machine at the time that gravity had reversed. The machine had tilted and had fallen over. His right arm could be seen lying limply on the ceiling. His body was obviously tucked underneath the machine.

Death was a strange mystery that had constantly followed Namrips everywhere he went after his father's death at the age of nine. He was terrified of death. He didn't know what was in the hereafter. He had never considered himself particularly religious. However, he wasn't an atheist either. It was an uncomfortable thought that he continuously tried to postpone.

He remembered thinking about what death would be like when he was ten years old. He had tried to imagine himself dead and ceasing to exist. This had produced such intense fear in him, he had sworn that he would do all conceivable to live as long as possible before dying. He wanted to find a way to live to two hundred years old if possible. Even though he recognized that the thought was childish, it was probably what had carried him through so many life-or-death situations in the war.

When he could not comfortably avoid the thought of death, he found himself reading about different religious philosophies. In his studies, he found himself reading a lot of texts about Buddhism. He tried to wrap his mind around the concept that the Buddha had taught that could end all sufferings; that concept was to eliminate desire. Even if it were all false, it was an interesting idea. What would it mean to desire nothing? As soon as he woke up in the mornings, he already desired a big plate of pancakes with butter and syrup on top. At noon, he desired a delicious steak.

He desired to live a comfortable life. He didn't want to suffer in pain. He wanted to find love and to have children. He wanted to pass on his knowledge that he had accumulated to his son. He wanted to show his son how to survive in the wild. He looked forward to the days that he could come home from work and have a family there waiting anxiously for his return. This placed him far from the ideals of Buddhism (or perhaps what he interpreted Buddhism to say), but it would always be an interesting thought that he carried with him everywhere he went.

The cubicles, as we have seen, had not been bolted to the ground. So they had fallen as well. They were lined up in front of Namrips' office. The lady who had been sitting in the first cubicle had been writing on a sheet of paper. When the gravity had reversed, it had happened so quickly that she hadn't had time to move her head. The desk that she was using had landed on top of her head. Her pen had jammed inside of her eye.

Namrips moved the desk off of her head. He remembered having had so many conversations with her. It was always a weird feeling when someone who he knew well died; it was hard to come to grips with the fact that that person would never have another conversation with him.

A little further down a woman was moaning in pain. When the gravity had reversed, she had extended her arms upwards in an attempt to protect her head. She had successfully protected her head, but her arm had broken from the force of the fall. Namrips could see a bone sticking out of her bleeding arm.

The woman was obviously dizzy as well. Her head was swaying back and forth as she moaned in a low voice. Her left hand was under her broken right arm in her lap. She was a brunette. She had come to work that day wearing a red skirt with a black blouse and red jacket. She had placed her red jacket on the back of her chair before gravity had reversed, and her red pumps had already fallen off of her feet and were lying at a small distance from her. He knelt down beside her.

"Hey, it's me, Namrips," he said gently. She didn't look at him. She simply continued moaning.

"Angela, do you know how many fingers I'm holding up?" Namrips held three fingers in front of her face. She stared at his fingers for a moment, but she didn't answer. "Can you spell your name?"

"A-G-L-E," she mumbled.

"Angela! I'm going to put a tourniquet on your arm. It is bleeding pretty badly." He knew that she was too concussed to understand what he was saying, but he wanted to be as gentle and as informative as possible. He took his red tie off. He stood up for a moment and looked around. He spotted her purse. The handle was visible, but the purse was underneath the desk that had fallen. He pulled it out and opened it. He found a large hairbrush. He knelt back down, and he put his tie around Angela's forearm next to her elbow. He made it as tight as possible. Then, he enclosed the brush in a knot and began twisting it as much as possible so that Angela was no longer bleeding as heavily.

Namrips lifted her up and carried her to the center where Johnny and several others had begun putting other injured people. After he had left Angela there, a man by the name of Josh walked over to Namrips and spoke in a low tone, "I think it's better if we throw the injured people out the window. If we try to help all of them, we'll all die together."

"If I hear that you've thrown a single person out the window, you'll be the next one flying with the birds," He said sternly. "Do you understand?" Josh looked shocked. He didn't respond. He simply walked away muttering under his breath.

Namrips ran back to the cubicles. There was a blonde girl with a broken ankle. Her name was Amy. She had come to work wearing a very slender black-and-white striped dress that looked more like an extra-long shirt than a dress. The dress hugged the curves of her body tightly so that it didn't take too much imagination for a man to know what her body would look like naked.

Just before gravity had reversed, she had knelt down to look for a pen that she had dropped. As she had picked up the pen, she had seen a quarter. She had gotten down on her hands and knees to grab the quarter. That is when gravity had reversed. This caused her to fall back-first towards the ceiling. However, she naturally turned her body as she fell so that her feet made contact first. That is how she broke her ankle.

Her ankle was swollen, but it didn't seem to be bleeding. "Hey, Amy," Namrips said as he came closer. "I'm going to pick you up and take you to the center of the ceiling. That is where we are putting all of the injured people."

"Alright, but please be careful," She responded. "I can't move my ankle. It hurts."

Namrips picked her up and then took her to the center of the ceiling where the group of injured people was getting larger and larger. Most of the injured people seemed to have concussions. Very few people had broken bones. Most of the people had bumped their heads as they landed on their backs.

He ran back to the cubicles where he saw Peter who was knocked out cold. Peter was about five feet eight inches tall. He had dark brown hair. He was wearing a red button-up shirt with gray dress pants, a black belt, and black shoes. Peter had landed awkwardly on his shoulder and had dislocated it. This had happened just after his head had already slammed into the ceiling knocking him out.

Namrips knelt beside Peter and noticed that he was still breathing. He also took notice of how lucky Peter had been; his friend, James, had cracked his head on the fluorescent light bulb that was just five inches away from his head. The people in the next five cubicles had also gone head first into the same long bulb. Namrips picked Peter up and carried him swiftly over to the center.

Amy was the only one who had a leg injury – a broken ankle. Five survivors had broken arms. Four survivors had dislocated shoulders. Twenty people had only concussions without counting those who had concussions and other injuries. This means that there was a total of thirty injured survivors. There were twelve uninjured people – a grand total of forty-two people who had survived up to this point.

"What good is this if we all die here?" Josh asked in a very loud voice. He was obviously irritated. He was constantly touching his ear, brushing his pale white hands through his thick brown hair, and rubbing his pudgy face. As Josh's foot was tapping the ground, a thought crossed Namrips' mind that this was what Josh needed to lose some of his gut; tapping his foot was probably more exercise than Josh had done in a week.

"Listen, Cheese-puff!" Namrips snapped. "I don't have time to play games with you. If you wanna throw yourself out that window, I won't shed any tears. I might even clap. It would be more courage than I've seen from you the entire time I've known you. But don't you dare suggest that we should throw anyone out, or I swear I'm gonna walk right over there and knock you out cold."

"I'm not even talking about that! Haven't you thought about the oxygen levels? I've been thinking. If gravity reversed, shouldn't oxygen be falling towards the sky too?"

"Oxygen isn't just going to disappear, Namrips explained. "Gases don't behave like solids. I assume that it will take several hours for oxygen levels to fall enough for us to feel the difference. You have to consider that we are talking about all of the oxygen all over the planet. If gases acted like solids, clouds would fall to the ground at the same speed as a person from the same height. Oxygen levels are thinner in the higher levels of the atmosphere, not non-existent. It will take a certain number of hours for oxygen to switch places with the outer atmosphere and become so thin here that we begin passing out."

"If that is true," Josh retorted, "that proves my point. We are going to die in a few hours when the oxygen runs low."

"The point is that we aren't dead right now. We are assuming that gravity reversed. What if gravity didn't reverse, and several hours from now, we are still breathing normally. We will be happy that we climbed up to the first floor and survived."

"If gravity didn't reverse, how do you explain that fact that we are walking on the ceiling?" Namrips sighed deeply. "Who knows? If we give up, we will die for sure. If we keep moving, there is some glimmer of hope that we can survive."

"What about the Earth not having any water? What about the moon floating away? What about the Earth getting farther from the sun?" Josh was throwing his arms around wildly as he spoke.

"What about you shutting up, or I'll shut you up. Don't say another word, or I'll break your jaw in so many places that you won't be able to speak unless we survive, and you make it to a hospital where they do facial reconstructions."

"You do know that Namrips was in the Army Special Forces, right?" Johnny chimed in. "Please, don't say anything else because I really don't want to see if he'll do it."

Josh stood there for a long moment as if he was fighting with himself on whether he should say something else. Josh was feeling a mixture of emotions. He was afraid that the threat was legitimate, but he was also angry for being treated so rudely. *How does Namrips know so much about science? He thought. I bet if a scientist were here, he would laugh at everything that Namrips just said! It's probably all wrong! Stupid gibberish. He doesn't want to comment on the moon and the water because he knows that I got him there.* However, through this tantrum of thoughts, Josh managed to stay quiet, which was better for him because Namrips would have fulfilled his threat simply to prove to everyone that he was a man of his word.

"We need to climb up towards the Earth," Namrips declared. "The window in my office is already broken. If someone can climb up and break the next window, we can tie the end of a rope to something firm. Then we can pull the injured up to the next floor and continue."

"Aren't the windows supposed to be unbreakable?" Johnny asked, "How did you break your window?"

"No," Namrips replied slightly annoyed. "About six years ago, there was a fire, and they had all of the windows replaced so that they could be broken. That way, the rescue teams could save people by taking them out through the windows if they couldn't use the elevator."

"I didn't know that."

"Yeah well, now you do. There is at least one box on every floor that says, "Break glass in case of fire." Inside that box, there is an ax. We can break the windows with that ax. The rope is more difficult. I think that we have to take off our clothes to form a rope unless someone can come up with a better idea. I really don't want to use electrical wires because we've already taken a lot of time gathering the injured. I have no idea how long it would take to break the ceiling up to get enough electrical wire to make it work."

"I guess we got to take our clothes off then," Samantha said. Johnny didn't say anything. He simply removed his yellow shirt. Samantha, one of the uninjured survivors, was wearing a black blouse that didn't take much effort to remove. Her white bra against her dark skin made it obvious that their clothes were coming off. Everyone quickly joined in and began offering up their shirts.

Namrips received everyone's shirt and one dress (there was only one woman wearing a dress – Amy). He tied all of the knots and made sure that they were the tightest knots that he had ever tied in his life; he wanted them to be unbreakable. If the rope broke, it wouldn't be because Namrips' knots failed. They also removed shirts from those who were unconscious or dead. This gave them a total of ninety-seven shirts (or if you prefer, ninety-six shirts and one dress).

      Several uninjured survivors went together to find the ax. They found four axes. However, next to the fourth one, they also found the door to the janitor's closet. Namrips had to get on Johnny's shoulders leaning against the wall to get the axes and to open the door to the closet. Johnny kneeled down, and Namrips got on his back with his crotch against the back of Johnny's head while maintaining contact with the wall to keep from falling. Inside the closet, they found a ladder.

      They carried everything back to where they had put the injured people. Namrips cleared his window ledge of glass. Then he began beating the walls with the ax looking for the support beams. This particular skyscraper had been made with hollow walls where the support beams were. The walls were four feet wide. When Johnny saw inside of the wall, he asked, "Why can't we take the injured through the wall to the next floor?"

      "Can you imagine carrying someone on your back inside of the wall? It would complicate things worse rather than make it easier."

      "If someone falls, they'll die."

      Namrips shook his head. "If they fall inside the wall, they'll die as well. The difference is that if they fall outside, they'll fall asleep when they run out of oxygen. If they fall inside the wall, they'll crush every bone in their body as their body smacks into every support beam along the way."

"What about the elevator?"

"You do know how an elevator works, right? The elevator needs gravity to work. It's probably stuck on the top floor. And if you think we're going to climb up the wire like they do in the movies, you got another thing coming. It won't be any easier nor any safer."

"Why can't we climb up the stairwell? It just seems so dangerous climbing up outside with the sky below us. Isn't there a way to climb up the stairwell?"

Namrips paused for a moment. His eyes shifted up as if he was considering it. He was trying to picture the stairs on the ceiling. How would it be possible to move up the stairs if they were on the ceiling? "Let's take a look at the stairwell. Maybe, we can come up with a better plan."

They carried the ladder over to the door to the stairwell. Namrips climbed up the ladder and opened the door. He looked inside. The stairs were made out of concrete. From the position of the ceiling, it would be like going up a series of very steep concrete ramps. As the stairs led up or down to the next floor, the ceiling was at an angle; at the point that the stairs stop so that the person has to change directions to continue going up or down, the ceiling forms a flat 'platform' before joining to another ramp. Only one person would need to climb up. Once that person made it to the next 'platform', he or she could tie their 'rope' to a fixed position. The handrail would do just fine for that purpose. There was also a pipe that ran vertically through the stairwell that would prove to be useful.

"You know something, Johnny," Namrips admitted. "I think you're right. My idea feels awfully stupid now that I'm looking at the stairs."

They quickly brought everyone over to the stairwell. Namrips climbed inside. Being on the ceiling of a stairwell was almost the weirdest sensation he had felt in his life – second only to seeing the sky below and the Earth above when he had looked out the window. Samantha climbed in immediately afterwards.

Everyone knew that Namrips was the most athletic of all of them. Perhaps, it was because they all knew that he had been a soldier and had fought in the war. However, they were equally aware that Samantha was more athletic than any of the other men. Both Namrips and Samantha had been chosen unanimously to go first.

Namrips tied the ax to the 'rope' to give the end enough weight so that it would be easier to throw. It took a few tosses for it to make it around the handrail just above them. As he pushed the 'rope', the ax lowered to their position. Namrips grabbed it and untied it from the end. Then he climbed up being careful to hold on to both sides.

Once he reached the handrail, he held on to it with one hand and removed the 'rope' with his other hand. He shoved the end into his pants so that it wouldn't fall.

Then, he grabbed the rail with his other hand with his feet dangling below him. He began to climb using the pipe that ran vertically through the stairwell as an aid. Once he made it to the top of the next platform, he asked Samantha to toss the ax up. She did so. He tied the ax to the 'rope', and then he tossed it up as he had done before. However, after having successfully tied it to the handrail, he motioned to Samantha to start bringing others.

In this way, they had to have patience. They continued to go up towards the Earth one floor at a time. At some points, they were lucky. Other people that were on other floors wanted to go up the stairs towards the first floor as well. Those who were trying to go up the stairs appeared and would make it easier to get to the next floor. However, they had unfortunately been right about the oxygen levels getting thinner. Once people started passing out, Namrips knew that it was likely the end of the line. He lay down and fell unconscious.

Chapter Three

Namrips woke up on a hospital bed. There was a seven-foot-tall Alien with blue skin looking down at him. He looked around, and he saw that he was in a room that was full of the same blue-skinned aliens. Their clothes were gray. They had seven eyes and four ears. They had two mouths – a smaller one and a bigger one. They had a small bump where the nose should have been with no nostrils. They had six arms on their torso and two legs. Their hair was long and black.

"Where am I?" Namrips asked. However, the aliens could not answer because they were incapable of speaking English. They had translation technology that permitted them to understand humans, but they simply could not make the types of sounds that humans make. They didn't seem to be dangerous. One of them removed the IV that was in Namrips' arm.

Namrips was wearing the same gray uniform that the blue aliens were wearing. They had evidently put clothes on all of the humans. It wasn't ugly, but it wasn't exactly stylish either. It was kind of meh. Namrips supposed that that was the point; it was meant to be neutral. It was fitting clothes for these seemingly emotionless aliens that surrounded him. Someone needed to inform the aliens that this wasn't going to fly with humans.

The room had hundreds of beds lined up in each row. There were hundreds of rows of beds. There were thousands of humans on the beds with IV's in their arms. Some of them were awake, but others were not. The ceiling was at least twenty feet above their heads.

Namrips saw one young man yelling at the expressionless blue alien. He was in the next row seven beds to the right. He was saying something about how his personal freedoms were being infringed upon, and that he knew that it was all part of a government conspiracy. Namrips even heard him claim that the blue aliens were probably on the US Government's payroll. "This is where my tax dollars are going!" He screamed.

A little closer to Namrips in the same row, there was an eighty-seven-year-old white-haired lady giving the aliens an earful. "Get thee behind me, Satan!" She hollered. "Don't you touch me. My God will strike you dead. You damned wretched demons!"

One of the blue aliens was wearing black instead of gray. It had symbols on its shoulders that Namrips assumed was its rank. It approached him and gave him a device. The alien did not even try to speak. It simply motioned to its ears implying that he should put the device in his ear. He put it in his ear, and he immediately began hearing a recording.

It said, "Your planet was attacked by a race known as Theadlians. They have an antigravity technology that they have used against your people as a weapon. We were able to arrive in time to keep them from killing everyone on your planet. They have a mother ship in orbit around Earth firing an antigravity beam at Earth. Their plan is to kill off all intelligent life and, then, populate your planet with their own race. Both of our races are able to breathe oxygen, which is what makes Earth so attractive for us. However, we want to live on Earth in peace with humans; they want to kill humans off. We are willing to help humans fight them off if humans will agree to interact peacefully with us in the future. If you accept to join our army, give this recording to the one who gave it to you. He will give you a translator that allows you to understand us; when we speak in our language, you will hear it in English. If you do not accept, put the recording on your bed, and you are free to leave the hospital. A spaceship will take you to a safe location."

Namrips removed the device from his ear and stared off into space. He was trying to make a decision. If he didn't join the army, what would life be like on Earth? Surely, a lot of people were dead. He wouldn't be able to go back to work. What would he eat? Would he have to live the rest of his life in a pressurized chamber that had oxygen? On the other hand, if he joined the alien army, they would surely feed him. Life could never be the same on Earth; if they didn't defeat these Theadlians, they would wipe out the human race. With this in mind, Namrips handed the device to the blue alien that had given it to him. He was immediately given a translator. It was an earpiece that resembled a Bluetooth. "Welcome to our team," the alien told him immediately afterward.

Just then, he saw Johnny walking with Samantha towards the exit. "Give me a moment. I want to say hello to my friends."

"Make it quick," the alien responded.

"Johnny! Samantha!" Namrips called out. Samantha's eyes immediately lit up. "Namrips!" She said in surprise.

"Hey!" Johnny called out.

Namrips quickly ran up to them. They were standing in front of the exit. "Did y'all listen to the recording?"

"Yes," Johnny replied immediately. "I don't want to fight in any army. I'm not a fighter."

"Me neither," Samantha said. "We're on our way to the spaceship. When they realized that we were turning down the offer, they gave us another recording telling us where to go next. What did you decide to do?"

"I'm gonna fight. Where are we now? Did the other recording tell you that?"

"Yeah," Johnny said. "We are on a spaceship that has a gravity simulator. The Earth still doesn't have gravity. The other spaceship is going to take us to a base on Mars away from the fighting."

"Why don't you come with us?" Samantha begged. "You've already done enough fighting in your life. It's time you settled down. You never know. Maybe, you'll meet someone special, and you'll have a family."

"And raise a son on Mars?"

"Why can't it be a daughter?"

"Son or daughter, it doesn't matter. I'm gonna fight. I won't raise a child on Mars without trying to get Earth back first."

When Samantha realized that her hints were falling on deaf ears, she decided to be a little more direct. "Listen, I don't like being so direct, but I want to be with you. I've always been attracted to you. I was thinking that if you come to Mars with me, we can be together."

"You are very beautiful," Namrips began. "But there are some things that are more important than sex."

"I'm not talking about sex! I'm talking about having a relationship. You are someone I could totally see myself marrying in the future."

Namrips chuckled. "Do you wanna know how I see the future?"

"How?"

"A gun in my hands. Killing Theadlians. Getting our planet back."

"Fine! If you don't wanna be with me that's fine. But when we were working together, you sure acted like you wanted to be with me!"

Namrips squinted his eyes at her. "That was before Theadlians came and turned our world upside down."

Tears were forming in Samantha's eyes. "I'm leaving with Johnny!"

"Leave already! What are you waiting for? Don't let the door hit you on the way out!"

By the time that the conversation finished, Johnny was looking sheepishly at the ground. Samantha grabbed Johnny's arm and stormed off with him. The "door" disappeared, and they walked through the hole into a hallway. The "door" reappeared.

Namrips walked back over to the soldier who had accepted him. "What do I do next?" he asked.

"You need to get some nutrients," the alien replied. "Then I'll take you to a base on Earth that we've set up. It is pressurized and oxygenated so that we can live there. The bases are being built right now. They are digging holes into the ground using lasers. Gravity is still reversed, so the bases will be made so that we can walk on the ceiling without a problem."

"When you say that I need to get some nutrients, you mean that I need to get something to eat, right?"

"We don't eat."

Namrips eyes widened. "That's nice, but we humans do."

"Humans have to get used to our style of life for now. Don't worry, we'll give you enough nutrients for you to survive."

"Are these nutrients given in an IV?"

"No, we usually give them to you in a drink. If an IV is needed, we can do that."

Samantha was walking with Johnny. She had tears falling down her face. She was really hoping that Namrips wanted to be with her. She had really felt like he had been flirting with her recently at work. She didn't understand why he would choose to fight if he really liked her.

Johnny was rambling on about some old movies he had watched a long time ago. They were science fiction movies about Mars and what it was like living on the red planet. In one of them, there was a person who was born on Mars. When he had tried to come to Earth, he began experiencing problems with his heart. In another, a person was left behind on Mars and had to survive until a rescue mission could come to save him.

Samantha wasn't really paying attention to him. Her thoughts were on Namrips. She wiped the tears from her eyes as they entered a room that was on the right side of the hallway. This whole time that they had been talking, they had been walking down the hallway. There were a few people in front of them going to the same room.

As soon as they entered the room, they were impressed with how white it was. There were several hundred other humans there as well. It was perfectly white and perfectly clean. The room was massive. However, the only defining characteristics of the room was a drain in the center, what looked like water sprinklers above them, and holes on one of the walls.

As soon as everyone was there, the "doors" appeared (they really didn't have doors – it was a spot on wall that appeared and disappeared). Then, lasers were shot out of the holes. Samantha saw blood from her stomach mix with the blood of those around her. She looked down and saw a large hole in her belly as she fell to her knees. She looked at Johnny who was wide-eyed. His face became pale as he fell over dead. Then, Samantha fell over and died as well.

Chapter Four

Memories of his father flooded his mind at night. The blue aliens had given Namrips a room and started him in training, but at night, he had nothing else to occupy his time - only memories of his father. In times past, he could have turned on a television or read a book in order to keep the memories from coming, but now, he was defenseless against reminiscing. His mind was like a double-edged sword that could kill the enemy, but it could also be used against himself. Sometimes, he wondered why he couldn't just turn his brain off. *This is why people drink alcohol*, he thought to himself. *It is so they can turn off their brain.*

After he finally fell asleep, he dreamed of a strange planet with intelligent fungus. They were called the Funglians in his dream. They communicated telepathically. It was a message of hope. Namrips didn't think such a species could exist, but he didn't believe that the seven-eyed blue aliens existed either - until now. One of the blobs of fungus transformed itself into the shape of Namrips. It had twnety eyes and beige skin, but it maintained the shape of a human with two arms and two legs. "Life as you know it is over, but life isn't over," it said telepathically. Then, he woke up from the dream.

One of the blue aliens entered the room, and told him to get dressed. Namrips had to begin his first lesson to learn about their attacker, the Theadlians. The following is the presentation that he watched.

"There is a galaxy that is six hundred million light-years away known by humans as Hoag's Object. There was a planet that was in the yellow nucleus called Thead. When Thead was still a young planet, it had a large ocean. The planet sustained a very large variety of plant life. However, conditions slowly changed over millions of years. The planet began to turn into a large desert, and the plant life began to die off.

"Over millions of years, this had created the perfect conditions for the evolution of the race of extraterrestrials called the Theadlians. There had existed a certain green creature that would resemble the gastropod known by English speaking humans as the slug, but they were three feet long.

"Their skin could perform photosynthesis like plants. However, it was able to survive in harsh conditions due to its ability to eat anything. Their mouths produced a strong acid that could eat through iron, so they didn't need teeth to chew. Their mouths were also lined with a certain mucus

that was constantly being replenished that prevented the acid from destroying their own mouths.

"One could imagine how this organism quickly became the dominant life form on Thead. After several million years, the varieties of species had exploded. There was one particular species that had grown upwards and had a height instead of a length. It was about five feet tall. The bottom still moved around like a slug. However, tentacles had evolved out of the body. There were three on each side giving a total of twelve tentacles. This is the organism that would become the ancestor to the Theadlians.

"After millions of years more, the Theadlians had finally evolved. They still had the strong acid in their saliva. However, their skin had also developed a poison as a defense against predators. This poison paralyzed those who it came into contact with. They had twelve arms that came out of their torso – three arms on each side. The arms had evolved from the boneless tentacles and had excellent flexibility. Their hands had four fingers, and the palms of their hands had what looked like a little cup. The fingers were fat and stubby.

"During their evolution, their bodies had learned to store high concentrations of energy. This was due to their ability to combine photosynthesis with the absorption of raw inorganic materials. Therefore, the palms of their hands began to emit light like lightning bugs as a way of discharging the *extra unneeded energy. Therefore, when the Theadlians had evolved their intellect, they began to learn how to control the discharge of energy and focus it. They invented a certain gadget that fit around their hands like a glove. This device was capable of taking their natural energy and converting it into a powerful laser. To humans, it would look like they were firing lasers out of their hands as a weapon.*

"*They never lay down; they slept in a standing position. Obviously, this was not difficult because they didn't have any legs. They slid across the floor like slugs. They had four eyes on all four sides of their heads – sixteen total – and two nostrils where a nose should be. Their ears were two holes – one on each side of their neck.*

"*Another interesting detail about the Theadlians is that they are hermaphrodites. Therefore, finding a mate is relatively easy for them, and they generally can lay one hundred eggs at a time. Thus, they quickly spread across their planet.*

"*In order to counteract the overpopulation, they began to spread out to other planets and moons. They constructed bases on seventeen other planets. However, they had a special affinity for the planet where they had evolved. They considered it their holy land.*"

With this, the presentation came to an end, and Namrips was a bit baffled. The first step to defeating an enemy was to understand them. He also had to watch videos of Theadlians mating. Then, he had to watch the eggs hatch. It showed the developmental process of maturation. However, he found it odd that a race of extraterrestrials that had become so advanced seemed to be barren of a real society. If the images that the Nemodians (the blue aliens) were showing Namrips of the Theadlians were accurate, the only thing that the Theadlians apparently lived for was procreation.

Was it possible that a race had ventured across seventeen planets without creating music or writing a single book? How can you create spaceships that fly into space and not have schools, books, institutions, and politics? The only conclusion that Namrips could come to was that the Nemodians were deliberately hiding this information. However, it didn't bother him too much. He understood that if they shared that information, it would make it more difficult to kill them on the battlefield. They had to be monsters in their eyes. The American Army hadn't shown its soldiers pictures of German soldiers with their families during World War II. The Germans hadn't looked at pictures of Americans with their families either.

Therefore, Namrips felt that it was perfectly reasonable to assume that the monstrous looking Theadlians had families and culture. He was enthralled by the question of what their society would be like and how they interacted. What would the Theadlians' music sound like? What kind of chemicals did they abuse to get drunk or high? What kind of literature did they produce? What was their political system like? Did they embrace democracy, or did they have kings?

    The blue extraterrestrials that had claimed to have saved the Earth were called Nemodians. Namrips was not told what galaxy they had come from, which bothered him more than not being told about the Theadlians' culture. Someone who is honest has nothing to hide. He wanted to see videos that showed how the Nemodians' society was. He wanted to see something that showed him their home planet. The only thing that Namrips could deduce was that, perhaps, they were a race that had become so advanced that they had lost contact with their mother planet after having traveled for so long amongst the stars.

    One thing that Namrips knew was that the Nemodians had begun setting up bases all over the Earth almost immediately after the reversal of Earth's gravity. Oxygen levels were regulated inside so that people could breathe inside their facilities. If one left the facility, he or she needed two things: something to fly and oxygen.

    The Nemodians told humans that it was impossible to make gravity go back to normal until they destroyed the Theadlians' mother ship that had the antigravity ray. This was impossible to do easily because it was heavily guarded. They needed to win the war. The Nemodians explained that gravity could only return to normal if they defeated the Theadlians.

Namrips was taken to a training facility where he was to learn how to operate the alien weapons. That is where he met Fiki who was a Nemodian. Fiki seemed to be void of personality like many of the Nemodians. Namrips couldn't figure out if it was their seven eyes and monstrous appearance, or if it was that they really were almost like biological robots. Every once in a while, he detected some emotions, but it was very rare.

His room was almost as void of life as the Nemodians' personality. There was a simple bed with gray sheets. The walls were black with red writings in the Nemodian language. Their alphabet looked like hieroglyphics to Namrips, and he couldn't make heads or tails of it. There was also a little screen on the wall next to where the door was.

Namrips would wake up in the mornings and be taken to a place that looked like a cafeteria. There, he received three bowls of liquid. The Nemodians had liquids that were blue, pink, and black whereas Namrips and other humans had brown, white, and yellow liquids. Namrips deduced that the brown liquid was a protein mixture (not only because of its color, but also because it was such a thick liquid). Namrips couldn't deduce what was in the other liquids.

The brown protein mixture was the worst tasting. If he hadn't known how important it was to his survival, he would have refused to eat it. He felt like he was trying to eat muddy water, and sometimes, it would clump up in his throat as he swallowed it. It took all of his will power not to vomit when eating it. The white liquid didn't taste great, but it wasn't unbearable either. The yellow liquid actually tasted pretty good. Namrips quickly learned to fight with the brown liquid first, wash it down with the white liquid second, and end enjoying the yellow liquid. The yellow liquid made him think of chicken noodle soup.

The cafeteria was humungous. Humans were brought in like cattle. Hundreds of humans were lined up and received their bowls of liquid nutrients one at a time. Then they walked over and sat down at one of the tables. The tables were fifty feet long each, and there were more than two hundred tables lined up in the cafeteria.

After the first night that Namrips had spent in his new room at this facility, he woke up to the sound of someone entering his room. "Wake up," a Nemodian had commanded. "I'm Fiki. You have been chosen to be my student. You will accompany me everywhere, and I will train you to be a Nemodian."

Namrips didn't question it. Therefore, he quickly got used to getting up early and going with Fiki to the cafeteria before accompanying Fiki everywhere. Namrips immediately realized that he was getting special treatment. The other humans were all gathered together like grunts. They didn't get too much contact with the Nemodians. Namrips was isolated from them and had to be with Fiki at all times.

"What is going to happen to the Earth?" Namrips asked Fiki one day. "Why don't we just attack the Theadlians and get this over with?" Fiki stared at Namrips with a confused expression on his face. "You know. The moon should be spinning away from the Earth. The Earth is on the brink of destruction, but we are just standing around here training. Time isn't really on our side. If we don't get the Earth back immediately, it will be destroyed, and we'll lose our planet."

"That's not how this antigravity technology works," Fiki answered. "They want to use the planet. They don't want to destroy it. The gravity only reverses in a designated area where the ray hits. The moon is still in the same spot because it never ceased to experience the Earth's gravity."

"What happened to everything that flew out into space?"

"We collected what we could. If no one collects it, theoretically, it would begin to spin around the Earth. It would fall up until it reached the spot where the antigravity ray is not affecting the Earth. At that point, it would experience Earth's gravity while equally being rejected. Therefore, it would just spin around the Earth and form a huge cloud of dead people and sundry objects." Namrips nodded his head showing that he understood. "But that didn't happen because y'all, the Nemodians, picked most of it up."

"We picked up as much as we could. However, we assume that the Theadlians were trying to pick it up as well. If they had let the objects accumulate, it would have blocked the sun. That would have been counterproductive to their cause. We picked it up so that it wouldn't fall into their hands."

After eating breakfast, Fiki usually took Namrips to their temple. In the center of the temple, there was a thirty-five-foot-tall statue of a Nemodian. The statue was in color and, therefore, was blue with a gray uniform. The bottom four arms were folded across its body. Its top right hand was holding an object. Its top left hand was holding a sword in a position as if preparing to strike someone dead.

The object in the statue's top right hand was a square stone slab. There was a red circle made of red triangles that fit snugly inside the square stone. Inside the circle, there was a teal triangle made of teal squares. Inside the triangle, there was a blue square made of blue pentagons. Inside the blue square, there was an orange pentagon made of orange hexagons. Inside the orange pentagon, there was a green hexagon made of green heptagons.

Finally, at the very center, there was a purple heptagon made of solid purple lines.

    The temple was built in a large circle so that anyone who visited it would always be looking at this statue. There were no chairs inside the temple. There was no priest. There was no service of any kind. There were only Nemodians surrounding the statue. Some of them were sitting on the floor; others were standing. All of them had their seven eyes closed. Occasionally, one of them would open an eye and immediately close it again.

    "The objective of this is concentration," Fiki explained whispering. "Look at the image. Memorize it. Then, close your eyes and try to retain the image in your mind. When you learn to control your thoughts enough to maintain the image in your mind with all of the details that you see, you will be able to learn how to access The Great Dimension. The Great Dimension has knowledge. Those Nemodians who learn such concentration are called wise ones. You will meet one of the wise ones soon."

    "What is The Great Dimension?" Namrips inquired.

    "It's a dimension very similar to this one," Fiki answered. "It is called The Great Dimension because all other dimensions proceed from it like an echo."

    After temple, Fiki would take Namrips to their shooting range. There, he would shoot a large variety of weapons. He shot different types of laser guns, laser cannons, and specialized weapons. For example, there was a specific weapon that was called the crusher. It would increase gravity at a specific point until the object was crushed by its own gravitational pull.

    In the evenings, Namrips would go back to his room and study. He would use the screen on his wall like a computer. It was an interactive artificial intelligence that was designed to teach Nemodians who were recently born about their place within the Nemodian society. In Namrips' case, he was being taught the Nemodian language and Theadlian evolution. Little by little, he was beginning to understand some of the red writing on the wall.

    He still couldn't understand all of it, but what he did understand said, *"We are the masters of the universe. We will liberate all races with knowledge. Nemodians are the most evolved race. Everyone should become Nemodians. We will travel amongst the stars until Nemodians are the only race."*

    One day after training, Namrips was walking with Fiki in a hallway. The lights were on the "floor" because they were convinced that gravity would begin pulling people towards the Earth again soon; they felt certain that it wouldn't take long to win the war. With this in mind, the entire facility was made so that they could easily turn the "floor" into the ceiling. There were ten floors underground. Stairs had been placed on the "ceiling" so that when gravity worked again, they could still go up and down from lower floors to higher floors. However, in the meantime, they were using levitation devices to move up into the Earth and to go down to the surface of the Earth.

"How old are you, Fiki?" Namrips asked.

"In this life? Or all together?" Fiki replied with his own question in an innocent tone.

Namrips' eyes widened. "Wait. What do you mean in this life or all together? What else could I mean?"

"I'm two hundred twenty-six years old in this life. However, Nemodians can live several lives. I'm really not supposed to tell you this, but it's true. This is my third life cycle. I lived three hundred ten years in my first cycle. I lived three hundred twenty years in my second cycle. I suppose that makes me eight hundred fifty-six year old."

"I'm confused. What do you mean by cycles? Have you died twice? Is that what you're telling me?"

"I suppose it depends on what you mean by death. There is a death that we do not know what happens any more than humans. However, if, by death, you mean that moment when your body begins to decay, yes, I've died twice."

Namrips scratched his head. "If your body began to decay, how did you revive? Did you reverse the decay, or did you get a new body?"

"I got a new body."

"If that is the case, then you can live forever. Just get a new body when you get old."

"If things were that simple! In theory, we can live forever. However, it doesn't work that way in real life. When you die, you have to get to your new body before Jeggolith gets you."

Now, Namrips was really confused. "Jeggolith?"

"You have to promise that you won't tell anyone that I told you this! If they find out a human knows this, I'll get in big trouble. They might even revoke my permission for rebirth."

"I swear. I won't tell anyone."

"When you die, your soul leaves your body. There is a monster that exists between our dimension and The Great Dimension. The monster is called Jeggolith. If he finds you, he eats you and carries you away. If he carries you away, it is impossible to be reborn."

"How do you avoid him?"

"You have to go to your new body as quickly as possible. We clone ourselves. The body is prepared close to death. If you die before the body is ready, you are pretty much screwed. If you get to your cloned body before Jeggolith gets you, you wake up in your new body. However, you don't remember very much from your life in the previous body because most of your memories are stored in your neurons. When you change bodies, you have a new brain, and therefore, most of your memories get erased. So we prepare a video, and we write a letter to our future selves describing what we want to remember."

Namrips was looking at Fiki with bewilderment in his eyes. "You said that you don't remember very much. So you do remember something. Do you remember what it was like being dead?"

"Sometimes, you remember more, and sometimes, you remember less. I remember my last death because it was so traumatic."

"Your death was traumatic? How did you die?"

"No, not my actual death. I died of old age. I saw Jeggolith."

"So, you remember what it was like being a ghost?"

"Yes. I remember feeling so much fear. I didn't think that I was going to make it back to my body. He chased me all the way to the moment where I entered into my body. One of his claws sank deep into my soul. Because he is an inter-dimensional being, his claws leave permanent marks in your soul."

"What does he look like?"

"He is red and orange. His size is indefinite. He can appear to be two inches one second, and the very next moment, he can be the size of the moon. He has an indefinite number of arms, legs, and claws. He can appear to have one, and then, he can appear to have one million. He has thousands of eyes looking at you. If he opens his mouth, you smell the stench of millions of rotting corpses. If he touches you, you feel the burn of a fire that is hotter than any star in the universe."

Namrips sighed deeply. "Okay. I got it. I would prefer not to meet this beast."

"You don't have a choice. Everyone meets him one day. We just try and deter it as long as possible."

"If memories are in the brain, then you shouldn't remember anything at all. But you said that you don't remember very much."

"The soul can't form memories. However, it experiences everything your body does. In some cases the brain somehow gains access to the quantum realm and reads it like a book. We don't know how this happens, but we know that it happens. When this occurs, the brain can recreate some experiences that the soul has had in another body."

As soon as Fiki finished his sentence, an explosion was heard. The entire building began to shake. Namrips and Fiki fell down and began sliding towards a hole that was in the floor just ten meters from their position. When they arrived at the hole, because what was made to be the ceiling was actually the floor, there were many electrical wires hanging there. Namrips and Fiki grabbed a hold of some of the wires.

Namrips looked down at his feet. Below his feet, he could see Fiki dangling around and the blue sky further below. There were spaceships flying around below their feet. He assumed that they were Theadlians who had initiated an attack on their base. If Namrips lost his grip, he would plummet down into the blue abyss.

Namrips' hands were beginning to slip. He felt weak. He wanted to go to sleep. *How is it possible that I could want to sleep at a time like this?* he asked himself. Then, he remembered that the oxygen levels outside the facility were too low to breathe normally.

As soon as Namrips began to feel dizzy, he knew it was likely the end of his life. He didn't have enough strength to climb up. He was losing his grip on the wire. He felt himself sliding down. Then, he fell.

For Namrips, his fall felt like an eternity. He was just conscious enough to know that he was falling. However, he was not mentally alert enough to keep track of time. He felt his eyes closing shut. All he could do was listen to the sounds around him. He heard Fiki shout, "I got you!" What did those words mean? He couldn't interpret them. Then, he lost consciousness.

Fiki had grabbed Namrips has he fell. Nemodians were capable of surviving for a long period of time without oxygen. So Fiki was still strong. Fiki was trying to pull himself up with two of his arms, so he still had four more arms that he could use to carry Namrips.

He had almost made it to the hole when the Theadlians made another pass and began shooting at them. Fiki threw Namrips up into the facility. Then, the wire broke having been hit by one of the lasers. Fiki plummeted into the abyss.

Fiki was patient as he fell. He didn't scream. He knew that Nemodians always did everything that they could to save their own. Therefore, he fell in silence as he looked around himself absorbing the beauty of nature. At least, it was beautiful to Fiki. In reality, the Earth looked terrible. Trees were dying everywhere. There was no water on Earth (except what Nemodians had brought with them into their facilities). There were no wild animals wandering around. The Earth had become a barren wasteland.

Soon, a spaceship placed itself under Fiki as he fell. It changed its velocity to match Fiki's. Then it slowed up just enough to accept Fiki on board. Then, they went back to the facility where they recovered Namrips' body. They administered oxygen to Namrips, and he woke up.

Chapter Five

There was still a battle that was being fought outside when Namrips woke up. Theadlians and Nemodians were flying around in their spaceships shooting at each other. Spaceships were blowing up and falling up into the sky on fire. If one were in orbit around the Earth at that moment, he or she would have seen large fireballs being ejected into space.

Everyone was on edge. "It looks like your training is going to be cut short," Fiki told Namrips. "We are probably going to get into the fight. You need to put your oxygen mask on in case we have another mishap."

"I'm on it," Namrips responded. He ran to his room and put on all of his battle equipment. This included a small oxygen tank that was only to be used in an emergency; it also included body armor and weapons. Alien body armor could deflect lasers. However, just as there is a limit to how much a bulletproof vest can deflect, there was a limit to how much energy being emitted by lasers their body armor could deflect.

Six hundred million light years away, Planet Thead had been converted into millions of meteors that orbited around their star. About ten light years away from the Theadlian star, there was a planet that was slightly larger than Thead had been before it was destroyed. On the surface of the planet, there was a large hole that lead down under the surface of the planet. At the entrance, there were twenty Theadlian soldiers who were guarding against invaders. This was presently the Theadlians' headquarters.

Inside, there was a network of tunnels that were full of Theadlians sliding around like slugs from place to place busily fulfilling their daily functions. There was a general of their military standing in front of what humans would interpret to be a computer with thirty Theadlians operating it keeping track of something on the screen. We could not possibly understand what that something was because we cannot read the Theadlian language.

Speaking in the Theadlian language, one of the Theadlians reported to the general, "Sir, we've identified the position of the Nemodians! We have star-fighters that are currently engaged in a battle with them!"

"Where are they?" The general asked.

"They are on a planet in a galaxy that is six hundred million light years away. Our intelligence says that they have found a race of pathetic beings called humans. It seems that they killed off billions of humans. The remaining humans are so stupid that they are willing to fight for their attackers. We can safely say that humans are our enemies because they are under the Nemodians' control."

"So, you are telling me that humans have become allies with the Nemodians."

"Affirmative."

"A race that stupid is better off dead anyway. Kill them all. Open a portal and send Fleet Z-393. I want the fleet to create a blockade. Then, I want another fleet of one trillion infantry soldiers to open portals and enter their base on Earth immediately. Don't waste any time. I want the element of surprise to be in our favor."

"If humans surrender, should we have compassion on them? They weren't the ones responsible for destroying Thead."

"We will take no prisoners. Everyone is to be executed."

The sirens sounded. If one had been in an aircraft flying above the surface of their deserted looking planet, he or she would have seen one trillion Theadlians coming out of the holes in the ground like ants come out of their mound after having been disturbed by the foot of an inconsiderate boy. Perhaps, you know the sight. If you have ever kicked a fire-ant bed, you've seen the sea of red that is quickly produced by the angry ants. This was a sea of green but no less angry.

It is hard to imagine one trillion of anything. Having seven billion people on Earth is considered overpopulation. One trillion is more than one hundred times greater than that. When *Charlton Heston* played the part of Moses in *The Ten Commandments*, it was considered an achievement to depict the scene where the Jews had their exodus out of Egypt. We are dealing with a scale one million times larger when we speak of trillions. That sea of Jews walking towards the Promised Land wouldn't fit on your television screen if we turned it into Theadlians marching out of their holes.

Once the Theadlians were lined up in formation, a commander spoke to them. He was using a technology that amplified his voice, but it was nothing like a speaker. It was more like teleportation, but instead of moving solid objects, it moved sound. In this way, he was able to project his voice to every Theadlian without the closest Theadlians having to be blasted by the sound. Every Theadlian heard his voice at the same comfortable level.

"My fellow Theadlians! Remember how the Nemodians came to our planet not too long ago. We did not ask them to come. They decided to use our planet as an experiment. They destroyed our holy land. Many of us lost family that day. I remember when the Nemodians fired their missiles directed at Thead. I saw our precious planet explode. My father was down below worshipping the Great Tirix. I remember seeing the pieces of our planet flying off in every direction. I was unfortunate enough to be on a spaceship nearby. We tried to attack the Nemodians, but they escaped. I swore that day that I would do everything in my power to kill every single Nemodian in existence. I know that there are Theadlians here today that share this same sentiment! Down with the Nemodians!" A roar of cheers was heard. Many Theadlians were beginning to chant, "Down with the Nemodians!" However, others were simply yelling wildly.

If one trillion Theadlians was quite a sight, the sound of one trillion Theadlians was just as impressive. It is certain that the most distant places on their planet could hear a low rumble. On top of that, some of them had begun firing their lasers into the air. Therefore, anyone watching from a distance could see the lightshow.

The Theadlians were ready for war. They were driven by their hatred for the Nemodians, but who could blame them? The destruction of an entire planet is a pretty terrible thing to be a part of. However, the Nemodians weren't all bad, and there are always two sides to a story.

We need to backtrack for a moment to understand how this all came to be. There was a specific Nemodian by the name of Nogar. Before he even knew that his name was Nogar, his first memory of his existence was in a laboratory. One day, he woke up surrounded by a liquid inside a glass tube. There was a mask over his face for breathing. He watched as the liquid drained. Then, the tube opened.

When Nogar left the glass tube, he felt disoriented. He had a hard time standing on his feet. He fell to his knees. He was naked. He didn't have any genitals. Nemodians don't have gender in the truest sense.

Nogar didn't know it at the time, but he was a clone. Nemodians had removed their genders from their genetic code when they began cloning themselves. Therefore, there was no such thing as sexual desire amongst them.

There were several other Nemodians that were naked that had recently been released from their tubes that surrounded him. A high ranking Nemodian stood in front of them saying something that he couldn't understand. It seemed that he was trying to give him directions about what he should do. As the Nemodian spoke, a rapid succession of images began passing through his mind that helped him interpret what the high ranking Nemodian was telling him.

He realized that he was supposed to get his clothes from a specific place. Everyone was supposed to wear identical clothes. He grabbed his gray uniform and put it on. Then he was telepathically shown the way to the cafeteria to get something to eat. He obeyed the telepathic message.

He sat down to eat. He looked at his tray. The food wasn't solid. There were three small bowls of various liquids. One bowl had a blue liquid. Another bowl had a pink liquid. The final bowl had a black liquid. He didn't question it. He simply drank the three bowls of liquids.

When he finished his meal, he stood up and went to his room. He didn't know where his room was. It was the telepathic messages that allowed him to find it.

His room was simple and clean. There was a small soft bed with gray sheets. The walls were black. There was writing all over the walls. The writing was in red. There was a small screen on one of the walls.

The telepathic messages continued to guide him. He was guided to stand in front of the screen. It was evidently a computer. He touched the screen and it came on. He was then guided through the process of using the computer. He was shown many things, and he watched many videos. He began learning the Nemodian language and about the Nemodian culture.

It took two years to complete his training. When he finished, he continued to sleep in the same room. However, he was finally given his job. Nemodians could not decide what they wanted to be. They were told what they were allowed to do.

Nogar was a special Nemodian in every sense of the word, *special*. Nemodians have different sources of DNA that they use for their clones depending on the job that the clone will receive in the future. Nogar was cloned from the DNA used to produce leaders. However, every so often, they make modifications to the DNA. It is done as an experiment to help their evolution along. If the change produces a positive result that they like, they begin to incorporate the change into all DNA for all Nemodians that they want to have those traits. Nogar's DNA was experimental. They had made modifications to the genes that make the brain. It was believed that the changes would make Nemodians more intelligent.

Therefore, Nogar was given the job to be director of a new scientific project. He was given a team of scientists under his command that were supposed to make an antigravity ray that could reverse the gravity on any planet that it was pointed at. However, Nogar was under constant surveillance because of his genetic capacity.

Nogar was successful in creating the antigravity ray, and he finished it way ahead of schedule. It only took him three Earth months to create the ray. However, they needed to test it out to see if it worked correctly.

"We need to test it out," Nogar had told General Fiki.

"What's the problem?" Fiki had asked. "Just pick a planet and test it out."

"We can't do that."

"Why not?"

Nogar squinted his seven eyes at Fiki. "There might be inhabitants. We could kill life. We should send someone to scout the planet first. If I get a report that says that the planet has no life on it, then I can test it out on that planet."

"Sure," Fiki answered in a dismissive tone looking away from Nogar.

Reports were made of several planets. Then, Nogar was given a list of uninhabited planets that he could test his antigravity ray on. They went out to one of the planets and began making preparations for the test run.

Nogar was standing in a spaceship far enough away to be unaffected but close enough to see what happened. Cameras had been placed on the planet, so they could see what someone would see as soon as gravity was reversed. It was a rocky planet, but it had no liquid water. The planet was twice as large as Earth. It was covered in mountains and volcanoes.

They turned the antigravity ray on and watched their screens. Video footage was being transmitted to the screens live. They watched as the cameras flew off the surface of the planet into the sky. As they predicted, all of the cameras began rotating around the planet when they reached the height where the ray stopped affecting the gravity. Therefore, the cameras were being rejected and pulled by the same force.

The Nemodians began clapping. However, something else began to happen that they weren't prepared for. The planet began to be ripped apart. They could see large chunks of the mountains beginning to get yanked off of the surface.

They immediately turned the antigravity ray off. Nogar ordered an investigation to see what went wrong. When the science was settled, and they knew how to fix the problem, Nogar chose another planet that was said to be uninhabited. This planet was deep inside of Hoag's Object.

The Nemodians arrived and immediately began firing the antigravity ray. Because the Theadlians live in underground tunnels, they cannot be seen when scouting the planet, and Nogar didn't see any Theadlians flying out into space. The Theadlians were inside their tunnels worshipping the Great Tirix when their gravity reversed. None of them were seriously injured because they didn't build the ceiling of their tunnels very high. However, calls for help were immediately sent out to the Theadlians that were on other planets at the time.

The Theadlians didn't actually live on Thead anymore. It was the planet that they went to pray. The planet had turned into a large desert. All of the Theadlians presently lived on one of the other seventeen planets controlled by their race.

Theadlian spaceships arrived quickly and began firing at the Nemodians' ships. As soon as

Nogar realized what had happened, he told the soldiers under his command to turn off the antigravity ray. However, General Fiki arrived with a fleet shortly afterwards and began firing back at the Theadlians.

"Call Fiki now!" Nogar yelled. Fiki appeared on a screen in less than ten seconds. "Fiki call your soldiers off! We can still negotiate with them. We were told that the planet was uninhabited."

"We can't call our soldiers off in the middle of a battle," Fiki responded.

"Yes, we can," Nogar pleaded. "It was a mistake."

"The Theadlians are a waste of space anyway."

Nogar's seven eyes widened with shock. "You knew! You knew that the planet was inhabited."

"No, I didn't. What makes you think that?"

"You even know the name of the race on the planet. That means that you already knew they existed. When did you have time to find out who they are, what they're called, and that they are a waste of space? You obviously already knew that they existed."

Fiki smirked. "Okay, I lied to you. It doesn't matter. We are about to destroy their filthy planet." The screen went blank. Nogar was furious.

"Turn our spaceship around!" Nogar commanded. "Fire!" Everyone looked at Nogar as if

he were crazy. "Fire!" He screamed again. The Nemodians under his command began to look at each other. They didn't know what to do. They were supposed to obey Nogar's commands, but they were also forbidden to kill other Nemodians. Nogar ran over to the control panel and began pressing buttons.
    Several missiles were fired. Several Nemodian ships blew up. Three soldiers ran up behind Nogar before he could do more damage and arrested him.
    Shortly after that, Fiki ordered all of his fleet to fire all of their missiles at Thead. This was three hundred thousand seven hundred ninety-nine missiles. Thead was annihilated. The planet broke apart into meteors flying around space. Then, the Nemodians disappeared through a wormhole that they closed off immediately so that they couldn't be followed by the Theadlians.
    Therefore, dear reader, you be the judge. If nothing else, we can at least understand the hatred of the Theadlians. However, this means that Namrips was in a predicament. He wholeheartedly believed what the Nemodians had told him. He believed that the Theadlians had the antigravity ray, when, in reality, the Nemodians were the ones who had reversed the Earth's gravity. The Theadlians weren't even close to the Earth when the Earth's gravity reversed. However, the Nemodians had known that the Theadlians were searching for them. Therefore, when they went to Earth, they made the decision to

blame the Theadlians knowing that they could use it to their advantage.

Now, one trillion Theadlians stood ready to exact revenge. Each Theadlian had devices on their twelve hands. These devices had two functions: they worked in tandem with each other to create a force field to protect the Theadlians from the lasers of the Nemodians, and they fired lasers utilizing the energy that naturally came out of their hands.

With the device that they wore on their hands, the lasers were powerful weapons that could incinerate steel. Therefore, a battle between *Superman* and the Theadlians would result in the death of *Superman* if such a battle were possible. If *Thanos* from *The Avengers* had really existed, the Theadlians would have killed him easily and his puny army. We are talking about one trillion soldiers that can survive off of the energy from the sun that they absorb and the dirt beneath them. We are talking about one trillion soldiers that naturally fire lasers using their body energy.

They opened up portals all around their position. One trillion Theadlians slid like slugs through millions of portals. The portals took them into the base where Namrips was stationed on Earth. A laser caused a Nemodian's head to explode as its thick black blood sprayed all over the place. Another laser burned a hole through a Nemodian's chest. Another Nemodian's upper left arm fell off. The top of a Nemodian's head disappeared exposing its brain that was a dark gray color. The battle had begun.

Namrips was lucky because he was always with Fiki, and Fiki was always heavily guarded because he was a general. He was not the highest ranking general, but even lower ranking generals were always heavily guarded. "We are under attack," Fiki explained. "We are going to go to our post. If the Theadlians make it to us, we have to stonewall them. We will be the last line of defense." They went with a unit of one thousand soldiers that joined together with ninety-nine other units; therefore, they were one hundred thousand in total. More than ninety thousand were Nemodians. The rest were humans who had signed up to help in the same way that Namrips had done.

They went up into the Earth to the ninth floor. They set up a barricade in front of a large door that was fifty feet wide and twenty feet tall. Namrips did not know what was behind the door because he had never ventured this far. However, given all of the effort they were putting into protecting whatever was behind it, he could deduce that it was very important. The hallway was eighty feet wide, and it was three miles long. Needless to say, this was an enormous hallway that was part of a massive facility.

Why would someone make a hallway three miles long? What would such a hallway be used for? These are the types of questions that Namrips was asking himself. This particular hallway wasn't even the largest that they had at this facility. There was another hallway that was seven miles wide. Someone might stop here and wonder if there was a mistake. '*Surely, she meant to say long!*' They will say. Yes, seven miles wide. There is no mistake; its width is in reference. Its length was an impressive thirty miles long. Its height is the least impressive – just one mile high. These hallways were like runways where aircrafts could take off and land.

However, the door that they were guarding had a secret behind it that Namrips would soon discover. It wasn't a secret held from the Nemodians. They all knew what was behind the door. It was a secret held from Namrips. It wasn't a *secret* because they didn't want Namrips to know. It was a *secret* because the Nemodians were experts in psychology, and they understood that people cherish being let in on a *secret*. When you let someone in on a secret, you make that person trust you more. You make that person feel *special*. They wanted Namrips to feel special so that he would be easier to control later.

"Now, we wait," Fiki declared as they settled into position.

"What's behind the door that we're guarding?" Namrips asked.

"I can't tell you that," Fiki whispered. Then he lowered his tone even farther and said, "I can't tell you here."

It made Namrips feel better to know that he would eventually find out what was behind the door. Something inside of him already knew what it was. If Fiki couldn't say it openly, it had to be something that humans weren't allowed to know. So, he assumed that it was most likely something to do with what Fiki had told him about before – the forbidden knowledge. It made him a little excited when he considered the fact that he had such a friend.

They could not see the battle that was being fought outside, but they could hear some of the explosions. From time to time, they felt the ground shake beneath them. This made Namrips more nervous as he waited for their own battle to begin. They waited for what felt like ages.

Then, it finally happened. A large explosion shook the ground at the front. Namrips could hear shots being fired. His mind was racing, and he could feel his heart pounding in his chest. The Theadlians were advancing.

As the battle raged, the ground was rumbling. Namrips could not see the Theadlians yet. However, he could see lights flashing in the distance. He could hear explosions and feel the ground shake beneath him. He heard humans screaming in the distance. He could differentiate the different types of screams. His time in the army had taught him that when someone screams in pain, it sounds different than when they scream in fear and likewise if they scream in anger. The screams that Namrips heard were screams of pain. Something was happening in the battle that was causing terrible pain.

    If we could jump about two miles down the hall where the battle was taking place, we would see the reason for their screams. As the lasers were not penetrating the force fields implemented by the Theadlians, humans and Nemodians had tried to come close and stab the Theadlians. In some cases, they were successful in stabbing the Theadlians, but most of the time, it was impossible because, as was mentioned, the Theadlians had arms all around their bodies to defend themselves. Regardless, the Theadlian invariably managed to spit on the attacking human or Nemodian. The person would immediately begin screaming in pain as the acid from the Theadlian ate a hole into the person's body. Sometimes, their arms fell off. Sometimes, their face became disfigured, and their eyes fell out of their sockets. In other cases, the person would lose his legs. In some instances, however, the person had a large hole in his legs, stomach, arms, chest, etc.

    One man ran up close to a Theadlian and grabbed two of its arms. His hands immediately fell limp. The Theadlian hugged the man who immediately became paralyzed from the poison that was on the Theadlian's skin. Then the Theadlian spat on his shoulder knowing that the man was exactly where it wanted him to be. It gleefully watched as the man screamed in pain. Unable to move, he just stood there as the acid destroyed his shoulder. His right arm was half attached and half disconnected. So the Theadlian decided to rip the arm off completely. As blood began to spurt out, the Theadlian began to play tug-of-war with another Theadlian with the human as the object being tugged on. They ripped him in half as more blood gushed out, and the man died.

Nevertheless, Namrips could not see all of this happening. He could only hear their screams. As a war veteran, he knew that the screams were from humans suffering in pain. *Have you ever heard someone screaming as their flesh was burning in a fire? Have you ever had a severe burn?* It is hard to imagine how bone chilling the screams were unless you have heard a burn victim screaming in pain as a flame consumes their body. The sensation of the acid on the skin was worse than being burned by a fire as the acid ate away the flesh and then the bone. *Have you ever broken a bone?* The pain was like first having the flesh set on fire and then having the bone crushed by a hammer.

Namrips looked at Fiki. He couldn't figure out if Fiki was worried or not. Fiki seemed like an emotionless stone. Namrips, on the other hand, was worried, and his face showed it.

Chapter Six

When the Nemodians had recovered from the initial shock of it, they began firing back. However, their lasers were being deflected off of the Theadlians' force fields. The Nemodians, on the other hand, were falling dead in droves. The Nemodians' black blood and the humans' red blood painted the floor and the walls. Because the Nemodians outnumbered the human combatants, it was mainly black blood. One of the Nemodian's head disappeared, and its blood gushed out of its neck.

Some of their arms fell off, and blood flowed out like a fountain. The floor became flooded with their thick black blood. In fact, the floor became so slippery that some people died after slipping down. Either they bust their head on the floor, or they were left slipping around trying to get back on their feet. If the latter was the case, they got shot before they had made it back on their feet.

The slippery floor did not seem to affect the Theadlians at all. They easily slid along the floor like slugs. Since they had no legs, the situation became an advantage. Imagine one trillion Theadlians entering through the portal little by little. The floor was already soaked with blood before even five thousand of them had successfully come through the portal at Namrips' location, and there were millions that had come through the portals by this time in the battle.

It was like being under heavy machinegun fire but replacing the machineguns with lasers. If you can imagine such a terrible sight, after hundreds of dead humans and Nemodians had already fallen, their dead bodies also continued to get hit by lasers turning their bodies into mush. Therefore, the floor not only was soaked in blood, but there were also areas of mush that had previously been humans and Nemodians. It was like an organic soup made of mashed humans and fried Nemodians. If you looked carefully, you might have seen a heart floating in the blood, the small intestines laid out like a misplaced rope, half a brain sitting in a puddle of black and red liquid, dismembered hands and legs, or any number of other body parts scattered about like lungs, noses, eyes, and fingers.

Once the Theadlians slid over the dead body parts of those who had fallen from the initial wave of attacks, the next line of defense was behind huge steel barriers. They stuck their heads out and began firing all at once. However, the Theadlians' lasers quickly destroyed the steel barriers and those left standing there were quickly left without protection.

Lasers were crossing paths in both directions. If anyone had been in the center of it, he or she would have become ground meat.

However, the Theadlians were not dying; the Nemodians had been reluctant to turn the frequency up on their laser guns because a higher frequency would use up the energy core faster. On the other hand, any human or Nemodian who was shot by a Theadlian's laser spilled large quantities of blood and died. The Theadlians continued to advance slowly sliding along the floor.

The battle finally came into view for Namrips. He saw the Theadlians firing lasers out of their specialized gloves. They slowly slid across the bloody floor. Humans and Nemodians were trying to hide behind the steel barrier while shooting at the Theadlians. However, as the steel barriers weren't actually much help, they began to resort to turning the frequency on their guns up. That is when Namrips finally saw a few Theadlians die. A Theadlian was hit in the head by five lasers in rapid succession. Its head was ripped off its shoulders and it slumped over as its green blood began to ooze out of its neck.

They say that when one faces death, that person's life flashes before their eyes. For Namrips, it was his father. He never met his mother because she died while giving birth to him. His father had taken care of him until he was nine years old. When his father was in the hospital dying of cancer, he explained to the young Namrips that he couldn't receive any of the typical cancer treatments because he had HIV. Namrips had never known that his father had HIV, and he stood in shock. He didn't understand why all this was kept secret for him. He loved his father dearly, and he wasn't ready to take on life as an orphan. Therefore, when death confronted Namrips, the face of his father was the only thing he saw. It symbolized the years of anguish he had spent deprived of the only parent he knew. It symbolized his hatred for the foster home that he moved into after his father passed away.

"Turn the frequency all the way up on your gun," Fiki told Namrips.

"But doesn't that use up the energy core faster?" Namrips asked.

"Yes, but we don't have a choice. The lasers aren't penetrating their force field. We need a higher frequency to penetrate it." Namrips obeyed.

"Set up the cannons and open fire!" Fiki yelled out. Namrips was positioned close to the cannon. He watched as they took aim and began firing the laser cannons. Three Theadlians turned into green goo that splattered all over the floor mixing their green blood with the red human blood and black Nemodian blood. They continued firing the cannons; there were four cannons total. Several Theadlians exploded in one place; then, they exploded in another place.

The Nemodians also decided to use the energy necessary to put up a force field. They had become desperate to stall the coming onslaught as long as possible. The force field wasn't exactly impenetrable, but they stopped dying in droves, and the Theadlians even seemed to get pushed backwards a little bit. Even though the Theadlians didn't actually move backwards, those on the frontlines had died making it look like they had.

Whereas the Theadlians had force fields around each individual, the Nemodians had a general force field that separated the frontlines from the Theadlians. An occasional laser penetrated this force field that stretched out between them like a defining line; this laser would take the head off of an unsuspecting Nemodian or human, remove a leg, incinerate an arm, or make a hole in a torso.

Namrips also opened fire for the first time in the battle. His laser was on the highest possible frequency. It took between four to seven shots in the same place to penetrate their force fields and create a hole in the alien. Namrips, who had been a sniper in the army, made every shot count. Four shots – dead. Six shots – dead. Five shots – dead.

The floor was becoming a puddle of blood near Namrips position like it had done farther down. The difference, now, was that there was finally green blood mixed in with the red and black. The cannons continued firing destroying several Theadlians at a time. Lasers continued to cross paths going both directions. The floor rumbled beneath them. Blood and body parts littered the floor.

However, every time they killed off a bunch of them, another wave of Theadlians came in. They didn't know that there were one trillion Theadlians that were coming through the portals. At this point in the battle, the majority of them were still waiting on the other side of the portal.

Anyone who has stared death in the eye has learned that even in the most impossible situations, there is hope. The forces of death surrounded Namrips, and he waited patiently to see what would happen. In the meantime, he survived keeping his head above water as the tempest-tossed waters threatened to drown him in the bottom of the sea. If death had a face, it would be one trillion Theadlians slowly sliding in your direction.

At this point in the battle, the Theadlians made their own adjustments. The Theadlians wanted to get rid of the laser cannons, so they brought in shrink rays. If you shrink people, they can continue living if they have an oxygen tank. Therefore, shrink rays were not typically used on people in wars. If the enemy knew that shrink rays were going to be used, they could simply bring oxygen tanks so that they wouldn't suffocate when they shrank. The reason they needed oxygen is that the atoms of someone who had shrunk couldn't form chemical bonds with normal atoms rendering oxygen from the environment useless to them (When they shrank, there was usually a pocket of oxygen that they could breathe for a few minutes, but soon after that, they would begin suffocating).

Nevertheless, using it on devastating weapons like the laser cannons made a lot more sense. They had tried to shoot the cannons with their lasers, but they couldn't do enough damage to them due to the force field protecting them. However, the force field wouldn't block the shrink ray. They aimed it at the cannons and shrank the them to a size so small that they could no longer be seen.

The Nemodians had enlarger rays, but they had to identify where the cannon was before enlarging it back to its proper size. This was not an easy task. Therefore, while the Nemodians were using their computers to identify the exact location of the cannons, the Theadlians were able to advance more easily.

Eventually, the Theadlians were able to get to a distance of fifty meters from Namrips. At that moment, the shrink ray missed the cannon and hit Namrips. He shrank down to a size smaller than a bacterium.

Namrips looked around himself and saw that he was surrounded by bacteria. He immediately began shooting the bacteria with his laser gun. The bacteria were coming towards him from all directions. He watched as his lasers set them on fire and burned them into oblivion. As he was doing this, he began to feel light headed, so he turned his oxygen tank on and put his oxygen mask on.

    Namrips completely sterilized the area. After about ten minutes, there weren't any bacteria or viruses in his vicinity. So he tried to look at the battle and interpret what was happening. The difference in size made it extremely difficult to know what was going on. That is when he saw a wave of blood headed in his direction. When the wave of blood absorbed him, he began testing his laser gun in the blood to see if it still fired. It fired and incinerated several red blood cells. Then he began shooting at the bacteria that were in the blood.

Chapter Seven

When Fiki could not see Namrips anywhere, he knew what had happened. However, he didn't have time to unshrink him due to the intensity of the battle. He would have to wait until the battle was over.

Theadlians continued to advance, and the bloodbath continued. The Theadlians knew that they needed to get behind the force field in order to kill more Nemodians and humans. They continued shooting their lasers out of their gloves, and the occasional shot would penetrate and kill a human or Nemodian. However, they also lined up and pressed forwards. Imagine a multitude of Theadlians from one side of the hall to the other. Imagine this multitude extends down the hallway as far as the eye can see like a sea of Theadlians. The strategy is obvious – to overwhelm them with numbers so that it was impossible to kill them all before they got behind the force field. As they moved forwards, many Theadlians slumped over dead with their green blood oozing out onto the floor. Other Theadlians exploded when hit by the laser cannons that were firing at their frontlines as quickly as they could.

Namrips was swimming in blood. It would be easy to imagine that Namrips was surrounded by a red liquid, and therefore, couldn't see very far in the blood. That would be half true if Namrips had been his normal size (if Namrips had been his normal size, it would have been mostly black). Namrips was smaller than the bacteria, and red blood cells are what give human blood its red color (Nemodians had black blood cells giving their blood the color black). Therefore, swimming in blood was almost like swimming in water, and Namrips could see just fine because the blood cells were larger than Namrips.

When the Theadlians slid past Namrips' position, neither their acid from their saliva nor the poison on their skin could harm Namrips. His body was too small for the chemicals surrounding him to interact with the chemicals on or inside his body. All he had to do to stay alive was kill all of the surrounding bacteria and destroy whatever was left of the dead's immune systems. So he turned the frequency down on his laser gun to conserve energy since a lower frequency would work just fine for this purpose.

The Theadlians finally crossed the force field. However, as soon as this happened, the force field was immediately moved back. The Nemodians and humans who were in front of the new force field were left without protection, and therefore, they were annihilated within a few minutes. Within those few minutes, it was reminiscent of the initial moments of the battle where lasers were quickly flying back and forth crossing paths. Blood flowed like a fountain. Intestines rolled out of some of their stomachs onto the floor. Dismembered hands, feet, and heads could be seen spread across the floor. Eyeballs, chunks of flesh, fingers, toes, and spinal cords floated in the growing river of blood.

    Fiki had obviously retreated back to a safe position before the force field was moved back. When Fiki had seen that the Theadlians were going to take the position, he had moved back along with the laser cannons. However, this process of retreating and changing the force field's position continued repeating until it became very obvious that the Theadlians were definitely going to win this battle. They had moved all the way back to one hundred meters from the door that they were guarding. The Theadlians were still lined up from one side of the hallway to the other and extended down the hallway as far as they could see. If they could have gone three miles down, they would have seen that there were still Theadlians who were on the other side of the portal.

    Fiki positioned himself behind one of the steel barriers and began shooting at the Theadlians again. The Cannons continued destroying Theadlians moving forwards on the frontlines. When the Theadlians had advanced so far that they were threatening to cross the force field again, Fiki stood up and extended his upper left arm to tell those who were operating the laser cannons to retreat again. As he did this, a laser came through the force field and took his arm clean off. Fiki's black blood came gushing out of the stub that was left. Fiki used his lower right arm to pull out his flamethrower. The flamethrower was a ten-inch tube with a two-inch diameter. A hot blue flame came out of the top and burned the arteries in the stub closed. Then he put the flamethrower away.

    As he retreated with the cannons, he saw a human whose laser gun's energy core had stopped working. He immediately dropped his laser gun and grabbed hold of his AR-15 that had been hanging around his shoulder and neck by a strap. The human began shooting with the AR-15, and the bullets ripped through the Theadlians' heads. The force fields couldn't stop bullets; they were made to stop lasers.

    This human's name was Arthur. He was one of those people who have a basement full of different types of guns. He was also an alcoholic and lived in constant depression. When the Earth's gravity had reversed, he had been sitting in his living room drinking a bottle of vodka. There was an empty bottle of Jack Daniel's laying clumsily in front of the television. His half-empty bottle of vodka was in his left hand. He was wearing a white sleeveless shirt and blue jeans. He had his black cowboy hat on his thick dark hair and sweat running down his chubby face. He was sitting in front of his couch on the floor with a black pistol in his right hand. On that day, he had slid the muzzle of the pistol into his mouth. His index finger had tightened around the trigger. He had been prepared to take his own life. And he would've done it if it hadn't been for the gravity reversing at that moment. The gun had slipped out of his mouth as he fell towards the ceiling.

  When he had woken up, he had considered it a second chance at life. He had decided to join the Nemodian army and fight the evil Theadlians in order to redeem himself by saving the Earth. He had only asked if he could bring his AR-15 with him to the battle. The Nemodians permitted it. However, when others had seen him with his AR-15, as humans are wont to do, they wanted one too. Therefore, there were three humans still alive in the battle who had AR-15's. Arthur was one of them. As soon as the other two humans who had AR-15's saw Arthur easily killing Theadlians, they threw their laser guns down and began shooting the Theadlians with their AR-15's.

  Fiki and the Cannons finished their retreat to fifty meters away from the door that they were guarding. However, they didn't move the force field back yet because the Theadlians were momentarily being pushed back. Nevertheless, the Theadlians advanced closer to the force field when they successfully shrank the cannons again. It took too long to unshrink them back to their normal size, and a wave of Theadlians came through the force field. The force field was immediately moved back to Fiki's position, and those outside of that position had to retreat as quickly as possible. The other two humans who had AR-15's died, but Arthur made it to safety and began firing his gun again. He had a lot of bullets, but not nearly enough to kill one trillion Theadlians.

    Arthur was shooting his AR-15, and Theadlians were spilling their brains and guts all over the floor. The laser cannons were annihilating the Theadlians, and their body parts and blood were littering the floor. Because the Theadlians didn't have legs, the base of their body dragged across the floor. Therefore, with so many Theadlians that filled the hall (almost three miles minus fifty meters), Arthur was standing in blood that was calf deep. There wasn't a single inch of the floor that wasn't covered in blood. The blood was a mixture of red, black, and green. There were eyeballs, fingers, limbs, and intestines floating around. Arthur could feel his feet stepping on body parts. As it squished underneath his foot, he would wonder what body part it was. If it felt like it was hard, he knew it was either an arm or a leg. If it was very squishy, he figured that it was either a stomach, liver, pancreas, or intestines. If it was neither very squishy nor hard, then he would assume it was a heart.

Namrips was still swimming around in the blood. He had to be on his guard. Bacteria would come towards him in large quantities. It seemed like he never got any time to rest. There were brief moments where he wasn't being attacked by bacteria, but then, white blood cells and antibodies would come upon him suddenly. Then, there would be more bacteria in the area before he could even destroy the white blood cells.

Fiki slipped down in the blood. When he stood back up, he was no longer standing behind the steel barrier. A laser came through the force field at that moment and took Fiki's lower left arm off. His black blood spurted out.

He torched the stub with the flamethrower like he had done with his upper left arm. Fiki stopped bleeding. He tried to shoot his laser gun immediately afterwards, but it stopped working. The energy core had been used up. Fiki immediately called for another retreat. They pulled the laser cannons back to within twenty-five meters of the door. Fiki pulled out a device and entered a password. It was a special weapon called the DNA-scrambler.

Suddenly, the lights began to turn on and off all throughout the facility. An alarm was sounded. Death had spread its wings. *Was it possible that everyone at the battle would die*? The DNA-scrambler was almost like a self-destruct button. The weapon would equally affect Nemodians as it would the Theadlians.

Fiki walked back to the door and stood there watching the end of the battle unfold. The Theadlians successfully shrank the cannons again. This time there was no attempt to unshrink them. The Theadlians arrived at the force field and passed over to the other side. Fiki watched as they grabbed one of his best lieutenants. One Theadlian pulled on his middle arms as the other pulled on his legs until he was ripped in half across his waist. His blood quickly poured out onto the floor.

There was a particular weapon that was made for this specific purpose – making a last stand. The most powerful force field used a lot of energy and couldn't last very long. Therefore, it was saved for these moments and was combined with what was called a laser grenade. A laser grenade was an object that could be thrown like a grenade; it immediately started firing lasers in every direction as it hit the ground. The force field protected them from their own grenade. It continued to fire these grenades like a grenade launcher until the energy core ran out. It almost looked like a technological version of the shields that knights used hundreds of years ago. It had a steel cross inside of a steel rectangle. The four spaces were full of a blue glow – the force field. If someone was holding it and knelt down, this person could fire the laser grenades without worry that the lasers from his or her own grenade would kill them.

    The remaining Nemodians and Arthur ran to the door with Fiki and pulled out this grenade launcher. They all knelt down and began firing the grenades simultaneously. Theadlian heads exploded. Holes formed in their chests. Their arms fell off. Their blood oozed out. This pushed the Theadlians back for a moment, but again the Theadlians came back advancing. There were too many of them. Their energy cores ran low. Their laser shields and laser grenades became weaker. The Theadlians shot and killed many of them. There were only five left: Fiki, Arthur, and three more Nemodians. They were trying to hide behind their weakened laser shields shooting out laser grenades. The Theadlians knew that they had won. The lights were still turning on and off. They shot their lasers and killed three Nemodians. Arthur looked over at Fiki. They knew that they were about to die. A laser took Fiki's only left arm off.

    However, the Theadlians suddenly backed off. They looked sick. Something was going on inside them. Their arms were slowly transforming into carrots. It wasn't just the Theadlians who were nearby; all of the Theadlians were transforming into various fruits and vegetables. The Theadlians were in a panic trying to go back to their planet through the portal. They knew that they had been hit with a DNA-scrambler.

Fiki quickly burned the arteries closed where his final left arm had been. Then, Fiki analyzed his three right hands. The tips of his fingers looked like they were transforming into broccoli. In fact, his blue skin was turning green all over his body.

Arthur's body was turning red. He had leaves that looked like they belonged to a tomato plant growing out of his neck and wrists. "What's going on?" Arthur cried out.

"It looks like you were given the DNA of a tomato plant," Fiki answered.

"Is there a way to reverse it?"

"Yes. We are going to go to a Nemodian hospital close to the moon."

Arthur's terrified expression disappeared and was replaced with a smile as soon as he heard that there was a way to reverse it. He was thinking about how close he had been to death. He stared at the Theadlians who were still trying to escape through their portals. He looked down at the bloody floor.

Then he looked over at Fiki. "I better get a medal of honor for this battle!" He exclaimed.

"Excuse me?" Fiki asked surprised at what he was hearing.

"We would have died if I hadn't had my AR-15. I basically saved the day."

"You saved the day?" Fiki raised his eyebrows.

"Yeah. My actions are the reason you and I are alive right now."

Fiki put his top right hand on his chest. "You saved me?"

"Yes. It's crazy, right? We, humans, are resourceful. The Nemodians are lucky to have us as an ally."

"You think so?" Fiki walked over to where Arthur was standing. He pulled out his flamethrower with his upper right arm and grabbed Arthur with his two lower right arms. Before Arthur could interpret what was happening, Fiki stuck the end in his face, and the hot blue flame shot out and consumed his face. Arthur immediately began to scream in pain and squirm trying to break free, but Fiki tightened his grip and continued to watch Arthur's face melt. "Before you die, I want you to know that humans are lucky that we are going to exterminate you from existence. You are lucky to have been in the Nemodians' presence before going extinct." Whether or not Arthur heard and interpreted Fiki's words was unclear, for he died immediately afterwards.

Fiki tossed his dead body, and it splashed as it landed on the blood-filled floor. Fiki's words would seem to imply anger, but he had said it with a voice that was void of emotion. It was like a psychopath who murdered while honestly believing that he was doing nothing wrong.

"Computer," Fiki said, "search for Namrips and enlarge him."

"Searching," the computer responded. Namrips was farther down the hall. He was still swimming in the blood and shooting bacteria. The Theadlians had successfully abandoned the area by opening extra portals.

It took about five minutes for the computer to identify Namrips' location. When the computer found him, it enlarged him to his natural size. Namrips was lying on his back in a puddle of blood. He sat up and looked around. He realized that he was back to normal. He turned his oxygen off and removed his oxygen mask.

Even though Namrips had been a soldier and had fought in the war, the sight of the floor being covered in blood and body parts sent a chill down his spine. He had never seen such a sight before. *Where is everyone?* He wondered. It was hard to believe that they were all dead. He saw only Fiki walking towards him, and Fiki was missing his three left arms.

"What happened?" Namrips inquired.

"The Theadlians were winning," Fiki answered. "They killed everyone. I had to use the DNA-scrambler to drive them off."

"Why are you turning green? Why do your hands look like broccoli?"

"If I don't get to the reversal station within two hours, I'll become broccoli – literally. The DNA-scrambler has this effect on all living beings in the area where it goes off. It gave me the DNA of broccoli. It didn't work on you because you were smaller than the radiation waves used to manipulate the DNA."

"What happened to your left arms?"

"I got shot three times. It was a crazy coincidence and, perhaps, good luck. Every time I got shot, the laser took one of my left arms."

Namrips squinted his eyes at Fiki. "Why would that be good luck?"

"Because it didn't take my head off, and I prefer my right arms." Namrips almost detected a slight chuckle in the voice of Fiki.

"Where is the reversal station?"

"We have one inside our mother ship in proximity to the moon."

"Let's go, then! I'll take you."

Fiki put a hand up. "Wait."

"What?"

"I don't have a body prepared in case of my death. I need a clone just in case."

Namrips sighed deeply. "How long will it take?"

"Not long. That's what's behind the door here. We were protecting the clones and, therefore, future lives of many Nemodians."

"But if your DNA is all screwed up now, don't you need to wait until you reverse it before creating a clone?"

"I'm not going to clone myself. I'm going to take a generic clone. Nemodians have taken the best genetic qualities of our race, and we have clones that are made from a designated batch of DNA. I just need to prepare it so that I am linked to the clone and, therefore, facilitate the change from one body to the other if I die."

Namrips thought for a moment. "And what if I die?"

"Don't worry. Don't tell anyone. We'll prepare a clone for you too."

"You're going to clone me?"

"No, I don't know how to do that. I would if I could because I'm sure you'd prefer to continue living with a body that is almost identical to your current body. But continuing as a Nemodian is the next best thing, right?"

"So, if I die, I have to become a Nemodian." Namrips stared up at the ceiling.

"It's better than not having a body."

Namrips took in a deep breath and exhaled. "That's true."

Fiki gave Namrips a pat on the back. "In your next life cycle, you won't think anything of it. You'll love being a Nemodian."

Fiki opened the door and they walked inside. The clones were inside large glass transparent tubes of liquid floating inside. Namrips could see them through the glass. There were thousands of them lined in rows. Most of them were Nemodians, but some were other alien races. The bodies that were designated to specific Nemodians had a red light on them. If they were free to be used, the light was green. There was a whole section of human clones lined up together. However, they all looked identical, and they were all female.

"Why do you have human clones here?" Namrips asked.

"I didn't know that we had them here," Fiki answered. "It looks like you have a choice to make. You can either become a Nemodian or a human woman."

"I think I'd rather stay human," Namrips said.

They found a Nemodian clone that was not designated to any particular Nemodian. Then, they identified the human clone that they were going to use. Next, Fiki entered inside of a machine, and Namrips pressed a button. His body was scanned, and he felt a jolt of electricity inside his body. He was able to see and feel as if he was inside his new body for a brief second. Then, it stopped. Namrips did the same immediately afterward. However, Fiki had to press the button with his elbow because his hands had completely converted into broccoli by that time. They were now linked to a new body in case they died.

Fiki was completely green by the time they finished. He could not move his arms at all. His three right arms had completely converted into broccoli. They ran quickly to a spaceship and flew to the mother ship that was close to the moon. They didn't leave their new bodies on the base on Earth. They had loaded the bodies up onto the spaceship. This was actually very easy to do. The bodies were already placed in position so that the desired body would be sucked into a long steel tube and naturally placed on a spaceship.

When they arrived at the mother ship, Fiki's legs had become broccoli. So Namrips had to carry him inside. "It's an emergency!" He cried out. "I need to get him to a reversal station for the DNA-scrambler!"

Fiki's face was covered in broccoli. He was unable to see or speak. The transformation was almost complete. He had about ten minutes left before there would be nothing left of his own DNA and, therefore, no way to reverse it.

Chapter Eight

Namrips was standing in a waiting room. He was pacing back and forth. He was worried that Fiki would die and have to face Jeggolith again. From what he understood, there was no guarantee that he would be able to make it to his new body if he died. On top of that, if Fiki died, there was a good chance that he wouldn't remember Namrips even if he did make it to his new body; Namrips would lose his best friend. The only way to keep his best friend was for Fiki to survive with his current body. Of course, Namrips would be happy for Fiki if he made it to his new body. However, it wouldn't be quite the same without his best friend.

The doctor came out and saw Namrips pacing back and forth. He walked over to him. If it were a human doctor, he could have looked at the expression on his face, and he would have known if it were good news or bad news. However, the doctor was a Nemodian. How could he understand the expression of an entity that had seven eyes? It wasn't just the seven eyes that threw him off. It was also the two mouths. It was like they were expressionless. Perhaps, Nemodians could discern different emotions amongst other Nemodians. Perhaps, humans were emotionless for them. However, none of these speculations were helping ease the angst that Namrips felt at that moment.

"Fiki will recover," the doctor said. "He is sleeping right now. He still looks like broccoli, but we successfully reversed his DNA back to normal. Within a few hours, he should be blue and back to normal."

"What about his left arms?" Namrips asked.

"After he wakes up, we will place robotic arms on his body to replace his lost arms."

Namrips took a deep breath. "When can I speak with him?"

"He should wake up within the next hour. You can go in and see him in an hour."

"Thank you, doctor." Namrips smiled as the doctor walked away.

After this conversation, Namrips waited exactly one hour. Then, he entered Fiki's room. Fiki's eyes were closed. He was still a little green. His face was completely visible. His right arms still looked like broccoli. It was impossible to know if anymore of his body looked like broccoli because black sheets covered his body.

Namrips looked at his friend and sighed deeply. "Is that you, Namrips?" Fiki asked without opening his eyes.

"Yeah, I'm here," Namrips answered.

Fiki opened his eyes and looked at him. "I almost died," he said.

"How do you know that?"

"I've died before. That tunnel is always there when you get close to death."

Namrips' eyes widened. "There's a tunnel?"

"Yes, but don't go down the tunnel if you die. We don't know what's on the other side. No one knows. Once you go down the tunnel, you're gone."

"Then, what should I do?"

Fiki closed his eyes for a moment and opened them again. "Go to your new body. Stay here as a ghost until you find your new body."

"But if I go down the tunnel, can I avoid Jeggolith?"

"Probably. But you don't know what's on the other side of that tunnel. You know what's on this side. It's better to take your chances with Jeggolith and stay with the living. There could be an even more dangerous creature on the other side."

"What if it's heaven?" Namrips inquired.

Fiki laughed. It was the first time Namrips had heard Fiki truly laugh. "What if it's hell? What if it's just another phase of life similar to this one? No one knows."

After a few hours, Fiki was up and walking around. His skin had returned to the typical blue of the Nemodians. There was no sign of broccoli anywhere on his body.

A doctor came in the room. "It's time to get you some robotic arms," he said. "Come with me." Namrips attempted to follow along, but he was told to wait in the waiting room.

When Fiki came back, he looked like his normal self with the exception of his three left arms being robotic. "If you keep up the way you're going, you're gonna look like a cyborg before long," Namrips said smiling.

"What's a cyborg?" Fiki asked.

"It's a living being with both organic and robotic parts."

Fiki looked at Namrips and squinted his seven eyes at him. "By your definition, I'm already a cyborg."

"I was thinking a little more robot and a little less organic."

"That's not a very good definition." Fiki looked away and began walking. Namrips followed.

"Why?"

Fiki turned his head to face Namrips again. "It's too ambiguous. All I know is that you don't define me as a cyborg because you feel like I should have more robotic parts. How many robotic parts should I have before I can be classified as a cyborg?"

Namrips scratched his head. "I don't actually know. I don't remember. I'll find out and get back to you later."

"I have a friend that has all six arms, his legs, his heart, and his lungs that are all robotic parts. Is that enough to be a cyborg?"

"I suppose." Namrips let out an exasperated breath. "I told you I really don't remember enough about the topic!"

"So why did you talk about it?"

Namrips face was beginning to turn red. "It was a joke."

"I'm not good with jokes."

"I noticed."

Fiki looked away and smiled. *Is that emotion I see?* Namrips wondered to himself. He felt like he was noticing more emotion ever since Fiki had almost died. *Death can definitely change a man,* Namrips thought.

"Listen," Fiki began and stopped walking. "We have to get nutrients, and then we have to report. We are going to attack the blockade that the Theadlians set up. Our goal is to break through it and initiate an attack against the mother ship that is in charge of the Theadlian fleet in our area. Another thing, we are no longer going to use lasers when fighting against the Theadlians. We are going to use AR-15's."

Namrips waved his hands in the air. "Wait. What? We are going to use human guns? But I thought alien technology was superior to ours."

"I'm not an alien; I'm a Nemodian. And, yes, Nemodian technology is superior. However, humans have never fought against Theadlians. So, Theadlians have not invented a way to protect themselves against bullets. I saw a human pull out an AR-15 and kill hundreds of Theadlians before he died. The bullets go right through their force fields."

"How are we going to get human guns here? Are we going to go back to Earth and collect them?"

Fiki started walking again with Namrips following closely behind. "We already have the AR-15's here on the mother ship."

Namrips' eyes lit up; he was shocked at this revelation. "How did Nemodians get human guns?"

Fiki waved a dismissive hand. "We collected everything that flew out into space when gravity reversed. Don't you remember the conversation we had about how we had to collect everything that flew out into space so that it would not fall into the Theadlians' hands? We confiscated the rest of the guns from military facilities on Earth."

"Yes, but Nemodians thought to do all of that just after the gravity reversed?"

"Obviously." Fiki's voice sounded slightly annoyed - more emotion; Namrips wasn't used to seeing so much emotion from Fiki. "That's why we're having this conversation now."

"So, we're going to receive an AR-15 before we go on our mission?"

"Yes."

Namrips was almost scared to ask any more questions. He got the weird sensation that Fiki wanted to wrap his hands around his neck and remove his life force for all the inquiries he was making. "And what will we do after that? I mean after we initiate the attack on the Theadlian mother ship."

"If we survive, we're gonna go to the seventeen planets under the control of the Theadlians and wipe them out completely so that they can never harm anyone ever again." Namrips continued following Fiki to their ship. They walked down a long hallway. After walking for fifteen minutes in silence, they stopped in front of a door. Fiki pressed a button and the door disappeared. They walked inside.

They were standing before all of the clones that they had loaded up before leaving the Earth. The tanks that contained the clones were in the shape of a cylinder. The bodies were floating inside a liquid and were hooked up to breathing machines. Their mouths were covered by a breathing apparatus with a tube coming out of it. The tube arrived at an oxygen tank placed at the back of the cylinder.

"We need to release the Nemodians who recently died and received new bodies," Fiki said.

"I thought they woke up as soon as they got to their new bodies," Namrips said.

Fiki looked at Namrips and closed his eyes for a moment. He opened his eyes again and spoke gently. "I didn't tell you that. I said that they wake up in their new bodies. I didn't tell you when they wake up. It can take a week for someone to wake up. We can help facilitate the process of them waking up. If a week passes, and they wake up naturally, there is an emergency release. The Nemodians will be released by the computer. However, if they are still sleeping, we can wake them up and release them now."

"Ah, I see. How do we release them?"

"I have to put in a code in the computer over there. Then you can press the button that I'll show you." They walked over to a control panel. Fiki entered a password. "You see that red button over there?" Fiki said indicating with the hand where it was. "Press it."

"Got it," Namrips said and pressed the button. They stood there for a moment staring at the clones. At first, nothing happened. They simply stood there motionless as if basking in the sun on a secluded beach absorbed in the tranquility of the tempestuous ocean.

Then, they began to notice that their eyes had opened. The liquid slowly drained as the Nemodians began to get used to standing there. Then, the oxygen masks fell from their faces. Next, the transparent glass slid open and allowed their naked bodies to step out. Watching this scene sent a chill down Namrips' spine.

It was weird looking at the naked Nemodians. Namrips' eyes were fixated on where their genitals were supposed to be. It was so strange seeing that it was a smooth blue surface with no discernible part that could be interpreted as male or female.

"Where is their... you know... their private part?" Namrips asked.

"We don't have genders," Fiki answered.

"So, you just clone yourselves."

"Yes."

Namrips raised his eyes to the ceiling as if in deep thought. "How do you use the bathroom?"

"There is a very tiny hole there where urine can be released."

Namrips focused his eyes trying to detect the hole. "I can't see the hole."

"It is very tiny, and it is towards the back below the anus," Fiki answered.

Namrips stood there staring thinking about what this implied for the Nemodian society. It was a strange revelation. Namrips found it an unbearable thought to go through life and never feel the warmth of another body next to him. What a sad existence the Nemodians had that they would never know the pleasure of making love to another sentient being.

However, the thought went even deeper. Namrips was also aware that this meant that the Nemodians would never know the love of a mother. They were born in cold laboratories. They were self-made orphans. They had no parents. It wasn't that their parents had died. It was that their parents had never existed. They could not shed tears for their parents. Who amongst them could share the joys of having a family? Who could say that they had gone to their brother's concert? Who could say that they had gone to their sister's wedding?

Then, another set of questions came to Namrips. What did they do to pursue happiness? What made them happy? Did they have any guilty pleasures?

Fiki gave the newly born clones directions on where they could find their videos that they had made. He told them where they could find their clothes. Then, Fiki left with Namrips.

He took Namrips back to the Nemodian mother ship. They were walking down a long hallway. Fiki was walking very quickly as he was obviously thinking about his task at hand.

Namrips didn't even notice. He had his own thoughts keeping him busy. He had just seen how Nemodians were born. Watching a human come out of the womb of a woman would be a precious experience, but this was different. It made him wonder what life was. Were the Nemodians self-created biological robots? Or were they living beings?

Namrips had always thought that what made life so sacred was the capacity to love. However, it seemed that the Nemodians possibly lacked this capacity. Who were they going to love? They had no parents, no marriages, and no children. They had themselves, and that was it. Perhaps, they loved themselves.

  Namrips had lost track of time, and therefore, he had no idea how long they had been walking down the hallway before they arrived to another room. The room was so large that Namrips couldn't see from one side to the other. It looked like something you would see in a horror movie. They entered a protected area behind a transparent wall so that they would see everything that happened inside the room. It was massive and without any defining characteristics. The only thing that it had was huge tubes coming out of the ceiling.

  Fiki put in a password on a control panel. A little later, all of the clones arrived through tubes that were in the ceiling. They were the clones that had not received rebirth and were not dedicated to anyone.

  The liquid drained out of the tubes. Then, the transparent glass tubes opened. The clones began to open their eyes, and the oxygen masks fell from their faces – or at least it fell from those who had faces; there were several extraterrestrial races and humans mixed together. They tried to walk a little, but their legs trembled, and many of them fell to their knees. Then, a yellow fume filled the room until they could no longer see the clones.

  They waited for about fifteen minutes. The yellow fume had dissipated enough to see the clones. Namrips was staring in horror at what he was witnessing. The clones were squirming around as if possessed. They were becoming distorted in their shape. Their size grew five times larger. The Nemodian's skin color became gray. Spines grew out of their backs. Six arms became ten arms. Their muscles bulged. Their teeth and mouths became excessively large. Their teeth looked like those of a Saber Tooth Tiger. They roared louder than twenty lions combined. They beat their chests. Claws grew out of their fingers that were razor sharp.

    This was not all. The human clones gained four more arms and had six arms. They became five times bigger. Basically, all of the aforementioned changes applied to humans except the change of skin color. Whereas the Nemodians went from blue to gray, the humans became colorless. It was as if they took a bunch of scotch tape and used it for skin.

    There were three other races of aliens amongst the clones as well. There were four-foot-tall gray-bodied aliens with large black eyes called the Merkians. Before the change, they had two arms and two legs like humans. They underwent all of the same changes except the color of their skin; their skin became purple.

    There was another race called the Retagians that had the eyes of a fish and gills for breathing underwater. They didn't have a nose but they had an extremely large mouth. They had two legs, but they also had a tail that could be used like a fin to propel themselves underwater. They had ten tentacles on each side of their torsos instead of arms. When they changed, they also became purple. However, instead of getting four new arms, they got forty new tentacles.

Finally, there were the Funglians. It was the same race of extraterrestrials that Namrips had seen in his dream. Now, because the Funglians are a fungus, they have no definite shape to describe. They can change their shape according to their desires. They are Beige with brown spots. These Funglians became completely brown. They became five times larger. Then, they all combined into one large blob. Then, it began to grow eyeballs all over on every side.

"Is this ethical?" Namrips asked.

"What do you mean?" Fiki asked.

"Turning living creatures into monsters – is it ethical?"

"We control them. They are soulless beasts."

Namrips squinted his eyes. "How do you know that they don't have souls?"

"We give them souls when we attach ourselves to them and use them as future lives."

Namrips took a breath. "What if that process kicks a soul out of the body?"

"When we clone them, we have technology that allows us to prevent the entry of any new souls."

Namrips scratched his head. "I don't know. Something about it feels strange to me. You're using human clones too."

Fiki smirked. He looked at Namrips, and then, he turned away to look at the monstrous creation. "They are all soulless beasts."

"You are allowed to do all of this on your own?"

"This particular job was given to me today after I got my new arms. There are other jobs that others are doing that might scare you even more than this."

Namrips raised his eyebrows. "Who said I was scared?"

"I did." Fiki didn't wait for a response. "Do you want to see the dead body animator work?"

"The dead body animator?"

Fiki chuckled under his breath as if he was trying to fight against his emotions. "Biki got that job. You can think of it as recycling what's no longer in use."

"So, what is it? Does it make zombies?"
Fiki looked at Namrips. "It makes dead bodies move as if they were still alive. You can use them like undead soldiers."

Namrips looked nervously over at the monstrous clones. He closed his eyes for a moment and took a deep breath. He opened his eyes again and said, "This is all very strange."

"The CRCs aren't going anywhere. Follow me. I'll show you."

"What are CRCs?"

"What we just created. CRC stands for Controlled Robotic Clones."

With astonishment written all over Namrips' face, he asked, "Why are they called robotic? They don't look robotic at all. They appear to be deformed monsters. You should call them CMCs for Controlled Monstrous Clones."

"Like I said, they are soulless beings. They are biological robots. They have organic tissue, but they are not living beings. Let's go."

Namrips followed Fiki into a long hallway. They went to another similar room. However, this time, they did not enter the room directly. They entered directly into the area protected by transparent walls; they could see into the room, but the dead people couldn't get to them.

When Namrips looked through the wall his jaw dropped open. There were millions and millions of dead people walking around as if in a daze. They never looked at anything in a way that indicated consciousness. They were all blank stares.

"Where did you get all the dead bodies to do this?" Namrips asked.

"Biki was given access to all of the dead humans who died when the gravity reversed," Fiki answered. "We were able to collect them after they were ejected into space. We didn't kill them. They were already dead. We're just making use of their dead bodies. In the same way, we were able to collect human guns that were ejected into space. Then, when we went to Earth to help save humans from death, we collected the dead bodies that were inside of the buildings as well."

Namrips shook his head in disbelief. "So, you have technology that animates dead bodies?"

"It's actually a branch of nanotechnology. We control the nano-bots. The nano-bots animate the body."

"I'm speechless. Why?" Namrips looked at Fiki in the eyes; it was hard to make eye contact with a being that had seven eyes.

"We have superior technology. However, Theadlians have way more numbers than we do. If we can match their numbers, we can win with our technology. We simply found a way to increase our numbers. We also have an army of robots. However, those are too expensive to make. So, we don't want to waste the robots that we have and be left without them. We need a good plan of action."

"So, wake up the dead and make a bunch of clone monsters! Sounds like a terrific plan!"

Fiki looked at the walking dead before them. "Yes. Yes, it is."

"I was being sarcastic, but it isn't a big deal."

Fiki looked at Namrips and almost let out a smile but fought it back. "It's just until we win the war, and then everything will go back to normal."

Three hours later, Namrips and Fiki were in their starfighters. Each starfighter was occupied by the pilot, and that was it. They could communicate through the radio. There were one hundred fighters in their group. They had all of the normal battle equipment inside of their cockpits with the exception that their guns were AR-15's instead of laser guns.

They flew towards the blockade. Their space fighters were cloaked so that the enemy could not see them. They formed five groups. There were twenty space fighters in the middle of the formation, twenty fighters flying approximately ten thousand kilometers above them, twenty at about the same distance below them, twenty to the right, and twenty to the left. Fiki and Namrips were in the middle group.

Those at the top fired their laser cannons first. Ships in the blockade began to explode. The Theadlian ships began directing all of their firepower in the direction of those at the top of the formation because, even though they couldn't see the Nemodians' starfighters, they could detect where the lasers had originated. However, the Nemodians had turned on their space-time bender. Therefore, all of the lasers that the Theadlians were firing in the direction of the Nemodians were redirected towards themselves and more of their ships exploded.

As they got closer, the Theadlians became desperate. They couldn't see the Nemodians, and therefore, they had no idea how many Nemodians were coming their way. They were determined to get revenge at all costs, and since they hadn't originated in the Milky Way, they were willing to destroy it too if it would help them get revenge.

The Theadlians opened an inter-dimensional portal that released Jeggolith. That hideous beast that dwelled in the indefinite realm and was never definitely present came out of the portal towards the Nemodians and Namrips. It was a strange sight to see something that was neither there, nor was it not there. It neither moved, nor did it remain still. When it was brought over to the dimension of definite being, it emitted light, and therefore, it could be seen by everyone.

Jeggolith was flying quickly in the direction of the Nemodians' starfighters. It was fifty thousand kilometers in diameter at the moment it was released. It seemed to have millions of arms projecting out of its elongated body. Its thousands of eyes seemed to look in every direction. It opened its mouth wide and was about to eat the Nemodians' space fleet.

Just as Fiki had told Namrips, Jeggolith emitted such a stench that it would have been unbearable. The only reason that they could not smell it was because they were inside of their starfighters that had pressurized cabins; nothing could enter their space fighters. If they could have smelt it, they would have begun vomiting relentlessly.

Fortunately, the Nemodians had already prepared a contingency plan for such an event. Just as the lasers were getting twisted around and shot back at the Theadlians, the same would now happen to Jeggolith. However, it happened a little differently due to the size difference.

The face of Jeggolith began to look like a concaved disk. It appeared as if its face was reversing its direction while the outer rim was continuing to move in the same direction. From Namrips' position, he interpreted this phenomenon to be Jeggolith turning inside out.

It became more evident what had just happened when Jeggolith's face came out of its butt. It was now moving in the reverse direction towards the Theadlians who had released the beast. This did not scare the Theadlians at all. They simply absorbed it back into the inter-dimensional portal. They immediately decided to do something that would be more effective. They redirected the portal to a location just outside of where the atmosphere of the Earth used to end before things had turned upside down. Then, they released Jeggolith upon the Earth.

The scene was terrifying. The creature swallowed the Earth. From the perspective of those watching the Earth from afar, the Earth disappeared as it entered Jeggolith's mouth. Flames shot out of its mouth immediately afterwards. From the perspective of those on Earth, the sky filled with an orange glow. If a spaceship was flying around close to the surface of the planet, the pilot would have seen a blanket of orange quickly fly across the sky and block out the sun. Once the sun was blocked out, the only light source would have been the orange glow from Jeggolith. The pilot would have seen flames dancing out of the Earth as time slowed down. For those on the outside, it took less than two seconds for the Earth to disappear and see flames come out of Jeggolith's mouth. However, for our hypothetical pilot, time would have slowed down. Notwithstanding, this slowing down of time would not have been a relativistic effect. When time dilation is due to relativistic effects, the person experiencing time does not notice any difference. Inside of Jeggolith, our hypothetical pilot would have seen time slow down. He or she would have seen the flames shoot out of the Earth in slow motion. The person would have seen his or her spaceship begin to melt. Such a person would have felt the flame melting his or her bones as said person began to scream a scream that would have been heard into eternity. This person would have been acutely aware of the process of shedding the body until our hypothetical pilot had completely entered into the hereafter – the *other world*, which we consider death. In the blink of an eye, the Earth was gone.

However, this wasn't the end of the damage done by Jeggolith. It continued in its path. It suddenly increased in size to ninety-three million miles long. It devoured the sun, and pitch black fell over the solar system. The only light source was the stars; the closest starlight came from Alpha-Centauri.

Chapter Nine

"If Jeggolith is allowed to continue, he'll destroy the entire Milky Way!" Fiki yelled over the radio. "Namrips, chase it down! The blue button with a red circle opens the portal to send it back to the other dimension."

"Got it," Namrips responded. Namrips used a wormhole to get within proximity. However, the beast had shrunk back down to an infinitesimal size. So the wormhole simply got him close to where the sun had been just a moment before. He was hoping that he would be able to see just a speck of light to indicate its position. He began using the computer to search for its position.

As the computer searched for Jeggolith, Namrips began to think about what was happening. Seriously disturbing questions were beginning to arise. For example: *if the Theadlians wanted to wipe out humans so they could take over the Earth, then why would they deliberately destroy the Earth and put the entire galaxy at risk?* These types of questions were plaguing Namrips' mind.

Meanwhile, Fiki continued to advance towards the blockade with the remaining starfighters. They began firing the crusher, which intensified gravity in a targeted area until objects became crushed by their own gravitational pull. Theadlian spaceships began imploding. It resembled the crushing of an aluminum can. The edges began to crumple slowly until the spaceship suddenly got smashed as if two hands were on each side pressing inwards. Once all of the Theadlian spaceships that were in the blockade were completely crushed, they passed through easily. They notified the Nemodian mother ship immediately. Then, they sent the large cargo ship, which quickly caught up with the position of the Nemodian starfighters.

When they arrived at the Theadlian mother ship, they forced an opening in the ship by bending space-time at the point of the door in such a way that it was ripped apart. Thousands of Theadlians flew out as that area of the ship depressurized. The cargo ship entered through the hole and landed there. A force field was placed over where the door had been, and the Nemodians pressurized the area. Then, the main door to the Nemodian cargo ship opened, and they released the CRCs and the dead.

The Theadlians had already sealed the area off. However, it wasn't very difficult for the Nemodians to destroy their doors. Once they had opened the doors, thousands upon thousands of dead bodies walked through the doors of the ship and attacked the Theadlians. Soon after that, the CRCs poured into the Theadlians' mother ship.

The Theadlians were shooting their lasers at the dead. One lost an arm; another lost its head. A laser blasted a hole in a dead body's chest. However, this didn't stop them. The one who lost an arm continued marching forwards. The one who lost its head only stopped long enough to pick its head off the ground and continued attacking. The dead body with a hole in its chest took a step back as if it had been stung by a bee and, then, continued walking. The only way to kill them was to completely destroy their bodies.

When the dead arrived to where the Theadlians were, they began biting them and tearing chunks out of their flesh. The Theadlians screamed in pain. They tried spitting on some of the dead bodies, but the dead couldn't feel any pain. Their saliva was successful in destroying an area of flesh though. This helped facilitate the destruction of the dead bodies, but it was a prolonged process. Each dead body was killing between ten to twenty Theadlians before the Theadlians could dismember the zombie.

Whereas the zombies were like mindless beasts, the CRCs showed signs of intelligence. They came roaring past the zombies. When the Theadlians shot at them, they didn't feel any pain. They bled normal blood for their species that they had come from, but they didn't die. They were fast and strong.

They plucked Theadlians up by the hundreds shredding their bodies into little pieces with their claws. The poison on the Theadlian's skin didn't seem to affect the zombies or the CRCs. Therefore, the CRCs could pick the Theadlians up and rip their bodies into little pieces without any problem. Each CRC killed hundreds of Theadlians before being killed. The only question: Could they kill one trillion like this?

Meanwhile, Namrips was still searching for Jeggolith. When the computer identified the beast's position, it had made a circle and was heading toward Namrips. Jeggolith quickly increased in size. Namrips went in reverse as quickly as possible. Namrips' computer showed a distance for Jeggolith. The distance was closing in quicker than the speed of light, and as confirmation of this, the computer was showing a velocity of four hundred thousand kilometers per second. Because of this, Namrips knew that he had to go through wormholes in order to escape the beast.

At one point, Jeggolith's mouth had almost surrounded his spaceship when he hit another wormhole just narrowly escaping the jaws of death. This continued to happen for an extended period of time. It happened for so long, in fact, that Namrips had drifted unwittingly more than forty-nine light years away from Earth's position (before it had been destroyed). This was possible because of how large some of the wormholes had to be to escape the beast. However, because he had used so many wormholes to go so far, his energy core was running low.

    A red light began shining on his control panel warning him that his spaceship would stop working shortly. Jeggolith had shrunk down in size. Now it was growing rapidly again. It grew rapidly until its mouth was touching Namrips' spaceship. The metal set on fire. His ship was going to be lost. The beast moved into position; Namrips' spaceship was inside of its mouth.

    Namrips turned his oxygen tank on that was attached to his spacesuit. Then, he used the last of his energy to open up a portal to the other dimension. This meant that he was going to continue floating through space without energy. Jeggolith was instantly absorbed, but his spaceship had already been set on fire in the process. Namrips hit the eject button and was catapulted into the abyss of space.

    He was flying through space at a high velocity. There was a nearby star. He had no idea how much radiation he was getting. He didn't know what star he was looking at. Well, he really wasn't looking at the star; he was spinning, so he would see the star three times every second – not really enough time to truly look at it.

    Imagine flying through space all alone with just a spacesuit, an AR-15 strapped to you, and a small supply of oxygen. This was death before death. It wasn't like there was a highway with lots of people who could potentially save his life. If a planet was nearby, and he somehow arrived at the planet before his oxygen ran out, the atmosphere would destroy him before his body was crushed against the rocky surface of the planet. Or perhaps, it would be a gas planet, and he would be crushed by the pressure of the gas as he plummeted to certain death. It really didn't matter; just about any scenario would result in his death.

There was a level of panic that Namrips wanted to have. His mind was racing with thoughts of his dead father. Namrips had been close to death many times in his life. However, situations like this absolutely terrified him. Loneliness was one of the greatest pains he had ever suffered. He would rather have died being tortured by an enemy than die like this. This was loneliness personified. He was looking into the depths of loneliness. Earth had already been destroyed, and here he was flying away towards a meaningless death. Who would remember Namrips? Who would talk about how Namrips had died flying in space? The human race was on the brink of being forgotten, and certainly, no one would ever tell Namrips' story.

He remembered the day that he became an orphan. He had cried so many tears that he could have filled the ocean - or so he thought. He had felt like his heart would explode. He had loved his father. Now, he would die an orphan, and he saw his father's face; he always saw his father's face when he faced death. *This is how humanity will go extinct*, he thought.

    Namrips started screaming with all his strength as if he was trying to empty his lungs of all contents. He clenched his fists and closed his eyes. Some of his veins on his neck were bulging out. Tears were streaming down his face, and snot was coming out of his nose. He was crying so hard that he began to hiccup. His mind was frantic. He felt like he was going to go clinically insane, but it didn't matter since no one would ever know.

Chapter Ten

While Namrips was flying through space, Fiki was overseeing the annihilation of the Theadlians. The zombie army had been destroyed. However, the zombies had killed millions of Theadlians before they were able to destroy all of the zombies. Then, the CRCs were even more difficult to fight.

This had caused the Theadlians to send out a distress call as the Nemodians had predicted. The Theadlians were determined to not lose their mother ship. Therefore, the rest of the fleet had left the blockade and entered the mother ship. They got off their individual ships and reinforced the numbers of those who were fighting against the CRCs.

What had started off as a fleet of one trillion Theadlians grew to ten trillion Theadlians after having received nine trillion reinforcements from one of their planets. This is what the Nemodians wanted because it brought their enemy to one single place where they could be destroyed together. The Nemodians jammed the Theadlians' communications as soon as they had received these reinforcements.

    The CRCs that had been created from Nemodian clones, Merkian clones, and human clones ripped billions of Theadlians into little pieces. The floor had turned into a green swimming pool of Theadlian blood with body parts floating on the surface. If a human had stepped inside of the Theadlian spaceship at that moment, he would have been thigh deep in Theadlian blood. However, that isn't what finished off the Theadlians. It was the CRC that had been formed from the Funglians that destroyed the rest of the Theadlian fleet.

    The legless, armless brown blob rolled off the Nemodian spaceship and into the Theadlian spaceship. It quickly began absorbing whatever it came into contact with. Then, it increased in size and expanded. Because so many Theadlians' blood was on the floor by the time this beast was released, it quickly grew in size until it arrived to the battle lines. It absorbed everything in its path; that included the other CRCs. Whenever it absorbed a living creature, it was suffocated and digested quickly. When the Theadlians shot lasers at it, the area that was shot would get destroyed, but it would also be quickly repaired and seemed to do no more damage than an ant bite would do to a human. The blob would then proceed to absorb and kill more Theadlians.

When all of the Theadlians in the their fleet had been completely killed off, the Nemodians hacked into the computers on the Theadlian ship and controlled it from the outside. "The Theadlians have been neutralized," Fiki said over the radio. "We have control of their mother ship."

"Good work," the voice of General Natalsauke said. He was the highest ranking general in the Nemodian army. "General Etifale will take the Theadlian mother ship. He is in charge of destroying the Theadlians on their planets. Now that we know what the Theadlians' weaknesses are, you can go on to more important work. General Etifale can easily kill all of the Theadlians with the CRCs. He will take the ship to the Theadlians with our ships cloaked. They will send out a victory message to the Theadlians as if it is coming from their mother ship and, therefore, from their own kind. We will employ holograms when the mother ship lands that make it appear that the Theadlians are emerging victoriously. Then, the Theadlian holograms will shoot at the Theadlians, and lasers will be fired from the cloaked ships. While they are in a panic not understanding what is happening, we will open their mother ship and release CRCs from the back. We will easily destroy them and take over all of their planets."

"Do you want me to go and assist him with this mission?"

General Natalsauke shook his head. "No. I want you to kill all of the remaining humans."

"What about their clones?" Fiki inquired. He was specifically thinking about how Namrips had chosen a human clone for his next life. "Some of the humans chose to return as humans instead of Nemodians."

"The clones are fine. We control what they will know. Their following life will be as Nemodians. Just make sure you kill all humans who were born on earth."

"What are we going to do about the fact that the Earth has been destroyed? The Theadlians released Jeggolith, and it destroyed Earth."

"We will search for a new planet and abandon this area. The Theadlians screwed it up for us."

"What about some of the other planets nearby?" Fiki was asking questions because he didn't like having simple jobs. He was trying to see if he could expand his duties farther than just killing the rest of the humans.

"Are you referring to Mars? Without the sun we can't use any of the planets in this solar system."

"No. I am talking about the planet known as Ross 128-b." If Fiki could help out with the battle going on there, he would be delighted.

"We are looking at all possibilities. General Timalog still hasn't secured the area. There is also a planet called Ademud that is in the Andromeda Galaxy that is fairly attractive to us."

Meanwhile, Namrips continued flying though space at a high velocity. He was unsure if he had fallen asleep or if he had stayed awake the entire time. How long would his oxygen last? How long had he been spinning through space like this?

Since he hadn't had any discernable dreams yet, he couldn't be sure if he had slept or not. All he knew was that he was staring into the blackness of space without any apparent hope of surviving. Then, he saw a bridge. *Ah*, it was a dream. *Let it come*, he thought to himself. It would be more interesting than watching the pitch-black canvas of space until he died. At least he could see something interesting before meeting his maker – or running to his clone before Jeggolith got to him.

There was a very wide river. The bridge that he had seen went over this river. The other side of the bridge had a forest. The side of the bridge that Namrips stood on had a large desert. It was a very strange sight, indeed, to see a desert end at a river. The water should have guaranteed life. It was as if his dream had cast reality aside in order to create a strange metaphor. Namrips was uncertain if his subconscious was capable of creating metaphors, but that was the only explanation he could think of as to why such a large river with such a strong current could be between a desert and a forest.

Namrips looked back at the desert and its lifeless sand dunes. There weren't even cacti like you might see in some American deserts. This was more like the Sahara. There were skeletons scattered across the sand. He could see steam raising into the air from the scorching ground.

Then, he turned and looked at the beautiful trees with large white fluffy clouds above them. There was a woman standing there. She had a child with her, and she was holding his hand. He was about five years old. The child had blond hair and reminded him of himself when he was that age.

Namrips turned around again. He saw the skeletons standing up. They began to dance around. They weren't the skeletons of human beings, but they looked very similar. They were larger than humans but had two arms and two legs. They were dancing and moving in Namrips' direction. Therefore, he decided to walk over the bridge to avoid a meeting with the skeletons.

The bridge was one of those bridges that you might see in a movie. It had rope on both sides, and the bridge itself was made up of wooden boards. When Namrips had made it half way across, the woman said, "My name is Kimberly," and they disappeared. Then, it began to rain.

Namrips was suddenly standing in the middle of the forest as it poured down rain. Water came up to his waist. Monkeys were in the trees taunting him. The water became blood, and the sky became red.

The trees became thirty-foot-tall monsters with tentacles. They reached out for Namrips. He knew it was a dream, and therefore, he wasn't afraid, but for some reason, he began to cry. He felt loneliness in the depths of his soul, and he knew that he was flying through space about to die alone.

He woke up with tears in his eyes. He screamed. No one could hear him; he knew that. No one would ever hear him again; he knew that too. That was part of the problem. So, on he went, flying though space alone – crying his heart out.

After about an hour of spinning, there was an object that he thought might be a spaceship, and it was coming up quickly. If there was one thing that Namrips knew, it was that it was neither a Nemodian spaceship, nor was it a Theadlian spaceship. He didn't recognize it at all. He only hoped that they would be friendly.

Namrips was accepted on board. When he entered a chamber, it immediately filled up with water. His spacesuit protected him, and his supply of oxygen allowed him to continue to breathe. Then, he was allowed to pass into the spaceship. He was met by a race of extraterrestrials that he had seen before. They were one of the three non-human extraterrestrial races that they had converted into monsters. They were called Retagians.

They had the eyes of a fish and gills for breathing underwater. Their skin was between blue and gray. They had no nose. Their mouths were very large. They had two legs, but they also had a tail that could be used like a fin to propel themselves underwater. They had ten tentacles on each side of their torsos instead of arms. They didn't have any hair, and their ears were like small holes on each side of their head.

Namrips was immediately met and escorted by two Retagians that he interpreted to be soldiers. They led him down a long hallway. There was no need for a gravity simulator. The water filled the ship. They swam along the hallway instead of walking. They entered a large room. There was a large group of Retagians there looking at Namrips.

"My, my, my! What do we have here?" One of them said. When he spoke, his lips didn't move with the words that Namrips was hearing. Namrips immediately realized that his translator in his ear was giving him an audible interpretation; the Retagians clearly didn't speak English. "A human dressed in Nemodian equipment. Do you like what they did to your planet?"

"What they did?" Namrips answered. "You mean what the Theadlians did."

The alien laughed. "Is that what they told you? Humans are so gullible."

"Listen. I don't know where you're getting your information from, but the Theadlians wanted to destroy humans so they could inhabit the Earth. Theadlians breathe oxygen like us."

He roared with laughter and slapped his leg at this. "Theadlians don't breathe oxygen. Nemodians breathe oxygen."

Namrips' eyes were bulging out of their sockets at this revelation. "Are you sure?"

"I'm positive. Listen. I know this is hard for you to accept. But think about it. The Theadlians don't even have an antigravity ray. The Theadlians were trying to kill Nemodians – not humans. Did you notice that the Theadlians never attacked Earth? Just after everything turned upside down, who showed up to save the day? The Nemodians have a long history of causing problems on other planets. Our intelligence tells us that the Nemodians had gone to the Theadlians' planet where they tested their antigravity ray. They ended up destroying their planet. The survivors swore to kill off all of the Nemodians. They followed them to Earth. Then, the Nemodians turned your planet upside down. The Nemodians apparently decided to kill two birds with one stone. They wanted your planet anyway. So, they hit it with the antigravity ray and blamed the Theadlians so humans would help them fight their war. I bet you, now that Earth no longer exists, they will kill off all of the remaining humans."

Namrips took a gulp of oxygen and shut his eyes for a moment. Then, he opened his eyes and spoke. "How can I know that you're not lying to me?"

"I don't care if you believe me or not. You can go back and get killed. It won't affect me. Tell me something. Did they give you a personal guide that has been giving you secrets that humans aren't supposed to know? Did they offer to connect you to a new body so you can live a second life cycle after this one?"

Namrips' face was turning red. "Fiki is my friend."

"He isn't your friend. It's a trick. He makes you feel like you are special by giving you secrets. Everyone knows that the Nemodians have that technology. We have that technology too. Most advanced intelligent species that are capable of interstellar travel have that technology. It isn't a secret. I bet he tried to get you to accept a Nemodian body. I could give you a Retagian body too."

"What are you – psychic?"

The fish-like alien laughed again. "I just know how the Nemodians operate. I've had to deal with their victims too often. They also took some of our people and cloned our race. So we aren't on very good terms with the Nemodians."

Namrips thought back to the monsters they had created using the clones. "If what you're telling me is true, what am I supposed to do now?"

"I don't care what you do. I don't have any reason to help the human race. I'm just telling you the truth."

"But I can't go back to Earth. Where are you going to take me?"

He thought for a moment; then he answered, "If you want to take your chances with the Nemodians, I can take you there. If you want to go to a planet that has oxygen, I know of a place where the Nemodians haven't gone yet. It's a dangerous planet, but it could be an opportunity for you to start over again. It's called Ademud."

Namrips sighed deeply. "Can you at least tell me where you got your information from? I need more information to help me make the right decision."

"I can introduce you to the Nemodian who gave me the information."

"I thought you hated the Nemodians. Why do you have a Nemodian here?"

His expression lit up. "Ah, but this Nemodian is very different from the others! Come with me." He swam away towards another hallway, and Namrips followed him. "I am King Thengstur by the way."

"I'm Namrips." They swam down the hallway for about three minutes. Then a door on the right side of the hallway slid open, and they entered a circular room. King Thengstur entered first followed by Namrips and twelve other Retagians.

"Call Nogar," Thengstur said. They waited for about twenty-one minutes. Namrips was growing impatient thinking that nothing was going to happen.

However, Thengstur and the other Retagians seemed to be perfectly content with waiting. It was as if they had nothing better to do than to wait. There was no conversation. They simply floated there in the water. Namrips couldn't see their eyes very well because he was looking at them through the water, but he got the feeling that they had closed their eyes and had gone to sleep. Well, it was better than waiting for death floating alone through space. So, he decided to close his eyes. He tried to remember the image that the Nemodians had in their temple.

Suddenly, a Nemodian appeared in front of them. It was a hologram. "Nogar, it's good to see you," Thengstur said.

"May we hope that it is always so," Nogar responded.

"As you can see, I have a human here. His name is Namrips. He was deceived by the Nemodians. They convinced him that the Theadlians had an antigravity ray that was used to destroy his planet."

"No," Namrips interjected. "Jeggolith destroyed my planet. The antigravity ray simply turned our world upside down and killed millions of people around the world."

"Jeggolith is an inter-dimensional creature," Nogar responded. "I doubt that it destroyed your planet. It can't touch our realm."

"I saw it with my own eyes. The Theadlians opened a portal and released it. I had to send it back to its realm. That's how I lost my ship and ended up floating through space until these guys here saved my life."

Nogar nodded his head. "That may be so, but I can promise you that the Theadlians didn't use an antigravity ray on Earth."

"How can you promise that?"

Nogar chuckled with a smile on his face. This was more emotion from one Nemodian than he could remember ever seeing before. "Because I invented the antigravity ray. The Theadlians don't have an antigravity ray. I invented the only one that has ever existed. If I had known how my race was going to use it, I wouldn't have invented it."

Namrips nodded with understanding. "I see. So you rebelled against them when you realized how they were going to use it."

"No. I was testing it out on planets that they told me were barren of life. We tested it on Thead. The Theadlians attacked, and I realized that General Fiki had intentionally lied and withheld that information. That's when I rebelled against them. Then, they arrested me."

Namrips jaw dropped open. "General Fiki?"

"Yes. Did you meet him?"

Namrips put his right hand over his heart as if hurt. "He's my best friend."

"No, he isn't." Namrips again saw true raw emotion in the eyes of a Nemodian. Even the fact that he had seven eyes couldn't hide the tears that he had at the corners of his eyes. If anything, it made his suffering all the more obvious.

"Why would you say that?" Namrips asked.

"He thinks he can use you. You might be his best friend, and I wouldn't doubt that, but he isn't YOUR friend at all. He doesn't care if you live or die. He destroyed Thead. He is the reason the Theadlians want revenge against Nemodians. He is the reason this war is happening. Then, he took my invention and dragged humans into the fight. Do you wanna know how you can tell if Fiki is lying?"

"How?"

"His lips are moving. That is the sad reality. You can't trust anything he says."

Namrips looked up at the ceiling with tears of his own forming. "So, what he taught me about the next life is a lie too?"

"I don't know what he taught you. You mentioned Jeggolith. That terrible beast exists. So, that much is true."

Namrips took a deep breath and exhaled dramatically. "Is it better to go through the tunnel of light, or should I go to my new body?"

"I don't know the answer to your question. The teaching of staying here and not going through the tunnel is definitely something that all Nemodians are taught. However, I've had my doubts about that."

Namrips smiled with pain in his eyes. "Thank you for being honest with me."

"Namrips." A tear was rolling down one of Nogar's cheeks.

"That's my name," he whispered under his breath. "I think."

"Sometimes, we deceive ourselves. We believe our own lies. We believe that we are better than we really are. We don't want to say that we don't know the answer to questions that frighten us. Not all lies come from malevolence."

"May I ask you another question? It's a little personal."

Nogar wiped away his tears. "Sure."

"You said that they arrested you. How did you escape?"

"I didn't escape. I was rescued. A Juliver by the name of Keejam came through a portal into my cell and rescued me."

"I suppose I can assume that Juliver is another extraterrestrial race."

Nogar laughed. He knew that humans knew very little about life beyond Earth. "You would be correct in your assumption. They live on planet Ross 128-b. In fact, I'm here with them right now. We are fighting a war with the Nemodians. I'm the only Nemodian that is fighting against the Nemodians."

Namrips looked away for a moment. There was a question that had been bothering him, and perhaps, he could get the answer now. "Where do the Nemodians come from?"

"What do you mean?"

"What planet do you originate from?"

"I don't think you want to know the answer to your question."

"If I didn't want to know the answer, I wouldn't have asked it."

"Don't forget that humans and Nemodians both sometimes lie to themselves. I have to go. I hope we can meet later." Nogar disappeared. Namrips couldn't understand why he couldn't answer his final question. It seemed like a simple question to Namrips. What did lying to oneself have to do with what planet the Nemodians came from?

Namrips decided that he would trust Nogar for now. He decided that he would go to Ademud and see if he could start a new life there since the planet had oxygen. Thengstur was a bit of an explorer and had wanted to look at the area, so he was more than willing to take Namrips there.

The Retagians filled Namrips' oxygen tank and gave him nutrients through a tube that was in his spacesuit. Then, they allowed him to go to their library while he waited to land on Ademud. The books were not made of paper like human books. They weren't like e-books either. The *books* were telepathic messages sent directly to the mind so that the *reader* experienced everything. Fiction and non-fiction were done this way. It was a technology that he hadn't seen employed by the Nemodians.

To use their *books*, Namrips sat down in front of a machine and closed his eyes. Telepathic images passed into his mind giving him options about what he wanted to *read*. When he heard the words, "*Keejam invents helmet of infinite knowledge*," he knew that he had found what he wanted to *read*. He remembered hearing Nogar mention the name *Keejam*. It had been presented in the nonfiction section. Then, he began to hear words while seeing the corresponding images in his mind.

****

There is a planet that is approximately eleven light years from Earth called Ross 128-b. There is a race of extraterrestrials that live there called the Julivers. They live in peace with another extraterrestrial race called the Nomedhecks.

Julivers have dark yellow skin. They are short and fat; their average height is approximately five feet. They have no hair. They have two black eyes. Their noses are not well defined, but they do have a large nostril that they use for breathing. Their mouths are very wide. It is clearly evident that they are vegetarians, for their teeth are blunt. Their ears are large and floppy like a dog might have. They have seven fingers and seven toes.

Their clothes are as creative as their buildings. They have all sorts of designs and color combinations. No two Julivers wear the same thing. They love different forms of art. This is evident from their clothes, their behavior, and their architecture.

There was a certain Juliver that had already lived many years; his name was Keejam. He was seventy years old by Earth's standards. However, one year on Ross 128-b is almost ten days long; therefore, seventy years is about 2,590 years. Keejam was 2,600 years old on his planet.

The planet is also tidally locked. Keejam lived in an area where the sun was always shining. Where Keejam lived, the temperature typically fluctuated between twenty-four and twenty-seven degrees Celsius (75.2-80.6 degrees Fahrenheit).

"I think that I've found out how to invent a helmet of infinite knowledge," Keejam told his friend, Suvone.

"That's impossible," Suvone answered immediately.

"No, it's not. It is very real."

"Do you even understand what you are saying? Do you know what is implied by infinite knowledge?"

"I know that it sounds crazy, but all information is contained within the quantum realm. I know how to build a helmet that could access that information and show it to you on command. This will be a helmet of infinite knowledge not infinite intelligence. You still have to interpret the information."

"I think that you are in over your head."

"I knew that I shouldn't have told you! Get out of my house!"

"Are you going to throw away one hundred years of friendship because of a stupid idea? Friends are supposed to be honest with their friends if they are doing something stupid."

"Friends are supposed to support each other! You make fun of everything that I do. You have never been a true friend, and I'm tired of it. Get out of my house!"

"It's not my fault that your ideas are always so stupid! I'm leaving. And don't ever ask me to come back because I won't." A section of the wall disappeared, and Suvone walked outside.

"Well, good riddance to bad rubbish!" Keejam exclaimed, and the section of the wall reappeared. "How dare he insult me like that!"

Keejam began to work on his invention constantly. He did not sleep for the first year (ten Earth days), but he did take breaks to eat a delicious salad. When he finally decided to sleep, it wasn't very much. It took him approximately ten years to finish building the helmet of infinite knowledge.

After he finished it, he put the helmet on his head. "Show me the closest alien intelligent life," he said.

He immediately saw a creature. Its skin was gray and scaly like a fish. It had four arms on its torso and tentacles like a squid instead of legs. Its eyes resembled the eyes of a fish. It had no nose, but it did have gills on its neck. It had a very large mouth and wide jaw. "This is a Nomedheck," a robotic voice explained. "They live on your planet in the ocean. Most Julivers do not know about their existence, but they sometimes make themselves known to a Juliver. They protect the Julivers from exterior threats, but they also see themselves as superior to Julivers."

Then, he saw a human. "This is a human. They live on a planet eleven light years away. They are intelligent, but they have not developed as much as Julivers. Their star is much hotter than Ross 128. Therefore, one year takes much longer to complete since they have to be farther from the star to maintain livable temperatures. Their planet spins whereas your planet doesn't. Therefore, they do not have constant light like Julivers have. They experience light and darkness in cycles. They call each cycle of light and darkness a day."

"Show me the future of my planet," Keejam said. After having watched his planet's future, he began to cry uncontrollably. He put the helmet on his desk and walked outside crying. He looked at the buildings. He saw all of the wonderful designs. There was one building that looked like a long snake that turned around in circles. There was another building that was in the shape of a pyramid. There was another building that was in the shape of the letter, 'U'. Every single animal on their planet was depicted in the shape of their buildings.

He continued walking down the street with tears in his eyes. The building that was in the shape of a pyramid was across the street. There was another building that had the shape of a pyramid at the base on the side of the street where he was standing. However, this building turned into a spiral at the top. It looked like the double helix that human DNA has. The top of this double helix turned into the head of two snakes.

    He walked inside. There was a large group of people standing around listening to poets at the center. There was a poet standing at the center of the crowd just beginning to recite her poem. The words of the poem were as follows:

> *"Death is a long, wide river.*
> *Inside, you start to shiver.*
> *At the bottom, it burns you.*
> *Your heart will do what worms do.*
> *Revealed are deeds that are true.*
> *Your skin peels and blood freezes.*
> *Eyes water and nose sneezes.*
> *Ghosts blow gently like breezes.*
> *Dead men do what he pleases.*
> *He is frightful, lives in fog.*
> *He hunts you with head of dog.*
> *You run quickly into bog.*
> *Panicking you trip on log.*
> *Eating your flesh is the hog.*
> *Upon the river, fog plays.*

> *It becomes infinite days.*
> *With us, the skeleton stays.*
> *In terror, the righteous prays.*
> *In the battle, their blood sprays.*
> *Storms come, and the heavens gray.*
> *The river is still freezing*
> *As the dead world is spinning.*
> *We sleep like the dead dreaming.*
> *Evil numbs hearts from feeling.*
> *Not knowing we go screaming.*
> *The poisoned waters stealing*
> *While Supreme River healing."*

Keejam couldn't bear anymore. He ran back out to the street. One block down was his house. Keejam ran back inside. He put the helmet back on. "How can the destruction be avoided?" He asked. After this, Keejam disappeared. All of his friends searched for him, but they couldn't find him anywhere. The police searched for him, and they couldn't find him either. They only found a letter that said the following, *"The destruction of our cities is coming close. It is almost unstoppable. Do not look for me. You will never find me. I have gone to seek help from the only ones that might be able to save us."*

Chapter Eleven

Nogar sat silently in his cell. There was a bed, but he was sitting on the floor with his legs crossed. His six hands were together in a praying position. The bed had black sheets covering it, and they were neatly tucked and pulled tight. The rest of the room was dark and empty. There was only a dim light that entered through a window that was on the ceiling twenty-eight feet above.

Suddenly, a blue circle emitting a soft light began to form to Nogar's left. He opened his eyes having sensed something strange. He could hear a soft crackle as a portal was being opened. He sat silently wondering who would be on the other side of this portal.

Keejam came through as soon as the portal was done forming. Nogar had never seen a Juliver before. He took notice that the entity before him seemed peaceful. His eyes were full of knowledge.

"My name is Keejam," the yellow-skinned entity whispered. "I know who you are and that you are kept here due to an injustice."

"How do you know me?" Nogar asked.

"There will be a time for explanations, but we need to get you out of here before we are discovered. Follow me through this portal, but first, put this mask on so that you can breathe." Keejam was already wearing a mask of his own, and Nogar obeyed. Then, he followed Keejam through the portal.

They stepped into a shallow pond, and the portal closed behind them. It was about two inches deep. "Okay," Keejam said in his normal voice, "I can explain a little more here. I invented a helmet of infinite knowledge. This helmet allows me to know what is going to happen based on the decisions currently being made."

"Interesting," Nogar replied immediately. "You accessed the quantum realm."

"Yes," he answered happily. "You really are the smartest creature in the universe, aren't you?"

"I doubt it."

"Very good." Keejam smirked. "You are humble. Therefore, you are trustworthy. You are right. You aren't the smartest. The Funglians are the smartest, but you are a close second. I have brought you to planet Fungus where the Funglians dwell. This planet is covered in water. In some places, the ocean is very deep, but we are standing in an area where it is shallow. There isn't any dry land anywhere."

Nogar nodded. "And I assume that these Funglians can help us in some way."

Keejam smiled. "They will appear here any moment coming out of the water. They are psychic beings. They probably saw our coming before we left your prison. Your people, the Nemodians, will destroy my planet soon. They are trying to take over the galaxy and be the only race. They want to eliminate the diversity of life. They see themselves as superior. I'm very selfish in this, you see. I only want to save my planet and my people. You are the key."

"And you know that the Funglians will help you because of the existential threat posed by Nemodians. You know that I'll help you because I want my freedom."

Keejam laughed heartily. "No, my child. I know that you will help because you don't have a selfish bone in your body."

"That's very kind of you to say," Nogar said. Just then, Funglians began to emerge from the water. The Funglians looked like huge blobs. As this fungus had evolved over centuries on this planet, a central intellect (or brain) developed; it was surrounded and protected by the outer layer of fungus. The central intellect gained control over the fungus cells that surrounded it, and they could move around and change forms. The brain developed eyes over the course of their lives. Whereas humans develop our eyes in the womb before birth, they developed them as their lives were being played out. So, some of these blobs that surrounded Keejam and

Nogar had five eyes, some had three, others had six, seven, eight, nine, or any other number of eyes.

When they saw the form of Keejam, some of them decided to try to imitate his shape. Others tried to take the form of Nogar, but the majority of them continued looking like blobs. However, instead of yellow or blue skin, they had beige skin with brown spots. They drew close to Keejam and Nogar, and they communicated with them telepathically.

"We know why you have come," one of them said.

"Will you help me?" Keejam replied verbally. They couldn't hear too well, but they knew what he said because they felt the vibrations of his mind.

"The power is already within your grasp."

"How so?" Nogar asked.

"There is a powerful machine on Ademud as Keejam already knows. Namrips and Kimberly need to reach that machine. This will not guarantee victory, but if victory is to be had, that is the path to have it. The machine uses quantum energy. The current user kills to obtain that energy, but we will supply the energy necessary through mediation."

Nogar shook his head. "I don't understand why y'all don't just build a machine and give it to us. You are obviously smart enough to do it."

"So smart you are," they replied, "but you have so much to learn yet. Of course, we can create the technology it uses, but we cannot create the journey that Namrips and Kimberly need to pass through. There is more going on than the Nemodian threat, and neither of you are aware of it. You will need Namrips, Kimberly, Erif, and those that are with them."

Keejam's eyes just about popped out of his head with this revelation. "There is more happening than Nemodians destroying everything?"

"So smart, yet so narrow minded, Keejam," they replied. "You built a helmet to know all, but you see only that which you ask it. You would destroy the Nemodians and let the fate of the galaxy fall into worse darkness that stands at the door. This journey will not end with fighting Nemodians. Keejam, use your helmet to identify the location of Namrips and Kimberly as soon as they are together on Ademud. Open a portal so that you can use quantum entanglement to be ever present with them through their journey. Then, close the portal. Wait and pray that they make it to the machine because that is the only path to keep peace in the galaxy."

Chapter Twelve
Kimberly
One Month Before Gravity Reverses On Earth

In order to understand the events that were to come, we need to meet Kimberly, who was already on Planet Ademud long before Namrips went there. Kimberly had been saved from the destruction of the Earth because she was taken from Earth one month before the Nemodians reversed its gravity.

Kimberly was thirty years old, and she looked a bit like *Alyson Hannigan* in *Buffy the Vampire Slayer*. She had red hair, green eyes, and glasses. Her nerdiness went farther than just her look. Most men are good at seeing beauty concealed behind a nerdy look and a pair of glasses. Kimberly was so nerdy that even the nerds had a hard time relating to her.

She could draw a detailed picture of something after simply glancing at it. She had scared her teacher one day when she was in the fifth grade. Her teacher had called each student up individually to show them their grade. The teacher knew that if she only called up the students who had bad grades,

the students would realize who had failed.
Therefore, she had called everyone up regardless of how good their grade was. When Kimberly had gone up, she noticed that the teacher had left her driver license and social security card sitting out; the teacher had been busy trying to adopt a child, so she had brought the documents to work that day. Kimberly had gone back to her seat. Then she had said, "Mrs. Haley, your social security number is a very interesting number." Then Kimberly had proceeded to recite the number. Needless to say, Mrs. Haley almost lost her mind.

    This had contributed to some difficult behaviors. First, it was what had given her a love for knowledge. She could read a five-hundred-page book in three hours if no one disturbed her. While other children were out playing, she was inside reading or trying to take her computer apart. She had built her first video game by the age of eleven years old.

    Second, her room was so orderly, that people literally thought she had gone insane. If an interested man made it all the way to her room for a visit, he immediately felt like he had entered the *twilight zone*. One wall had the bed placed snuggly against it. The other three walls had huge bookshelves that were full of books from her ceiling down to the floor. There was only a space for the door and the closet. When someone entered her room through the door, the bed was against the wall to the left. The closet was immediately to the right (the closet had a sliding door).

On the wall to the right, one would have seen what Kimberly called information books. This included encyclopedias, dictionaries, thesauruses, computer manuals, mathematic books, science books, anatomy books, and history books in that order. Each section was alphabetized first by name, then by author name, then by publisher.

On the wall with the door (the door was at the corner next to the closet), there was a philosophy section. She had the works of *Socrates, Plato, Aristotle, René Descartes, Spinoza, Leibniz, Locke, Berkeley, Hume, Kant, Hegel, Kierkegaard, Nietzsche, Karl Marx, the Bible, the Quran, the Vedas* (Hindu scriptures), and many *Buddhist Sutras*. The most amazing aspect of this was that she could tell you who you were reading from and what page you were reading from if you cited a passage to her.

Across the room from the door, she had a section of fiction. You could find classical works such as *Don Quixote, Romeo and Juliet, Hamlet, Macbeth, Beowulf, the Iliad, the Odyssey, 1984, Frankenstein, Animal Farm, Of Mice and Men, The Scarlet Letter, Lord of the Flies, The Count of Monte Cristo, Dracula, Brave New World, Moby Dick, Oliver Twist, and The Strange Case of Dr. Jekyll and Mr. Hyde* to name a few. One should not imagine that just because we haven't mentioned a piece of classical literature, she didn't have it on her shelf. If we mention every book she owned, we would fill several pages. However, it is also worth mentioning that she also had some modern books on her wall such as *A Game of Thrones, It, The Talisman, Black House, all of the Dark Tower series, and Lord of the Rings*. Everything was in alphabetical order.

    Her desk was in the center of the room. Everything was evenly spaced. Her pencil was always three inches to the right of a stack of blank paper, and it was flush with the top of the paper. An eraser was placed exactly three inches to the left of this paper, and it was flush with the bottom instead of the top. One centimeter to the right of this, there was a pencil case where she put pencils and pens that were not currently in use. She always put her laptop under the desk when she went to sleep or left the room.

    This was not the most worrisome behavior, but for most normal men with normal intelligence, it was already too much. Therefore, seeing the posters of various anatomies all over the ceiling and wall above her bed was where it became a visit to the *twilight zone*. The first poster one would see over her bed was a human skeleton with one of human muscles next to it. Next to that, there was another of human organs like the stomach, heart, and lungs. However, once one studied the room a little longer and looked at the ceiling, that person would see posters of dissected frogs, pigs, dogs, cats, horses, snakes, deer, octopi, and a fascinating one of a chimpanzee that showed the similarities to human anatomy.

Third, she was very blunt with people. If she deduced a lie, she would immediately call the person a liar. This was probably what had contributed, more than anything, to the fact that guys did not want to go out with her. Unfortunately for Kimberly, she was so good at calling guys on their BS that she drove them all away.

However, in spite of all this, it would be hard to imagine that she would be chosen to go on an adventure to an unknown world. She knew nothing about survival. She would almost faint if she got the smallest little cut on her arm. Nevertheless, she was destined to meet Namrips on Planet Ademud, which is somewhere deep within the galaxy, Andromeda.

One day, she got a call from a potential employer who wanted her to reconfigure all of their computers. It was a large multimillion-dollar company. The company had recently had a failure due to a virus that had left the company paralyzed; they needed to get their computers up and running as fast as possible.

She left her home in Phoenix, Arizona at about five o'clock that morning headed towards Texas on a large interstate called I-10. Late that night, she was still driving through New Mexico. She was closing in on a city called El Paso, Texas when her life changed forever.

Her car was the only one on the interstate at the moment. Suddenly, she saw a large light in the sky descending down on her vehicle. As it drew closer, she realized that it was a UFO. She felt the impulse to stop her car and watch to see what happened.

The UFO stopped over her car and hovered there for a moment. She got out of her car and looked up at it. Suddenly, she disappeared.

Kimberly found herself in a new place. She was surrounded by twelve four-foot-tall aliens. Namrips would have recognized them as the Merkians that he had seen amongst the clones used for the creation of the CRCs; he also would have recognized them as the same aliens that had saved his life in the war ten years ago. They were not wearing any clothes. They were extremely skinny. They had large black eyes with no pupils (or perhaps it was because the entire eye was a pupil).

From Kimberly's perspective, they appeared not to have any gender. In fact, they were parthenogenetic. Parthenogenesis is the term used to describe asexual organisms that can reproduce without male fertilization. The Merkians had certain cycles in their lives that they laid eggs. It was similar to women's menstrual cycle, but instead of it being once a month, it was once every two years. They laid between one to three eggs in water. The eggs hatched in water, and after one year, they had to leave the water as they lost their ability to breathe there. Each Merkian laid eggs in this way for the first sixteen years of its adult life. Afterwards, Merkians spent the next thirty years raising their children (most Merkians began laying eggs at the age of thirty years old). Once their children were all thirty years old or older, they could live the next three hundred years developing themselves intellectually until they died.

The light was dim and Kimberly could not see much. She was lying on top of a large metallic examination table. They were studying her closely. She felt overwhelmingly tired. She was too tired to be afraid. She fell asleep right there.

Kimberly woke up inside a holding cell. She was sure that she was still inside their spaceship. She stood up and walked to the door. She pounded on the door while screaming, "Hey! Let me out! Bring me back to Earth! Please!"

The door slightly opened. The alien spoke telepathically without moving its lips, "We won't harm you. We just wanted to study your DNA. You will be returned to Earth soon."

Without thinking too much, Kimberly gathered all of her strength and forced the door open knocking the gentle alien to the ground. Some force within her was assuring her that she was making the right decision. She did not know if she could trust these aliens.

She grabbed the nearest object that she could find and she began beating the little alien in front of her. Evidently, they had left some metal tubes there because they needed to replace the tubes that had slightly begun melting next to their nuclear reactor. She hit it so hard so many times that it stopped moving. She stared at it for a moment wondering if she had killed it.

That is when fear struck her. If she had killed the alien, they would most certainly want to get revenge against her now. She had to find a way off the alien space ship. Kimberly ran looking to see what she could find. She entered a large room that had little circular objects on the floor that reminded her of the Star Trek teleportation devices. *Could these be used to send me to a different location?* She wondered to herself. She had to find out.

As she was stepping on one of them, five aliens entered the room. "Please, stop!" One of them cried out telepathically. "We know that you are afraid. We won't hurt you. Our friend is unconscious but not dead."

Kimberly did not know if she could believe the aliens or not. *What if they were lying just so they could stop her from leaving and kill her?* With this in mind, she lowered her hand on top of a button and disappeared.

Now, she was standing on an unknown world. Everything seemed so big. The trees seemed to reach the sky. She observed some butterflies that were flying about. They were humongous. The creatures were not the tiny bugs we would see on

Earth; they were the size of her home back in Arizona.

As she was observing the butterflies, she realized that they were gathering together. There was an army of them - millions of them. Then they began to encircle Kimberly.

As they were flying closer to the ground, Kimberly was able to see their razor sharp teeth! These were not ordinary butterflies! These butterflies were like vampires that wanted to suck her blood.

As the fear intensified, matters got worse. In the distance, she could see a multitude of large spiders heading in her direction. The spiders were even larger than the butterflies. In fact, they were much larger – five times larger.

As the spiders were converging on her, the butterflies were coming down to grab her. She knew that she was going to die. Her only question was, *would she die by being eaten by spiders or butterflies*? She closed her eyes and ducked her head. She placed her hands on her head and waited for the pain to begin.

After a moment, when nothing had happened, she opened her eyes. The spiders were attacking the butterflies. They had saved her life. The butterflies were interested in sucking her blood, but the spiders had made it in time to prevent it.

One very large spider had placed itself over her guarding against any butterflies. As the butterflies retreated, it said, "Come with us, and we will protect you." She obeyed.

While Kimberly walked with the spiders to their home, she pondered the reality that the beautiful butterflies were so deadly, and the horrendous spiders were the ones who saved her life.

Chapter Thirteen

The spiders' home was deep under the ground. When they realized that Kimberly was having a hard time keeping up with them, they invited her to climb onto one of their backs. Thus, she rode on top of Dill's back until arriving at their home.

Dill was the same spider that had placed itself over her to protect her against the vampire-like butterflies. Dill was the largest of all the giant spiders. Climbing up his leg was especially difficult. His leg was full of sharp spikes that could cut her if she wasn't careful. However, these same spikes also gave her something to support her weight as she went up.

Once she reached the top, it was all smooth sailing from there. The spiders moved swiftly into their underground tunnels. The tunnels got darker the deeper in their planet they went. They continued to move through these tunnels as the light from the planet's star slowly disappeared, and it got darker and darker until Kimberly couldn't see her own hands in front of her.

"Hey!" She cried out. "It's too dark in here. I can't see anything!" She heard a laugh. It sounded like the laugh of a wicked witch from an old movie. *Was it laughter from the spiders?* Kimberly wondered to herself. *Or was it laughter from someone else that was here with us?*

Kimberly was paralyzed with fear. She didn't know what to do. The spiders who had saved her life were taking her deeper and deeper into their planet. Apparently, they had the ability to see in the dark. Why would they save her life and, then, harm her?

Suddenly, they stopped moving. Kimberly was frozen stiff. Something grabbed Kimberly. It felt like two large arms wrapping around her. She could not see what it was, but she could feel its strength; it would have had no problem breaking her into little pieces.

She felt herself lift off the spider. She felt like she was flying in the arms of the giant creature that had grabbed her. Then, she was placed inside of what she interpreted to be a large cage; she couldn't see it, but she could hear it open, and she could feel it. It sounded like metal, and when she put her hands out to touch it, she felt the icy cold metal bars.

Suddenly, a dim light was lit. It was a small flame. A woman had the flame in her hand. Her skin was purple and her hair was lime green. She had a very beautiful appearance but wild-looking eyes that had the appearance of flames instead of pupils. She was wearing an orange robe that was lined with black fur. She also had matching fur slippers on her feet.

"I control these spiders," she said. "I control this world. You can call me Queen Death. Here you will be my slave until you die." She laughed. It was the same insane laughter that she had heard a moment before.

A large orange man who had more muscle than Superman on steroids stood beside her. In fact, there were several other identical looking orange men with bulging muscles. The could apparently fly; the one next to *Queen Death* was floating in the air. They all wore back pants with an elastic waistband; they reminded Kimberly of the type of pants worn by martial artists, and none of them had shoes or shirts.

She looked behind her in the cage, and she saw at least one hundred more people who looked like humans curled up on the ground staring at her. Bones were scattered on the ground. Rotting dead bodies had been placed at the back of the cage. Beside the stench of rotting corpses, there were feces at the back; there was nowhere else to use the bathroom. "This is where I'll die," she thought.

Chapter Fourteen

Kimberly drew close to some of the people who were in the cage with her. "Hey, I'm Kimberly," she whispered. "What's your name?" They stared in silence with a confused look on their faces. They whispered something between themselves. Kimberly could hear it well enough to realize that they were not speaking English. "I see," Kimberly said. "You don't speak English."

Kimberly sat down in the darkness. Queen Death had walked away. The dim light was gone. Therefore, it was completely dark again; she couldn't see her hands in front of her face.

Kimberly was now left to dwell in the darkness of her mind. All of her thoughts came flooding her head like a waterfall dumps water in the river below it. For example, she considered the fact that the spiders and Queen Death spoke her language. The people in the cage made it all the more obvious to her that it should not be expected to find extraterrestrials that speak her language.

The aliens in the spaceship were different because they were speaking telepathically; they didn't need to know her language. The only explanation that she could think of was that Queen Death had some sort of magical powers.

With this in mind, Kimberly considered the fact that Queen Death was manipulating the spiders. Maybe, they weren't magical powers. Perhaps, they were psychic powers. Did this mean that Queen Death could manipulate her psychologically? Is this why she felt the impulse to hurt the alien back on the spaceship?

She considered all of this and much more. She sat there in darkness not knowing if one hour had passed, or if several days had passed. She knew that she had fallen asleep a couple of times, but she didn't know how long she had slept. She could smell the stench of rotting bodies. She could hear the whispers of the people in the cage that spoke a foreign language.

Suddenly, a dim light was lit. There were ten orange men that looked identical to the muscular man that had put her in the cage. The one in front had a torch in his hand. They came to the cage and opened the door. They grunted something in an unknown language while motioning with their hands. It seemed that they wanted them to leave the cage. Multiple people had already stood up and were leaving. Kimberly stood up and began following them.

This is when Kimberly realized that those who were in the cage with her were not human at all.

They only looked similar to humans. She was able to see that their noses were like little stubs. She could also see that they didn't have ears in the same way that humans have ears; there were simply two little holes, one on each side of their faces. Their eyes were similar to cats' eyes. As far as their physical appearance, Kimberly couldn't detect any more differences with humans.

As they walked, other groups were brought from other cages. Most of them were the same alien race that had been in the cage with Kimberly. There was a multitude of them. She had no idea how many there were; all she knew was that more and more aliens were joining them every second as they moved through the underground tunnels.

Finally, they reached a massive underground room that had electric lights all around. There were many spaceships there. They were the same types of spaceships that the aliens who abducted her had. The mystery began to unravel when she saw a group of Merkians talking to Queen Death.

Bringing me to this planet was always part of their plan! Kimberly thought to herself. *They knew how I was going to react. Perhaps, they used mind control to make me react in that way.* She became furious inside. She wished that she had killed the little alien back on the spaceship. If she could have done it all over again, she would hit the little alien harder and for longer.

Kimberly's thoughts were broken up by one of the large orange men. He gave her a plate of food to eat. The food looked disgusting, but she ate it because she didn't want to die yet. She was hoping that she could find a way to escape and get back to Earth. When she finished eating, she was put to work. She was a slave being forced to build spaceships.

Chapter Fifteen

Kimberly was moving large metal bars from a pile and putting them onto a conveyer belt. They weren't too heavy, but doing it all day was tiresome. It seemed like she was being watched at all times. There were so many large orange men that Kimberly couldn't count them all. They were like supervisors.

Kimberly continued to work as she tried to observe everything about her environment. She needed to find a way to escape. Unfortunately, she could not find any realistic way of escaping. If she tried to run, one of the flying orange men would swoop down and grab her immediately.

Therefore, this was Kimberly's life for a very long time. She was incapable of discerning how many months passed, but she knew that it was more than one month. She worked every day as a slave looking for a weak spot that would allow her to escape. Nevertheless, she couldn't find anything to help her.

They usually only gave her very brief moments to eat. There would be times that she was on the verge of vomiting because of how disgusting the food was. Nevertheless, she controlled herself. She knew that she needed to eat well so that she would have enough energy to escape when the moment came.

One day, the ground shook beneath them. The electric lights turned off, and Kimberly's exceptionally visual memory came to her rescue. It is what had helped her become one of the most sought after computer programmers on Earth. She closed her eyes and imagined in vivid detail where everything was as if the lights were still on. She was able to move around with agility.

She raced toward one of the spaceships that were being prepared for takeoff. She ran inside. Inside the ship, she moved around more clumsily because she had never seen inside this spaceship. She ran into walls and stubbed her right big-toe. She was able to stumble her way into the cockpit where she looked for a place to hide herself. She felt around the wall and found a small door that seemed to be a storage place for cargo. She got inside and stayed there. She almost had to get in the fetal position in order to fit.

She waited there for what seemed like hours. The lights came back on. She could hear voices screaming that some of the slaves were missing. She couldn't hear everything from her position, but she understood that there was a fierce search for missing slaves.

She could also hear every time a slave was found. The slave would begin screaming in pain as each slave that was found was dismembered and fed to the beasts that guarded the exits. Besides the bone chilling screams, she could hear the beasts chewing on the bones of the dead slaves. *'Crunch, Crunch, Crunch,'* she would hear as someone choked on his or her own blood.

Finally, she realized that there was only one slave that they had not yet found. Most of the voices she heard were speaking in a foreign language, so she hadn't heard them say that there was only one slave. She couldn't put her finger on exactly how she knew it. She had absorbed enough of their language during her time there that she could sometimes pick up what was being talked about without understanding the details of what was being said. If she could have understood them perfectly, she would have known that none of the spaceships could leave until they found that last slave. She thought that if she stayed out of sight for long enough, they would eventually stop looking for her. In reality, they were going to search every inch until they found her.

Kimberly was petrified. She didn't want to make the slightest noise. She was hoping that she could stay in the same spot and go unnoticed, but her body was hurting from being in the fetal position for so long without much space to move around. However, she knew that her hopes of going unnoticed had vanished when she heard them begin searching on the spaceships.

She could hear some of them entering the spaceship that she was inside. She heard feet stepping inside the cockpit. She held her breath. *Please, don't look inside!* She thought. She felt tears beginning to form in her eyes. She knew that if they found her, she would be dismembered like the rest of the disobedient slaves.

Suddenly, the door to the cargo area where she was opened. One of the gray four-foot-tall aliens looked inside. It was looking directly at her. Tears were streaming out of her eyes at this point. She remained silent, but she wanted to beg for mercy.

Then a telepathic message came to her, "Don't worry." It didn't say anything else. Nothing else needed to be said. It closed the door. Then everyone left the cockpit.

It sounded like everyone was still searching around. She could hear Queen Death demanding that no one leave until she had punished the disobedient slave. The orange men were flying around and threatening the aliens. Kimberly took notice that she always heard Queen Death in English, but she heard everyone else in a foreign language that she couldn't understand. Therefore, she didn't know that they were threatening the Merkians. However, their yelling made her shake with fear. If she could have understood them, she would have known that they planned on killing any Merkians that were harboring the slave.

Immediately after this, Kimberly heard feet in the cockpit again. They seemed desperate. They were moving around pressing buttons and doing many other things as quickly as possible.

Then she heard an explosion and the spaceship began to move. They were taking off! She felt it move and shake a little. Then, one of the gray aliens opened the door and invited her to come out. She obeyed.

They were flying away. However, they couldn't get off of the planet. The orange men were attacking the spaceship. They were flying with it and punching it as it flew. The ship had taken too much damage, and they were losing velocity. The spaceship continued to lose its altitude until it crash landed in a large forest.

Chapter Sixteen

They had crashed in a clearing that was close to a waterfall. The spaceship was still capable of flying. However, the orange muscular men were pounding it so hard that it could not gain altitude. Once it had crashed, the orange men continued pounding it.

Every punch created a small dent. The metal used by Merkians was the strongest ever created in the entire universe. If it had been any other metal, the orange men would have crushed the spaceship like a tin can. Thus, they could not just break through and destroy them like they wanted to do; they had to weaken the metal by beating it for a prolonged period of time. Then, they would be able to destroy the traitors and the disobedient slave.

The spaceship shook with every single punch. The Merkians and Kimberly had all gathered together watching the exit. As they were looking at the door, they would occasionally see a new dent form. The Merkians had little devices in their hands; Kimberly did not know what they were for.

"Don't worry, Kimberly," one of them said telepathically. "If they break through that door, we're going to send them to a different dimension."

"Why are you going to do that?" Kimberly asked. "Can't you just kill them?"

"We don't like to kill," it responded. "Sending them to another dimension will end the threat without killing them."

"You don't like to kill? You wanna play like you're moral now? Then why did you hand me over to them as a slave to begin with?"

"We told you not to press the button. You handed yourself over."

Kimberly rolled her eyes. "You mean that it wasn't your plan all along for me to be taken a slave here?"

"No."

She shook her head. "I think so. You were manipulating me through telepathic means."

"No, we weren't. Queen Death was manipulating you."

"We were building your spaceships!" Kimberly's face was turning red. "You already came here long before I was taken captive."

"Queen Death is the only one who has access to the metal we need. It is the strongest metal in the universe. We have to come here to trade. So, we were already here, but we never had the intention of bringing you to this place. You did that when you pressed the button. Once we knew that you were under her care, we had to wait for the right moment. We turned the lights off using a special device that doesn't allow electronics to work. That gave you time to run. We simply increased our chances of success by providing some telepathic influence so that you would choose our spaceship."

Kimberly squinted at the alien. It sounded extremely unlikely. There was no way their version of things could be entirely true. "Why should I believe you?"

"You don't have much of a choice right now."

Kimberly was utterly confused. She didn't know if they were telling her the truth or not. She fell silent and stared at the door as more dents were accumulating.

After ten minutes of hearing the banging of the orange men's fists pounding on the spaceship, she saw a crack in the door. Light shined through. The orange men had finally weakened the door enough to break it. It only took a few more hits, and the door flew open. A blue light shot out of the device in one of the Merkian's hands and guided the door safely to the ground without harming anyone.

As the orange men came flying in, they began disappearing. Kimberly assumed that they were being sent to another dimension. However, the orange men realized what was happening, and the rest of them that hadn't been sent to another dimension left. They began beating the spaceship again.

The door was wide open but none of them wanted to come in knowing that they would simply disappear. Therefore, after about five minutes, one of the gray aliens was sent to the door. As soon as its head peaked outside, it attempted to point its interdimensional device. However, his upper body was incinerated and his legs flopped down on the ground.

The orange men continued to beat on the spaceship. After a while, Kimberly noticed that the area inside of the ship was getting smaller and smaller. Another one of the gray aliens tried to run out and shoot, but it was incinerated immediately as well.

The others were beginning to get worried. It seemed that there were orange men that were simply waiting for someone to leave so they could kill them immediately. On top of that, the area was getting smaller with each punch that the they landed on the spaceship.

The space within continued getting smaller and smaller until the gray aliens were completely separated from each other and from Kimberly. There were little tiny pockets where a person could be in the prone position, but the space was already too small to stand. Kimberly saw the walls enclosing around her. She was lying on the ground and the ceiling was almost touching her back. The path to the door was too small to try and crawl in that direction.

    She watched as one of the Merkians was completely crushed by the ceiling in front of her. First, the ceiling began to crush its arms. It began screaming, but it was pinned down and it couldn't move. Then, the legs got crushed. When the ceiling began crushing its back, she watched as blood spurted out of its mouth. She stared in horror as it squirmed until it stopped moving.

    Her area became smaller. She could feel the pressure of the ceiling clamping down on her arms and legs. Then, she began to feel as if an enormous weight sat down on her torso. She began suffocating. She couldn't breathe very well. One more blow would probably have begun breaking her bones. However, it suddenly stopped.

    It sounded like there was a fight. People were yelling in a language that Kimberly didn't understand. She couldn't leave to see what was happening; she was trapped. After about twenty minutes of fighting (and shallow breathing), the noise stopped. Suddenly, the ceiling was ripped off. She took in a deep breath; she could breathe normally again.

    She looked at the person who had ripped it off. He looked perfectly human. He had fiery red hair and large muscles. She looked around and saw that seven gray aliens had survived as well. Hundreds of orange men were stacked in a pile dead.

Did this man before me kill the orange men? She asked herself.

Chapter Seventeen

"Who are you?" Kimberly asked.

The man didn't answer. He had a blank stare that implied that he didn't understand the question. Then, Kimberly remembered that the *people* on this planet did not speak English. She motioned to herself, and then she said, "Kimberly." Then she motioned to the newcomer hoping that he would understand that she wanted to know his name.

However, he ignored her. He didn't ignore her to be rude; he had become engaged in a telepathic conversation with the gray extraterrestrials. They weren't speaking audible words, but Kimberly realized that the conversation was happening because the blank stare had left him, and he was staring directly at one of them with an expressive face that was changing as if someone were speaking.

Finally, one of the Merkians filled Kimberly in on what was transpiring. It communicated telepathically with Kimberly, "He says that his name is Erif. He says that we can find refuge if we follow him behind the waterfall. There is a cave behind the waterfall that leads to some underground tunnels. He says it isn't safe for us to be outside alone because all of the creatures that live on this planet are enormous. On top of that, most of them are controlled by Queen Death."

They followed Erif to the waterfall. Climbing the slippery rocks would have been dangerous. However, Erif had the power of flight. Therefore, he simply carried each one individually up to the cave. Then, they continued walking into the cave.

The cave was very dark. Because of this, Kimberly was about to refuse to go any farther. Her last experience in a dark cave was still burnt into her memory. However, as she opened her mouth to object, Erif's hand lit on fire. It was different than the way that Queen Death had held fire in her hand. Queen Death had held the flame in her palm whereas Erif's hand appeared to actually be on fire! It was as if Erif could turn his body into a flame.

There was something mysterious about Erif. It was more than the fact that she couldn't communicate with him in his language. It was more than his unusual powers. It was everything about him from the way he smiled to the way he walked. His face was typically expressionless as if he were some sort of emotionless being – or perhaps he had overcome his emotions and had become superior to them. His smile exuded kindness but seemed to lack any real sense of emotion. Even with all of the mystery surrounding him, she felt like he could be trusted.

They continued to walk deeper into the planet. After ten minutes of walking, they entered a very large area that had a multitude of little green creatures that Kimberly had never seen before. Their skin was emerald green, and it had a slight sparkle to it if the light touched their skin in the right way.

They were called Filoses. They were about four feet tall. Some had blue hair. Some had yellow hair. Some had red hair. Some had green hair; basically, their hair color could vary any color one could think up. They had three eyes that also varied as much in color as the rainbow itself. They all wore what appeared to be overalls. The males had four arms that were somewhat stubby and hairy as were their legs. Females had four smooth arms. Both males and females had a small button-noses and a wide mouth. Males had thinner lips, and females had thicker lips.

They seemed to be happy little creatures. They were all smiling, singing and dancing. Two of them ran immediately to greet Erif. They all spoke the same unknown language that Kimberly couldn't understand. Of the two that came to speak with Erif, there was a male and a female that Kimberly assumed were married. The male had blue hair and pink eyes. The female had long red hair and purple eyes. They kept looking at Kimberly as they talked about things that she didn't understand.

There were two children with them, which Kimberly interpreted to be their daughters. They had green hair and magenta colored eyes. There seemed to be a curiosity in their expression. It was as if they longed to know who the visitors were. As the gray aliens were able to communicate with them telepathically, their attention was quickly turning to the only mystery left – Kimberly.

"It's nice that everyone is happy here," Kimberly finally blurted out. "But I want to know what's going on. I'm the only one who doesn't understand what is being said."

One of the gray aliens communicated with her telepathically, "We understand. We already knew that you felt uneasy about your lack of knowledge. We asked Erif if he was willing to share his past with you, and he agreed. He is going to give us access to his memories. We are going to share those memories with you through telepathy. However, you will see it as if it is happening to you from Erif's eyes. All of the conversations will be heard in your language. Afterward, are you willing to allow us to share your past with Erif?"

It seemed like a genuine enough offer. Therefore, she agreed. They all sat down together, and she closed her eyes. She immediately began seeing what Erif's life was like.

Chapter Eighteen

Huge black pillars of smoke were rising into the sky. They were emanating from what appeared to be a village. The straw huts had orange flames dancing out of their roofs as they were being reduced to ashes. To an unthinking observer, it would seem that it was an ordinary village, but a trained eye would recognize that it was designed to look out in all directions and, thus, a refuge for wounded soldiers. The rules of war were clear in those parts; if civilians were caught housing soldiers by the enemy, they could be treated as soldiers.

Just to the south of these burning huts was an executioner with his axe raised high above his head ready to come down on the neck of an elderly man who had a mixture of gray and black hairs. Ten meters to the north of the execution lay headless bodies. Most of the bodies were soldiers who had been wounded in battle, but a few were dressed as civilians. Amongst these individuals without heads was a man who had been the father of the man who was about to be executed; his head that was full of white hair was thrown into a pile of other dismembered heads fifteen meters to the east.

The man with the axe raised was six feet and six inches tall. His arms and legs were chiseled, and his body was like a tree stump. He had a black veil over his face. He wore auburn leather armor that covered his body.

The condemned man who was about to meet his death was the father of the child who was presently screaming for the release of the condemned man. His head was laid over a tree stump. His hands were fastened behind him. His clothes were the usual rags worn by civilians. They appeared to be a juniper green. The man had no shoes on his feet and mud covered them.

The child that was screaming was being held tightly by one of the three high ranking officers who were standing by giving their approval of the execution. The child's deep-set blue eyes had tears streaming from them and sat upon his wide-set cheekbones. He had snot running from his triangular nose that protruded from his square face. His jawline was already developing well and adumbrated the kind of man that he would become. His narrow mouth trembled on his beardless face. His hair was a light brunette color; the ends of his hair rested upon his narrow shoulders. The child was about fifteen years old and had recently begun to develop his muscles. He was not terribly skinny but was well fed. You could see that this child would have the body of a warrior in ten more years if he were to live that long. He had on a dingy white shirt that was presently discolored with dust. His pants were the color of basil and reached down to one inch below the knees. His calves were exposed all the way down to his ankles where his feet were covered with his tattered-and-torn hickory-brown leather shoes. The child's face was raging with innocence but was currently being consumed by the flames of virulence.

    The commanding officer was set apart from the three officers with his sword raised high in the air; the lowering of the sword would be the sign to the executioner to finish his job. Both the commanding officer and the three high ranking officers were ten meters to the west of the execution, but the commanding officer was standing five more meters south of them. The officer in the middle had the boy in his grip. Another twenty meters west were one thousand soldiers lined up in formation with a dismal expression on their faces.

    The commanding officer was a tall man—about six feet and four inches. He had broad shoulders and a stout body. His eyes were a dark chocolate brown. His brown eyebrows were thick and attached in the middle to make a single brow; this uni-brow sat underneath his furrowed forehead. His face was square, but his jawline was not very well defined. He was wearing similar leather armor as the others, but as the commanding officer, he also wore a bronze chest plate to distinguish him from the rest.

One thousand five hundred meters to their east was a forest. There was another forest one thousand meters to their west. The forest to their east was much lusher and had many more dangerous animals that resided in it. They were in a clearing between the two forests that was considered to be the borderlands between the two nations. To the south was a large desert, and to the north were more forests.

There were flocks of birds circling in the sky to the east. A group of vultures was gathering together above them in the sky. The sun was shining brightly above them as if to overlook the pains of the soon to be orphan.

The commanding officer lowered his sword. The child screamed helplessly in response. The executioner brought down the axe. The lifeless body of the child's father flopped over onto the ground beside the tree stump while his head rolled three meters westward. The commanding officer turned his head towards the child and said, "Let this day be a reminder to you and your kind. Those who house soldiers will be treated as soldiers. Now be gone, you wretch!"

The little child was crying and hiccupping as little drops of snot were falling onto his shirt. His little chest was bobbing back and forth as one who could not breathe properly as he fell to his knees.

The child could not force himself to move. His heart was destroyed.

"If you do not leave now, I swear by the outer realm and the Great Dweller who gave us life that I will strike you down as I did your father and grandfather!"

The boy slowly, with trembling knees, began to stand up. He started in a westward direction. He went around the formation of soldiers to the north, and then maintained a perfect westward movement. His brain felt as if it were on fire, and his heart felt as if it were plunging to the bottom of a bottomless pit. His heart felt cold and empty.

He entered the forest to the west and left the view of the soldiers who had killed his father and grandfather. His mind kept reverting to the concept that he would never again wake up to the sound of his father's voice. He could hardly believe it. He continued onwards as he envisioned his father's smile and listened to his father's laughter.

The boy fell down near a tree as he continued to cry. His chest felt as if it would explode. He curled up into a ball as he sobbed tears of eternal misery and wailed from the depth of his fiery tomb in which he had been buried covered by the dirt of desolation. As his dejection intensified, and he could bear no more, he fell asleep.

In his dream, he saw a fire that was emanating from his heart. He was looking at himself from the outside. The fire appeared not to be hurting him, but on the contrary, it seemed to make him stronger. He could even feel the intoxicating sensation of the fire from outside his body, and he noticed that his muscles felt more vibrant. The fire encircled him and he became one with the fire. Then he saw a knife in his hand and an army of men before him. The leader of the army was the commander who had ordered the death of his father.

    His eyes glared as he looked upon the man. They were in a garden full of bourbon and centifolia roses. There were eglantine roses to his left, gallica under his feet, hybrid tea under the army in front of him, and red moss to his right. The bourbon and centifolia were in a circle that connected the other four that were set apart distinctly from each other and peppered the landscape within the other four groups. To imagine the scene, imagine a pie with four parts cut evenly. The centerpiece is its own circle distinct from the other four slices to make a total of five pieces. The roses occupy their own blocks, but the bourbon and centifolia that occupy the center, also reach out and mix with the roses in the other four "slices."

    On this scenery, the boy ran forward with his knife that suddenly extended into a sword. He slashed the sword around relentlessly as he approached the leader. He took off the head of the leader and then began to butcher every single soldier behind him. Within thirty minutes, the once beautiful field full of roses was bathed in blood. The roses were trampled and mostly dead. The stench of rotting corpses covered the elegant smell of the roses. The roses then turned into another form. The roses turned into countless dead bodies as if they had symbolized the four races of Planet Ademud all along.

    The boy woke up, but the pain in his heart had not subsided. He remained seated and looked at his surroundings. He saw something moving around on the ground. He took a closer look. It was some kind of bug. He studied it closely as it maneuvered into a small crater in the dirt. Suddenly, there was a quick thrashing motion caused by another creature that was hidden in the bottom of the crater. The hidden creature had taken a firm hold of the little bug and begun to eat it.

    He continued to be observant of nature and the creatures that inhabited the forest. This particular planet was known for its large insects that were bigger than some houses. However, it was more than just the insects; there were spiders, worms, and centipedes that were equally as big. The trees were also larger than any tree than one would see on Earth. Some of the trees were up to one kilometer in height. The area Erif was traveling through had less dangerous creatures. The four intelligent races of this planet would destroy all of the dangerous life forms that threatened their wellbeing.

    However, there were a few large insects that were considered innocuous due to their vegetarian diet. Because of this, Erif was able to watch them move around in the forest as he slowly walked towards an unknown destination. It was somehow relaxing to look at the various insects and study the terrain. It distracted his mind temporarily from the pain in his heart, and he did not feel so much like he wanted to die. It was a moment of relief from the fire that was consuming his heart. If he stopped observing nature, the hatred and despondency immediately returned. He had never observed nature before; he discovered his escape through a pure accidental observation of a tiny bug that had been eaten by another.

  He continued traveling west until he made his way to the end of the forest where the flatlands begin. However, it was growing dark and the sun was preparing to set. The poor child had not eaten all day and was painfully hungry. However, there was a more pressing matter that was putting the child's life in jeopardy; he had not drunk any water all day. A man can live a considerable amount of time without food but will die after three days without water. This was his second day without water, and there did not seem to be any relief on the way.

  The child continued to walk westward into the grass that was waist high. The sun was dipping below the horizon, and an array of colors was shining forth. In the distance, he could see small houses that peppered the land. He had never traveled so far away from his homeland. He had heard rumors that the Filos race dwelled in the flatlands. Everyone spoke of the Filoses in a negative light. Some said that they were incredibly stupid. Others said that they were oafish. Because of this, he would have passed the homes by without even considering to ask for help. Nevertheless, something happened that prevented him from continuing on his journey; a snake reached out and grabbed hold of his right ankle. Just as swiftly as it had latched onto him, it went away.

      The boy screamed in pain. Fears began circulating in his mind as his foot continued to throb. His eyes settled on a nearby house. He limped towards the house hoping that he would not die. He said a quick but fervent prayer to the Great Dweller. A mixture between being bitten by the snake and the fact that he had not eaten in a long time (not to mention his dehydrated body) caused him to collapse along the way.

      Again, the boy had a vivid dream. There was a man working in a large field; he was planting his crops. He tilled the land and then walked in straight lines where the trellis would later be built dropping seeds. The man went back to his house and waited. The sun set and rose again. The clouds flew across the red sky; the sun set and rose again. The cycle of life repeated. Spiders ate their prey; lions killed smaller quadrupeds. Antlions trapped ants; panthers hunted for food. Men died, and babies were born.

Then, he saw that the crop was growing out of the ground like tiny tree trunks (but they were not trees). The farmer fertilized and irrigated the land. As the vines grew and began to branch out, the farmer began the process of training the vines by thinning and pruning them; he put in the trellis and continued to irrigate the vines. He grafted in other vines that were desirable for the blend that he wished to create. Finally, when the time was right, the grapes budded out of the branches, and the man began to harvest them as they ripened.

    All of this was very pleasing to the child who watched with great interest. Then, something else happened. An envious neighbor saw that the farmer was becoming more successful than he was, for he had not planted anything. He had to live day to day on what he hunted and killed. So, he began to steal grapes from the farmer. When the farmer realized what was happening, he built a large fence around his vineyard. So the man made a fire and burnt up half of the farmer's grapes. The farmer became furious and retaliated. He went and set fire to the man's home. The people around that area had not known about the fact that the man had burnt up the farmer's grapes, but the man had gone around telling everyone how the evil farmer had burnt down his home, and he had nowhere to live. So the people in the region became furious with the farmer. They went and arrested the farmer and all his family with him. "Such a wife that you have that she approves of your deeds! Such children that you will raise that they will be like you!" They exclaimed as one voice. "Be rid of him and all like him! His family is a contaminant to our people. Destroy the problem at the root!" At that moment, the people executed the farmer and his entire family by beheading them.

The boy woke up. He was in a bed. He looked to his right and observed his surroundings. He was in a cottage—perhaps the very same cottage that he was heading towards when he collapsed—and he saw Filoses. There was a female, a man, and two children. There was a large pot for cooking stew, and there was currently a fire underneath it. The woman was stirring something in the pot. All of the beds were in the same room. The man was smoking a pipe and reading a book in his rocking chair. The children were two little girls and they were playing with their dolls mimicking the voices of each.

"Ah, ther he's! The laddy's awaken," the woman sung out to her husband.

"Tis be true, me deary wifey!" exclaimed the husband. "Whatcha say laddy?"

"Where am I?" He inquired.

"Now don't that be a bit of a silly question? Donchya think, laddy? Ain't it clear that ya be here wit ous here?" The man cried out in a joyful and innocent tone.

"Yeah, but where is here?"

"Wher else can here be but here? Here ain't never gone nowhere before! What's yer name laddy?"

"My name is Erif."

"I'm Valiant, and this be me wifey Chastity. These little ones be me childr'n, Fiery and Charmy."

"What happened to me?"

"From the looks of it, me think ya been bitten by a snake. Me childr'n playin' outside they were. Ya came on walkin' up kinda dizzy like and felled over, ya did. Ya foot is all black now. But I, worrying about all that, I wouldn't be doin' it laddy, for it'll be gone back ta normal 'n 'o'time 't'all. I been bitten by the snake before, I have."

Valiant was about four feet tall. He had blue hair and three large pink eyes. They all wore overalls, and Valiant's overalls were a merlot color. His four arms were somewhat stubby and hairy, as were his legs. He had a small button nose and a wide mouth. Chastity had long red hair, three purple eyes, pink overalls, four hairless arms, stubby legs, a small button-nose, and narrow mouth with lush lips (Valiant's lips were thin). Chastity was three feet and ten inches tall. Both of the two little girls had long green hair and magenta colored eyes. Fiery was a little older, and thus a little taller; she was three feet tall. Charmy was two feet and seven inches tall. Their facial features resembled their mother, and they wore purple overalls. The skin color of all

Filoses was an emerald green that seemed to sparkle in the light.

"I really want to be going as quickly as possible," Erif declared. "I do thank you all for the hospitality, but I have to travel to the west to find my people, the Seregine race." The Seregine race more or less looked human in almost every respect. The only physical difference was that some Seregines had greenish hair. The majority of the Seregines had hair colors that resembled human hair, but this was one little recessive gene that demonstrated the vast differences between them and humans. All Seregines were asexual. Everyone laid at least one or two eggs in his lifetime. The genetic variations that the race had were due to their ability to incorporate new DNA sequences into their genome through contact (in a similar way that bacteria share DNA). Each cell on the skin had pili that could incorporate new DNA. However, no one demonstrated the traits that they picked up. Instead, the DNA that was absorbed was taken and incorporated into the formation of the new egg giving the newly born Seregine differing features from his father.

"As soon as ya be well 'nuff ta walk, laddy, we'll be sendin' ya on ya way," Valiant responded. "At the moment, ya be needin' ta eat, ya do."

Once the dinner was prepared, they all sat together around Erif instead of at the table (which was their usual custom) so that Erif would not feel left out. They told local tales of the creatures that roamed that area at night. These tales were accompanied by the consolatory reminder that Erif was lucky to have been bitten by the snake, for otherwise, he would have been out in the open for the creatures to attack him. In the local tongue, they were known as tiskolas. They were said to be rather doltish creatures and did not break into houses. They only hunted that which they could readily see with the eyes. They flew like bats on wings without feathers but were fifteen feet long. He was also given the warning to be cautious once he left and to carry goatskin with him. If night fell upon him, he could cover himself with the goatskin and lie motionless until the morning. This is the same way that many men had remained alive when caught out at night before they could make it home. If one has trouble believing that a creature could be so stupid as to be fooled by goatskin, consider the June bug and its propensity to run into the same wall over and over without realizing that the wall is there.

    This was followed by the tale of the old necromancer that lived in the mountains. The necromancer frequently communicated with the dead relatives of those who wanted to know if their family members were still alive or dead. If someone did not return home after being out late, Filoses would go to the old necromancer to communicate with the dead to tell them if the Filos had died or was somewhere trapped or injured. Of course, the necromancer had no way of knowing what had happened to the relative if he or she was not dead, for he could only talk to the relative if he or she had died; the other dead Filoses would inform him if he or she was not with them.

    This led to a discussion of other powers that the necromancer allegedly possessed. The necromancer claimed that the dead could give him incredible strength to avenge them, and anyone who wished to avenge the dead could be bestowed with the same power if he, the necromancer, willed it. The necromancer claimed that the reason he never used the power was because he was an outcast from society and did not care to avenge anyone's death. Aside from that, the use of the power came with severe consequences that he was not willing to pay. Most of the Filoses did not believe that he had the power, but there were a few tales that had been circulating around of certain Filoses who had put it to the test and had avenged their loved ones through the power of the necromancer.

    Upon hearing of the powers of the necromancer, Erif's eyes lit up. His heart began to race. His palms began to sweat. His lower lip began to tremble. His throat became parched. His right eye began to twitch. His stomach began to flutter. His skin began to crawl, and his hair stood on end. With a trembling voice, he asked, "And how would I go about finding this necromancer?"

"Me laddy, tis be a man best left 'lone if ya want me 'pinion, he's," Valiant replied. "But if ya really desire ta find 'em, first ya haf ta make it to the mountains. If ya stay goin' west, see three mountains wit tallest peaks, ya will. Be goin' ta the big'n, slight to the north, and find a cave on the north side, ya will."

Erif continued to stay with the Filoses. He could not leave on his journey just yet; his foot needed to heal first. They continued to tell stories of things that occurred in that region. They would laugh together when a funny story was told, but once Erif finished laughing, his mind would revert to the fun times and laughs he had had with his father. This caused his moments of laughter to be quite painful, and thus, his laughing became briefer and less frequent. The boy did not want to laugh without his father. He missed his father. The last time he laughed with the Filoses, almost as quickly as he had begun, a tear formed at the edge of his left eye. It quickly gained mass and began to trickle down the little boy's cheek. It arrived at his jawline and posed for a moment as if to say goodbye. Then, it released its grip from the boy's face and fell towards the ground. It was one little drop of water falling to the ground but symbolized so much. It was one little teardrop, and it was full of memories of a dead father. It was as if his father and grandfather were united together in that little tiny salty ball of H_2O, and they were the ones who were falling towards the floor. The tiny little splash that the teardrop made was the execution of his father and grandfather. The boy trembled inside wanting desperately to forget everything that had happened that day.

Chapter Nineteen

Once Erif healed, he readied himself for his journey. The Filoses gave him a piece of goatskin to cover himself. To make it easier to carry and faster to hide, he decided to wear it over his shoulders like a cape and tied a string around the neck connecting the two sides of the skin. The Filoses also gave him food for his journey and wished him well. Erif was glad to have met them. They did seem to be lacking in intelligence as others had told him, but they were very warm and loving. It also struck him that they had a form of wisdom that comes from living experience and is in no way dependent on the being's intellectual capacities.

Erif traveled westward. The land was completely flat for miles and miles. His eyes could pick out many different cottages that peppered the landscape. The boy tried to keep his mind off of his father as he traveled. It was a very difficult task because of the nature of the landscape. In the forest there had been many different creatures for the eyes to feast upon and the mind to dwell upon. However, all he saw here was a brownish color grass that reached his waistline with an occasional cottage in the distance. If he could have removed the grass, he was sure that he would have seen many different insects and reptiles—perhaps spiders too. However, the grass covered it all.

As he continued to walk he looked up into the sky and suddenly realized that he had been wrong; planet Ademud was full of life for his eyes to feast upon. There were many different types of birds that flew overhead. Some were large and some were small. He saw one bird that had a wingspan of one hundred yards. The birds of Ademud were typically harmless for Seregines. None of the dangerous birds roamed these parts. He watched one land very close to him, and he stopped to admire its immense size. It picked something up, and then, it flew away.

It was such thoughts that he continued to try to maintain in his mind, but at times, he was unsuccessful. Sometimes, his mind would drift back to his father, and tears would roll down his cheeks. Even when he was distracted looking at the birds and the shapes of clouds, there was always a lingering sensation of dejection.

Erif stopped twice to eat the food that he carried in his large bag that was slung over his back. The bag had to be large in order to fit a jug of water. It was difficult carrying so much weight but necessary if the boy wanted to survive. He had timed his eating with the position of the sun. When the sun was at high noon, he ate his first meal. He ate his second meal about an hour before sunset. He continued to walk after sunset hoping that the tiskolas would not come to the area that he traveled upon.

The moon lit up the country side, and the stars filled the sky. He was as much enraptured with the stars as he had been with the clouds. He began to make out shapes in the constellations and, at times, stood still in wonder. It was as if the world was full of little diamonds that one had to be observant to see, or he would never realize the beauty that surrounded him. These reflections were interrupted by the sound of something in the sky.

Erif dropped to the ground and covered himself with the goatskin. The tiskolas were flying all around the field. They had seen him before he had covered himself, and now, they were encircling the area. Hundreds of them were shrieking so loud that Erif needed to cup his hands over his ears. The sound was deafening. One of them landed in the field near Erif. It paced around searching for the flesh that it had seen just moments before. Its feet came within inches of Erif as it wobbled through the high grass.

Erif could smell its foul stench. It was like someone had placed thousands of rotten eggs into a field of rotting corpses. Erif was about to gag. He could feel it coming. He knew that he was about to cough as he began to convulse, and his mouth opened wide. He pulled out his knife in a frenzy wanting to protect himself and knowing that he was about to be discovered. He threw off the goatskin putting himself in a standing position at the same time. He stabbed the creature in its face before it had time to react. Erif began coughing violently because of the disgusting smell.

At this moment, hundreds of other tiskolas took notice of him. He got back down into the grass and, once again, covered himself with the goatskin. He crawled away from the dead creature breathing heavily. Five other creatures landed in that spot searching for the flesh that they had seen. They found the dead member of their species and began to claw at it and eat it ripping its flesh off of its bones.

Several other creatures landed and began to fight with them for the food. *They apparently eat their own dead*, Erif thought. He continued trying to crawl away. That is when one of the creatures discovered him. Its feet bumped into him almost causing it to tumble over.

Erif froze. He did not want to stand up with his knife to kill it like he had done to the other, for how could he fight off so many when they were all already so close to him? He wanted to wait to see what would happen. If it were to attack him, the only thing that he could have done to stay alive would be to fight back. He was clinging to some little light of hope that it would not have to come to that; he felt certain that he would not come out of it alive.

The creature kicked at him. Erif wanted to cough again, but he was able to restrain himself this time. Then, the creature jumped on top of him. Then, it flew away. Erif drew the conclusion that the creature had thought that he was a rock. He breathed a sigh of relief and decided to stay there and not move until daybreak.

Erif woke up as the sun rose. He was sweating due to the heat. He continued on his way towards the west. For some reason, there was not a single bird in the sky. There were no clouds, and the sun was beating violently down upon the head of Erif. What was stranger was the fact that there was no sign of life anywhere. He could not see a single cottage on the horizon. There was no sound of any type of animal or bug.

Suddenly, Erif saw a man appear in the distance that seemed to be walking towards him. He continued to walk westward hoping that the man was friendly. As the man came a little closer, he saw that he was wearing a hood, and Erif could not easily see his face. Once he came a little closer, he saw a little bit of white hair protruding from his hood. Then, the man flew through the air until he came to where Erif was and hovered above him.

Erif was astonished at this and began to wonder if it was the necromancer. "Who are you?" Erif asked the hooded figure above him.

"I am Deeb, the necromancer whom you seek," the figure answered.

"I would like to communicate with my father and grandfather. Can you help me?"

"Is it not rather that you wish to take revenge upon the man who murdered him?" Deeb said as he glared down upon Erif below. Now that he could see the face of Deeb, he could see his long nose that looked fit for a witch and eyes that said everything from insanity to a deeply imbedded evil that had spawned from a wicked heart. His skin was excessively pale, and he had several warts on his wrinkly skin. The look was unsettling to Erif's nerves.

"I wish to speak to my father to receive guidance from him!" declared the child.

Suddenly, the shape of the necromancer changed. He was transformed into the most grotesque creature imaginable. It was like a dragon with slimy skin but not any ordinary dragon. Its head was sticking out of where it should defecate, and its face was equally terrible with large eyes that were completely red and had no pupils. Its mouth projected forwards fifteen meters with large sharp teeth that had innumerable brown stains on them. Its arms were pointed towards the sky as it floated in the air carried by two wings that were dripping with bile. Out of its mouth, bile shot forth in the shape of fire and rained upon the head of Erif.

Erif tried to run, but he began to slip and fall in the bile that had been emitted. The entire field was sopping wet with bile. The creature continued to hover above him roaring with laughter knowing that the child could not escape. The boy's feet became stuck in what felt like tar, and he began to sink as if he were standing in quicksand. Then, the dragon swooped down and picked him up into his teeth and carried him high above. Erif could feel the jagged teeth against his back and stomach. He could feel his back beginning to break. The teeth on his back were beginning to penetrate his skin. His entrails were beginning to expose themselves to the air.

Suddenly, Erif woke up in the field. It was all a dream. He shuddered as he considered its potential implications and if it were a foreshadowing of things that would occur; perhaps, it was a dream given to him by the Great Dweller. He also considered that it could have been a premonition given to him as a warning and that he could still change his destiny. However, he couldn't help but think that it was also equally possible that this night terror had come to him because his mind had been fluttering with fears the night before due to the tiskolas in the field and that the dream was nothing more than a nightmare that could be dismissed. It would be a shame if he did not have the opportunity to achieve his purpose because of a silly dream.

With this thought, Erif encouraged himself to continue on his way. The first sign to him that he was correct and that it was only a silly dream was that the sky was full of clouds and birds as it had been before. None of the ominous signs that he had seen in his dream were present in reality. The crickets were singing their songs. The insects were crawling through the tall grass. Erif could have spent a lot of time studying the scenery if he had the mind to do so. However, the dream continued to reverberate through his mind like an echo as his mind fluttered between his dream and the pain of not having his father.

Again, Erif stopped to eat when the sun was at high noon. This time, however, he did not make it to his second meal. As the day passed by, he became more and more aware of the mountain range before him. This caused him to quicken his pace hoping to arrive at the mountains before nightfall. His new friends, the Filoses, had not told him if the creatures also plague the mountain range at night.

As the sun dropped beyond the horizon, the boy continued his fast pace walk that was beginning to borderline a slow jog. With every second that went by, the faster he moved. He knew that those creatures would appear in the sky at any moment, and he was almost there. The grass had gotten smaller and smaller until it was ankle high. Presently, he was trotting along the rocks, and there was no more grass. The base of the mountain was still several more kilometers away.

Suddenly, he heard the shrieking in the air; the creatures were flying through the air so many kilometers behind him. Erif felt that he was too close to stop now. He only had a little farther to go. It would have been wise for him to lie down underneath the goatskin, but he was desperate to end his journey, and his impatience got the better of him. He was running now; he could not sprint such a great distance and certainly not over rocks, but he certainly could run at a decent pace.

Erif was angling his run slightly north so that he would come to the mountain where the necromancer lived. The tiskolas saw the boy running and flew in his direction. They were still a great distance away, and the real question was who would arrive at their destination first.

There were several hundred of the creatures flying towards Erif. The closest one was within one hundred meters now. It was as if everything went into slow motion. The creature swooped down and came within seventy-five meters, fifty meters, twenty-five meters, ten meters and five meters. Its mouth opened wide and its fangs were gleaming in the moonlight. Erif had turned his head to look directly at it as he was running. He could see its beady little eyes staring lustily at his flesh. The boy knew that he was about to die and wished that he had taken cover. His hand was clutching the knife as he was unsheathing it preparing for a fight. He would still die, for there was no way to fight off so many of them.

A person's life can pass before his eyes in the moment of death. Surely, Erif's thoughts went to his father and the moment that he would be reunited with him. He saw all the times that he laughed with his father. He saw his father and his grandfather standing before him clothed in light in a field of lilies. They stood in front of a golden gate. His father was wearing a golden robe that was shining brilliantly as if it was its own light source. The grandfather was dressed equally. The father walked over to Erif and gently put his right hand on his left shoulder and said, "Not yet, son. You have work to do."

    Suddenly, Erif was jolted back to reality and to the creature before him as a brilliant white light shined forth; the creature never made it to Erif. When it was a few inches away, the light shined and the creature was thrown backward and went tumbling on the ground.

    "Don't touch this lad!" cried a sharp voice from the source of the light. "He will sojourn with me for a time." Erif's eyes made out the figure at the source of the light, and it was the same man from his dream; it was surely the necromancer.

    He couldn't be evil, Erif thought. *He wouldn't have saved my life if he were evil.* Without saying a word more, the necromancer turned around and walked away. Erif continued to follow him until they arrived at his cave. The necromancer waved his hand at Erif signaling that he should follow him inside.

They sat down together, and then, the necromancer broke the silence, "I'm Deeb. Your father came to me last night and informed me that you were coming to receive guidance from him."

"Can you arrange that?" Erif asked. "I mean, can you arrange it so that I can speak to him?"

"The question to ask yourself is if you're ready to hear what he has to say."

"I'm ready! Please, I want to speak to my father."

"Drink this potion here and lie down." Deeb pulled a large spoon out of a stew pot with a liquid that appeared to be a juniper green. The necromancer put it to the lips of Erif, and he drank it. The boy immediately began to feel drunk.

"Wow, ders so many cullerrrrrs," slurred Erif as he laid down. Erif suddenly woke up as he was falling into a deep dark pit. The pit seemed to be bottomless. He was falling and falling and falling without any sign of a ground.

The necromancer appeared in the form of a dragon, but this time it was not an ugly dragon. It was an effulgent dragon and shining forth brightly. He caught Erif in his hand and set him down in a place next to an active volcano. He could see the lava gushing out of the volcano and a pillar of smoke raising into the heavens. There was no sun nor moon nor stars. There were two lights: the necromancer and the lava. Then, in front of Erif, appeared his father.

For some reason, Erif was acutely aware of his inner anger boiling within his heart that seemed to glide through his veins at the same pace as the lava spread over the land. It was somewhat intoxicating. There was a deeply imbedded sense of hatred for those who murdered his father that was just now circulating through his mind.

"My son," said the man before him, "you must avenge my death. But you must avenge, not only mine but all of our race's deaths that have occurred at the hands of the Delikies." The men who killed his father were known as the Delikie race. They had both men and women just as humans do; in fact, they were almost identical to humans in every way.

"How can I, one person, do such a thing?" Erif inquired.

"My son, you will be given incredible power. The necromancer has already made the necessary sacrifice of a bull. If you say yes, your capacity to lay an egg will be taken from you, for a sacrifice on your part is required. All of the dead have agreed to add their souls into the power that will be given to you. For this reason, once you receive their power, you are bound to do everything they ask you for the rest of your life. Once you receive the power, it cannot be taken from you on a whim, nor can this be easily repeated. They would have to find other members from the dead that are willing to participate, for the dead who have already offered themselves cannot be offered again. Thus, if you change your mind after receiving the power, they will hunt you down and kill you to retrieve the power given to you and give it to another."

It almost seemed strange that his own father would ask him to sacrifice so much. He had never known his father to be vindictive. However, he felt compelled to do it for the hatred that was steadily growing within his own heart. He felt as if the lava were running through his veins. He could imagine himself pounding in the face of the murderer who took his father from him. His life had already been robbed from him, and what was it to him if he allowed his life to be lived in subjugation to those who were helping him avenge his father's death?

"I'll do it!" Erif cried out. Immediately upon saying this, he was taken into the air by an invisible force. The lava also began to levitate at the same time. The lava joined up with his body in midair and began to enter into his bloodstream. Erif felt intoxicated by it all. It did not hurt; it felt good. It was all the power of thousands of dead men, women, and children. His muscles increased in size; he suddenly looked ten years older, and his hair turned fiery red.

Erif woke up lying next to the sitting necromancer who had his eyes closed and seemed to be meditating. "Was it a dream?" Erif inquired of the necromancer. He was shocked to hear his voice when he asked the question; it sounded much deeper than normal.

"Go look at yourself in the mirror," Deeb replied without opening his eyes. Erif ran to a mirror and looked at himself. His hair was fiery red and he looked twenty-five rather than fifteen. His muscles were huge. "Go test your strength," said the necromancer, still with his eyes closed. "And try to jump really high in the air. When you jump as high as you can, try not to come down."

The advice sounded strange enough, but with all that was happening, he knew that it would lead to some discovery of a power that he had been given. He walked outside of the cave into the night. He jumped as high as he could. He shot upwards thirty feet into the air and, then, began to descend. He tried to concentrate on staying in the air, but he continued to fall. Just before he hit the ground, however, he stopped and began to hover three inches above the rocks. Then, he allowed himself to drop.

He began to run as fast as he could eastwards towards the flatlands. He could not believe how fast he was running. He traversed several kilometers in a matter of seconds and reached the edge of the flatlands. The tiskolas were out scouting for food, and they saw Erif as he stood there staring off into the sky admiring the stars. Erif saw the creatures and that they were coming towards him. A part of him wanted to be afraid and run away, but another part of him knew that he was given greater power than those creatures could withstand. It would be a good opportunity to see what he was truly capable of.

Erif flew into the air to meet the tiskolas. As the first creature reached him, he ripped its head off with his bare hands. He punched another, and it went flying backward. The others surrounded him and attempted to peck at him. He became enraged, and his body began to glow a dark orange color. He extended his hands in front of himself, and fire ejected from the palms of his hands destroying every creature in its path. Once all the creatures were dead, he knew that he had exactly what he needed to avenge the death of his father.

Erif flew through the night sky towards the east—towards the Delikies. He made no stops along the way. He had to fight off several other rounds of tiskolas that had spotted him, but he easily killed them all in minutes and continued his way. Once he arrived at the edge of the forest at the clearing where his father had been killed, he laid down to sleep so that he would be ready to begin his slaughter in the morning.

In the morning, he immediately began to search for Delikie soldiers. Every time he saw Delikie soldiers, he would burn them up with the flames that would shoot from his hands. However, in none of the groups of soldiers that he killed, could he find the commander that had ordered the death of his father in spite of his tears.

At about midday, after he had killed thousands of Delikie soldiers, Erif saw a small Delikie village. He flew down and began to search through all of the civilians there. He did not want to kill civilians who had nothing to do with the death of his father. He only wanted to kill the soldiers and, especially, the one responsible for his father's death. He was walking around studying the faces of the individuals, but everyone there knew that something strange was going on; everyone in that village knew everyone else. Therefore, the face of Erif, being an unknown face, made several Delikies run to the mayor who then informed the military members that were there. There was a unit who had come home from the war in order to rest. The commander of that force with three hundred of his best soldiers suited up and went out to meet the strange man.

As they came into Erif's view, Erif recognized the commander. It was the same commander who had killed his father. He walked calmly over to the small unit of soldiers and said, "How can I be of service to you?"

"Who are you, and why are you here?" demanded the commander.

"You recognize me not!" Erif exclaimed in a happy tone. "What a pity, for I recognize you *perfectly* well." As Erif arrived at the word *perfectly*, his face changed from happy to hatred, and his tone changed equally. "You are the one who murdered my father in the clearing just so many days ago. How could you recognize me now that I have this power?"

"That's impossible. The boy's father that I ordered dead was a small boy – about fifteen years old."

"I AM fifteen years old. Now I have come to take your life!" At saying this, Erif ran forwards and attacked all of the surrounding soldiers without laying a hand upon the commander. He moved so swiftly that they could do nothing. He was taking their own swords out of their hands and cutting them in two with them. Not only did he have greater speed running, but he could move his hands so fast that they appeared to disappear.

As Erif finished this, he took the commander's sword from him and put it to his neck. "Do you see what I am capable of now?" He began. "A wonderful necromancer has helped transform me into this form to avenge the death of my father. Now, you will know the pain that you caused me." Upon finishing this statement, he raised the sword ready to cut the commander's head clean off of his shoulders.

At that moment a small child appeared in the distance running and crying, "No! Don't kill my father! Please, spare my father!" This took Erif off guard. It brought back so many memories. He remembered vividly the day that he had pleaded for the life of his own father. Now, here he was about to take away the father of an innocent child. It wasn't that child's fault that his father had made those decisions. In his mind's eye, Erif saw his own father with his hands tied behind his back. He saw the axe come down on his father's neck.

He saw all the times that he laughed with his father. He saw his father and his grandfather standing before him clothed in light in a field of lilies. They stood in front of a golden gate. His father was wearing a golden robe that was shining brilliantly as if it was its own light source. The grandfather was dressed equally. The father walked over to Erif and gently put his right hand on his left shoulder and said, "Not yet, son. You have work to do." His father had already spoken to him before the necromancer had gotten to him. *I have work to do; I need not die yet*, Erif thought.

At that moment, he looked deeply within his own soul and saw that he was being eaten up by hatred. The tooth of the dragon that had pierced his back in the dream was symbolic of his own hatred and that he was being devoured by it. The dream had come true, but he hadn't died in the dream. He was only pierced. Here he stood, pierced by the dragon's tooth. His entrails were metaphorically pouring out onto the land below him. However, he could still turn it around and live in peace. A tear formed at the edge of his left eye. It quickly gained mass and began to trickle down the man's cheek. It arrived at his jawline and posed for a moment as if to say goodbye. Then, it released its grip from Erif's face and plummeted to the bloodstained dirt beneath him. It was one little drop of water falling to the ground, but symbolized so much. It was one little teardrop, and it was full of memories of a dead father. It was as if his father and grandfather were united together in that little tiny salty ball of $H2O$, and they were the ones who were falling towards the bloody ground. The tiny little splash that the teardrop made was the execution of his father and grandfather.

"I won't do it!" Erif yelled out. "My father would never have asked me to give up my soul! You're a fraud, Deeb! I won't do it. Come and kill me if you dare; I won't do it. You speak not with the dead!" With those words, he allowed the little child to embrace his father. Then, he flew off into the sky taking the sword with him.

Chapter Twenty

There was a certain Delikie woman who was unmarried. She had dedicated her life to trying to understand the mysteries of magic and constantly looked for potions and spells that she could learn. Her name was Cheevell.

She had brown hair and a very beautiful face. However, she typically wore dirty clothes and did not pay a lot of attention to her appearance because she was too interested in learning more spells to cast. She would stand in front of a large pot of boiling water throwing in ingredients. Usually, nothing would happen. Every once in a while, she would successfully create a new potion.

She wasn't very good at magic. The running joke was that she was more likely to make a frog fart than harm anyone with a spell. She was more dangerous to the animals that she sacrificed in order to attempt more potions and spells. This was also known by all Delikies in the area. Everyone made fun of her to her face. She inspired no fear in anyone anywhere on the entire planet.

One day, when she was buying food at the market, a man tripped her. All of her fruits and vegetables fell out of her hands and went all over the ground as she fell face first. One of the women that were with the man burst out laughing.

Cheevell looked back at the man's face. He smiled at her. "You don't know who you are messing with!" She screamed. "When I find out how to create more powerful spells, I will make you all worship at my feet as my slaves!"

"Crazy woman!" The lady who had laughed exclaimed.

Cheevell began picking up her fallen groceries when, suddenly, they began floating in the air and put themselves into a woven basket and returned to her. The man who had tripped her and the women who had laughed had an expression of fear on their faces.

Deeb approached her. Deeb was well known by all the inhabitants, and he did strike fear in the hearts of those who saw him. Everyone knew of the powers attested to him. "Such a shame that everyone here doesn't recognize the jewel that they have before them," he said in a soft voice.

"The mighty Deeb!" Cheevell exclaimed. "It's an honor to be in your presence. I have modeled my life after your example."

"Yes, my daughter. I know who you are, and I know those who have hurt you. From hence forth, you shall be known as Queen Death. Everyone on planet Ademud will know who you are and will honor you as a queen."

Cheevell immediately looked over at the people who had laughed at her and smiled. "In very short order, I'll be seeing you again," she said in soft but scary tone.

Deeb took her under his care and began teaching her the secrets of talking with the dead. He taught her how to gain enough power to cast spells. She finally understood the reason that her spells constantly failed. She hadn't understood that she needed a source of power. Anything that you do always has a cost.

One day, Deeb approached her. "It is time for you to show your worthiness," he told her. "There is a certain Seregine by the name of Erif. I want him dead. If you can fulfill this duty, you will become my right hand. You will truly become Queen Death. Everyone will answer to you."

"I am already Queen Death," she responded. "If you are so powerful, why don't you kill him?"

Deeb was surprised by the answer. "How dare you respond to your master in that way!" He screamed in a threatening tone.

"How dare you think that you are my master! Do you think that I came here to become your pawn? I wanted a father figure. You called me daughter. Now, I see that you want a slave so you can be clean of all your actions. You don't want to take responsibility so that you don't have to pay the cost. Do you remember how you taught me that everything has a cost? I see what you do. You avoid the cost by getting others to do your work you filthy scoundrel!"

"I can kill you and raise another up higher than your level!"

She laughed. "Little do you know that I surpassed you long ago, you weak old man." Deeb raised his arm to cast a spell. Queen Death simply looked at him without moving a muscle, and he became frozen and couldn't move nor speak. "You see. You rely on words and movements to cast your spells. I am beyond that. Now that I have you frozen and unable to speak, you can do nothing to me." She reached her hand up to the chest of Deeb. Her hand went through his chest as if she were a phantasm. She pulled out his heart, and Deeb died there on the spot.

Suddenly, Queen Death's skin changed to purple. Her hair became green. Her dirty white clothes transformed into an orange robe. Her eyes lit up with flames inside. She had truly become Queen Death.

Queen Death immediately began creating an army that could serve her purposes. Planet Ademud was already known for its extremely large insects and bugs. So, she took advantage of these creatures and put them all under her spell. Then, she went around and turned all of the Delikies into large orange muscular men that could fly. She put a spell over them so that they could no longer think for themselves. They needed her command to do anything.

Then, she used them to entrap the Seregines. The Seregines were taken and put into cages. They were kept alive so that whenever one of her orange men were killed, she would have a sacrifice that she could make in order to bring her soldier back to life.

Then, she captured the race known as Primees. These are the people that almost looked human that Kimberly had met in her time being enslaved. They had cat-like eyes, holes for ears, and stubs for noses. Primees were used for slave labor. However, if she got in a situation where she no longer had Seregines, she had no problem using Primees for sacrifices.

Finally, she went to capture the Filoses. She had left the Filoses until last because Filoses were considered to be so stupid that she knew that they couldn't possibly cause her any problems. However, the orange men were sent back to her cut into little pieces. A certain Seregine had left one orange man alive to carry the dead back to Queen Death with the message that she was not permitted to harm the Filoses. That Seregine's name was Erif.

She raised her dead men back to life and immediately collected one million orange men. She prepared them for battle. Then, she went to search for Erif.

Erif had already taken the Filoses to a secret location inside of a cave hidden behind a waterfall. However, he knew that she would eventually find it if she looked for it. Therefore, the only way to keep her from looking for it was to go out and fight her army.

Erif stood waiting in a field knowing that they would come. As soon as he saw them in the distance, he didn't wait any time at all to attack them. He flew up and began cutting them into little pieces.

Erif killed thousands of them. The orange men were falling down into a pile. The field was turning red. However, Queen Death was only allowing him to win for the moment to see how he fought. She was standing at a distance watching him kill her army of orange men.

When she had seen enough, she ordered her men to stop attacking. Then, she used her magic to freeze Erif as she had done to Deeb. He was flying high above in the sky, but he couldn't move a muscle.

She brought him down close to her, and she looked him in the eyes. "You are the first one to cause me these kinds of problems," Queen Death declared. "Do you know that?"

"You're not the first evil murderer that has existed, and I'm sure you won't be the last," Erif responded.

"Why am I evil?"

"Killing defenseless creatures is evil." She laughed. "You killed defenseless creatures. So are you evil?"

"I killed your army that was going to massacre many innocent lives."

"I mean you killed defenseless creatures when Deeb gave you your power. And how do you know that they were going to be massacred? I like to think that they were going to have a better life than what they have now." Queen Death winked at Erif.

There was a look in Erif's eyes that was unsettling to her. This being before her had an unyielding spirit, and it scared her. "I made a mistake, and I repented of that mistake. You should repent of yours. If you repent, I won't kill you. Deal?"

"How are you going to kill me? I am the one that has control of you now. I could rip your heart out now."

Erif grimaced as he tried to free his hands. "I dare you to try it. Your filthy hand won't even make it within two inches of my body."

"Listen. I'm trying not to kill you. Don't make me angry. I wanted to offer you a position. If you help me maintain control over this planet, I will spare your life."

"Take your mercy and shove it where the sun doesn't shine you wicked filthy scumbag!"

Queen Death immediately reached her hand out towards Erif's chest. She was going to rip his heart out in front of him for his insolence. No one could insult her that way and get away with it.

However, just as Erif had promised, her hand didn't even make it to two inches from his chest. Her spell had frozen his muscles keeping them from moving. She had permitted only his mouth muscles movement so that he could speak. Nevertheless, she could not prevent him from using his ability to shoot fire out of his body.

Flames shot out of his body and burned Queen Death. As she fell to the ground, Erif was released from the spell. Then, he quickly killed the rest of her army that was with her, and he flew back to the waterfall and hid there with the Filoses.

Chapter Twenty-one

Kimberly was amazed by all of the details that she had learned about Erif. Once she understood that he was a simple orphan who had been given great power, she could perceive the depth of his soul. She felt like she could relate to his sufferings. Even though she never witnessed the death of her parents, she had suffered in other ways. Her parents were still alive as far as she knew. However, their divorce was a painful memory within her soul that she always carried with her.

She related to his pain because she felt like pain was universal. She had come to the conclusion that everyone suffers in different ways. She had never met someone over thirty years old who had not suffered in some way. In some cases, their suffering was plainly visible; in other cases, it was interior.

Her suffering was interior. She had a boring life in comparison to Erif. She had graduated with honors. She had a good job before the aliens had abducted her. She made plenty of money.

However, something was missing from her life. She was constantly lonely. She didn't know how to communicate with people. She longed to have someone that would hold her and love her. She would see attractive men and think about what she would do if those men were interested in her.

She had so much passion within her heart and no way to release it. She had slept alone in her apartment for ten years. She never went shopping. She simply went to work, ate her meals, went home and slept. This routine had repeated itself from the time she was twenty until she got abducted by aliens at the age of thirty.

There would be days when she sat in her room crying with her face in her pillow. She didn't know why she was crying. She just knew that she was lonely. There were many nights where she had cried herself to sleep.

She had started getting desperate just before getting abducted. She started thinking that none of the attractive guys would go out with a thirty-year-old virgin. So, she tried going out on a date with a three-hundred-pound five-foot-eight man. Half way through the date, she ran off crying. The man was a little confused as to why she ran off crying.

She had simply realized that there was no way she could ever kiss the pig in front of her. His name was Andrew. He was a prototypical slob. As he was eating, he was spilling food all over his shirt. His stomach was so big that he couldn't even tuck his shirt in; the bottom part of his stomach was hanging out. He had mustard stains under his lower lip. She could see the top of his butt crack above the top of his pants as he walked. It was too much to bear.

    When Kimberly and Erif had finished watching each other's lives using telepathic communication, they had both gained a great deal of respect for each other. The interesting thing about telepathic communication was that it permitted them to feel the emotions that the person had experienced. Therefore, they weren't just seeing what had happened, but they were truly experiencing what the other had experienced. In this way, Erif was able to experience the depth of loneliness felt by Kimberly; and Kimberly was able to experience confusion, hatred and fear that had been felt by Erif when his father and grandfather were executed.

    "You suffered so much pain," Kimberly said in a gentle voice as she looked at him with a loving expression.

    However, Erif looked at her with a confused face. "Don't forget that Erif doesn't speak English," a voice told Kimberly telepathically. "We helped you share information with our ability to communicate telepathically. But he is a Seregine. The Seregines don't have the ability to communicate telepathically."

    "So, if I want to talk to him, you have to help us?" Kimberly asked.

"For now. If he can learn your language, or if you can learn his language, you will be able to communicate without our help."

Kimberly looked up as she was thinking about something. "You called him a Seregine. What is that?"

"It is what they call themselves. It is their race. There are four intelligent races on this planet. This planet is called Ademud, and it is inhabited by Seregines, Delikies, Filoses and Primees. You were a slave with the Primees. The Filoses are the little green people with three eyes and four arms. Queen Death is technically a Delikie, but she doesn't look anything like them anymore. Erif is a Seregine, but he doesn't look like a typical Seregine anymore after his transformation. However, now that you saw the Delikies and Seregines in the telepathic communication with Erif, you can understand what they should look like."

"The ones who killed Erif's father and grandfather were Delikies, right? Why do they look so similar to humans? Shouldn't aliens look different?"

"Please, don't call us aliens. We are not from Earth, but we are still intelligent sentient beings. We are known by our races. To answer your question, the Delikies are basically human."

Kimberly's eyes almost popped out of her head. "But how is that possible?"

"I didn't say that they are human. I said that they are basically human. It's a long story. The long and short of it is that you share similar genetics because you share a common ancestor from several million years ago."

"How do you know this?"

"Our people have never lost the written records in what we call *Chronicles Of The Moldrekians*. That doesn't mean that our version of the history is complete. We simply have knowledge about your distant ancestors that were propagating their race across several planets. Earth was one, and Ademud was another."

"What do you call your race?"

"Some humans have gotten into the habit of calling us grays because of our skin color. However, we call ourselves Merkians."

"Who is our distant ancestor?"

"The Moldrekians are ancestors to the Delikies, Seregines, Primees, humans, Mogians, and us."

Kimberly gasped. "We share an ancestor with Merkians?"

"Yes. That is one of the reason we are interested in studying humans. Like I said, it is a long story." Suddenly, the conversation was interrupted. One of the Merkians communicated something to the one that Kimberly was talking to. "We have a visitor. A human has just arrived here from Earth. The Retagians brought him."

They stood up and walked towards the tunnel that led to the entrance of the cave. Suddenly, Kimberly saw a human walking next to a few Merkians. He was wearing a spacesuit. His helmet was under his arm. He had an AR-15 strapped to his body along with some other gadgets that she didn't recognize. He had something in his ear that reminded her of a Bluetooth.

As soon as his eyes fixed upon Kimberly, he exclaimed, "There are other humans that have survived like me!"

"Survived what?" Kimberly asked.

"You know! Earth's gravity was reversed, and later, the Earth was completely destroyed."

Kimberly covered her mouth with her right hand. "When did this happen?"

"Wait a minute. You really don't know, do you? How long has it been since you left Earth?"

Kimberly shrugged. "I don't know. I lost track of time. I know that it's been a long time."

"About three months ago, Earth's gravity was reversed. I survived. There was a race of aliens that rescued us called the Nemodians."

"They don't like being called aliens."

"Whatever. Like I was saying, the Nemodians rescued us. They have blue skin, six arms, seven eyes, four ears, two mouths..."

Kimberly squinted as she listened to these details. "They sound like monsters."

Namrips sighed. "They were actually pretty nice. However, I just recently found out that they may be the ones responsible for the gravity reversal. I'm still confused about that one. I'm not sure if I can trust the Retagians, but if they are telling me the truth, then the Nemodians are actually responsible. Anyway, I enlisted into their army because I thought they were the good guys. They had told me that the Theadlians wanted to exterminate humans. So, as we were fighting against the Theadlians, they released an inter-dimensional creature called Jeggolith. Jeggolith swallowed the Earth and the sun. So yeah, if you were thinking about returning to Earth, it doesn't exist anymore."

Kimberly took a large gulp of her own mucus in her throat as she was trying to digest the new information. "So, they're all dead?"

"Everyone that was on Earth at the time would probably be dead now. What's your name?"

"Kimberly."

"I'm Namrips."

"What kind of name is that? Were your parents high?"

Namrips looked at her shocked. "That's kind of rude don't you think?"

"I'm sorry. It just slipped out. I've never been good with people. Everyone says I'm a nerd."

"Don't worry. I'm not mad. Namrips is the name that my father gave me. He said that it had special meaning and that he would tell me what it meant when I was old enough to understand."

"So, what does it mean? Did your father ever tell you?"

"No, he died when I was nine years old."

Kimberly covered her mouth with both hands at hearing this revelation. "I'm sorry to hear that."

Namrips took a deep breath. "It was a long time ago. My father got HIV, but he never told me. I found out when he got cancer. I was asking why they couldn't do chemotherapy or something to help him survive his lung cancer. He said that they couldn't do that with HIV positive patients, and he just had to wait for death to come for him. I was blown away. I didn't care that my dad was gay. I was sad that he didn't tell me sooner."

"That's something that I've never understood," Kimberly said cocking her head. "How is it possible for a gay man to have children and a wife? I'm not homophobic. I just don't get it. I see it all the time."

"I'm sure that it would never happen if our society was more accepting of gay people so that they didn't have to live their lives in secret. But my dad was different. He was probably bisexual rather than gay. My mom died while giving birth to me, and he just dated men after that. I realized after my father told me about the HIV. I thought back to all the guys we had over at the house, and my brain put two and two together."

"To be fair, straight people get HIV too." Kimberly was trying to get away from the topic, but she didn't want to end it abruptly either.

"Oh, trust me, I know," Namrips chuckled. "I studied up on the disease as soon as I found out that my father had it. It was a lot for a nine-year-old boy, but I was determined to understand."

Kimberly seized this opportunity to change the topic completely. "So, what do we do now? I mean with the Earth destroyed and all."

"We have to make a new life on a new planet. That's all we can do."

"Well, that's easier said than done. This planet is full of insects bigger than my house was in Arizona. On top of that, there is a crazy witch called Queen Death that wants to enslave all living creatures on this planet."

Namrips coughed and, then, looked at Kimberly with a smile. "Life just keeps getting weirder and weirder. *Queen Death*? Witch? Insects bigger than a house? I can see the green guys with three eyes and four arms over there. I'm in hell aren't I?"

"Well, you ain't far from it on this planet. I think the devil has his second home right here."

One of the Merkians decided to chime in and began to communicate telepathic messages to both of them. "If humans are going to start over on this planet, you have to defeat Queen Death," it said. "However, you cannot come here to dominate like you did on Earth. You have to be willing to share with the other intelligent species on this planet."

"But Queen Death's magic is so powerful!" Kimberly exclaimed. "How can we defeat her?"

"First, you must understand that it isn't magic," The Merkian responded. "When a race advances beyond animal intelligence but still hasn't reached maturity in their intelligence, they start trying to explain the world around them. Magic is the way they explain what they have yet to understand. All sentient beings that have intelligence have certain psychic capabilities that need to be developed. These psychic abilities can be assisted by other technological devices to do things that appear to be magical to those who are unaware of this technology."

"Are you saying that Queen Death has some sort of device that permits her to do what we perceive as magic?" Namrips asked.

"She realized that Deeb had built a machine that allowed him to do things. He was simply permitting her to tap into this machine with her own psychic abilities. That way, he was able to monitor what she was capable of doing and maintain control. This also kept her in the dark so that she could never usurp his power. However, she found out about it from the same beings that had given the knowledge to Deeb. This allowed her to build her own machine that was more powerful than Deeb's machine. This is why magic will accompany sacrifices sometimes.

Death of a creature will create pockets of energy at the quantum realm that can be harnested with the right equipment."

"So if we destroy her machine, she will lose her powers?" Namrips inquired in a thoughtful tone.

"She will lose most of her powers. Her army of orange men will definitely transform back into Delikies."

"Where is the machine?" Kimberly asked.

"If someone puts such a machine where it can be easily found, that person is at risk of losing one's power. Therefore, the typical practice for a person like Queen Death is to hide the machine deep inside of the planet. The closer you come to the machine, the more obstacles there are that can kill you. You have to remember that this machine connects one's natural psychic abilities to the natural energies of the universe that is present in every atom. This technology is like a catch-all that permits one to do whatever their imagination is capable of dreaming up. That is why people see it as magic. Its powers can, sometimes, seem unlimited within the hands of a very creative being. Therefore, I cannot tell you what obstacles will appear. It completely depends on the imagination of Queen Death. This is probably why Erif still has his abilities even after Deeb's death. No one will likely try to find Deeb's machine. It is likely that such an adventure would lead to your death."

"But do you know where it is?" Namrips pressed further.

"We can take you there. We consider humans to be our brothers. We want to help you survive. I just want you to understand that we will likely die."

"Considering that you can speak to us telepathically, you must have some psychic abilities too," Kimberly observed. "Is that how you know all of this?"

"Like I said, all sentient beings have certain capabilities. You just have to discover them. We have technology that helps us communicate telepathically. It is the same type of technology used by Queen Death. However, we have certain laws guiding how we are allowed to use it because of its potential to harm others. Humans used to have this technology as well. That is how the pyramids of Egypt were built."

The Merkian turned to Erif, and it appeared that they were having a telepathic conversation. Then it turned toward Namrips and Kimberly. "Erif said that he cannot come with us because he has to protect the Filoses."

"So are we going to try to destroy the machine?" Namrips asked.

"Yes," the Merkian responded. "Let's be going, for death doesn't like to be kept waiting."

Chapter Twenty-two

Namrips, Kimberly, and seven Merkians were walking together. Namrips was carrying an AR-15. He still had all of his battle equipment. The only difference now was that his oxygen tank was turned off, and his helmet was connected to his belt.

Kimberly was still wearing the same clothes that she was wearing when she arrived. She was extremely dirty. Her pants had holes in them. Her hands were black. Her hair was all over the place and sticky. She desired so bad to take a shower.

The Merkians were carrying small devices in their hands. There weren't any buttons on the devices; they controlled them telepathically. The devices were black cone-shaped objects with a green light on the end facing away from the Merkians. The green bulb on the far end had a larger diameter than the side that the Merkian held in its hand. The devices seemed like they could do almost anything; they could shoot lasers, open inter-dimensional portals, levitate objects, create force fields, and just about anything that the Merkian could imagine as long as it didn't require more energy than the device could put out in one blast. The only limitation seemed to be that it couldn't do two functions simultaneously; it had to be used for only one thing at a time.

As they walked, Kimberly observed her surroundings. There were many insects that were the size of cars and trucks. There were centipedes as long as a football field. At first, when the insects got too close to them, Namrips started shooting them. However, the Merkians did not like this option as they were opposed to killing innocent creatures. Therefore, they gently asked Namrips to stop shooting them. Then, the Merkians started opening up portals with their hand held devices that sent them to another dimension momentarily. Then, the insect would reappear in this dimension at a different location.

They walked for several hours like this. No matter how dangerous the creature was, the Merkians were able to get rid of it. However, they finally ran into a problem that the Merkians could not solve with their handheld devices. *Quicksand* on Ademud was more like a yellow goo. It trapped its victims because of how sticky it was.

As they walked into the *quicksand*, they felt like their feet were being glued to the ground. As they tried to fight their way out of it, they sank more rapidly. It felt like it was alive. It was as if the yellow goo tightened around their legs, pulled them a little further down, released them slightly as it reset at a higher point on the legs, and pulled again repeating the process.

"Kimberly!" Namrips yelled. "Don't fight it! It sucks us in faster if you fight it!"

"I noticed!" Kimberly replied. "Can't you get us out of this with your technology?" She asked the Merkians.

"No," it replied. "We must pass through this."

"Why do we have to pass through this? What if it kills us?"

"It might kill us, but there is no other way." They continued to sink. All of the Merkians, Kimberly, and Namrips were all stuck in the yellow goo. Kimberly didn't understand why they could send huge insects through portals to other locations, but they couldn't get them out of this predicament. Perhaps, moving them through a portal would also move the quicksand through the same portal. That was the only reason she could think of at the moment. If that was the case, then they would still be sinking in the quicksand if they were moved to a different place.

"I always thought that I would die of old age on a bed," Namrips said to Kimberly. "Since gravity reversed on Earth until now, I keep thinking that I'm living my last moment. I constantly feel like I'm going to die."

"Do you think we're going to die now?" Kimberly asked.

"Yes."

"Why can't you lie and tell me, no?"

"Okay," Namrips laughed. "No, we aren't going to survive."

"That's not funny."

"Why do we do things like this?"

Kimberly looked at Namrips and frowned. "What do you mean by '*we*,' and what do you mean by '*like this*'?"

"By '*we*', I mean *we humans*. Why do we humans prolong our death? Here we are sinking to certain death. We are trying to be as still as possible so that we can live a few minutes longer before we are suffocated underneath this yellow goo."

"If you wanna die faster, you can lead the way by fighting the goo."

Namrips shook his head. "Obviously, I don't want to do that. But why? What is five more minutes in comparison with how long we will be dead afterwards?"

"What do you think happens after death?"

"My friend, Fiki, had told me about the initial phases. The Nemodians have technology that allows them to surpass death sometimes. However, it doesn't always work, and they don't know what happens after that. It bothers me."

"Why?"

Namrips sighed deeply. "We use our brain to think, right?"

"Yes."

"So what will our soul use to think? What will our soul use to see? What will our soul use to hear? What will our soul use to feel?"

"So, you think that there isn't a soul?" Kimberly was always very careful to phrase things properly by saying things like, "you think." She had read enough philosophy to know that everything always boiled down to *we think*.

"I think the soul, or whatever it is, senses and exists in a way that would be incomprehensible to us. Linear thought would be impossible. It makes me question the legitimacy of any afterlife without a body."

At this point the Merkians submerged underneath the yellow goo. Kimberly and Namrips were down to their necks. They knew that they were almost out of time.

"Did you know that I'm a virgin?" Kimberly asked.

"Why are you telling me this?" Namrips asked in a disgusted tone.

Kimberly's eyes were full of tears. "I'm about to die. So I decided to say it. No man has ever wanted me."

"Well, it's not for a lack of beauty."

"Why do you say that?" Kimberly asked unable to see anything through her tears; she had no way to wipe them away.

"I looked at you. You are physically beautiful. If no man wants you, it is probably your personality."

"Well, that's comforting."

Narmips frowned. "It's not an insult. Sometimes, more intelligent people have more complicated personalities. You just need to find the man that is on your wave length."

"Didn't you say that the Earth was destroyed?"

"Yes."

"So, that guy no longer exists."

"Yeah, he's probably dead. You're right." At this point their heads were slipping beneath the yellow goo. They took one last deep breath as they sank below.

Chapter Twenty-three

When Kimberly woke up, she was lying in a pool of sewage water. It was about three inches deep, so she was able to lay there on her back with her nostrils unimpeded. She sat up and looked around. She saw feces in the water floating around, rotting animals, and rotting corpses of human beings. It smelled so bad that she began to vomit.

She was surrounded by fog. "Namrips!" She called out. There was no answer. *Where am I?* She wondered. *Am I dead?*

When she stood up, she heard a sound. It sounded like a low growl. Something was in the water. She could hear the water moving in the distance. She looked in the direction of the growl. She stared as hard as she could trying to see what was being blocked by the fog in the distance. After a moment of staring, she made out the shape of a large squid-like creature that was thirty feet tall and had hundreds of tentacles.

Kimberly was so scared that her entire body began to shake violently. She began to cry uncontrollably. She didn't know what she could do or where she could run. She fell to her knees and vomited again.

    The beast was slowly moving in her direction. She could hear it sloshing in the water. She closed her eyes for a moment, and she imagined her mother's face. Her mother had always given her strength when she was scared. She imagined her mother reaching out her arm for her to grab.

    She opened her eyes and looked at the beast that was inching closer. Then, she took off running in the opposite direction. The sewage water stopped at a muddy shore. Kimberly continued to run onto the mud.

    Kimberly only thought that she was escaping the beast. In reality, she was running towards an army of *ants*. However, these weren't ordinary *ants*. Each ant was five inches long. These *ants* also had tails that resembled a scorpion's stinger.

    Kimberly stopped as soon as she saw them. She turned around and looked at the beast in the water. It was still inching towards her. Then, she looked at the ants again; they were stationary. No matter which direction she chose, she had to fight with something.

****

    Namrips woke up surrounded by flames. He looked around and saw nothing but fire for miles and miles. He heard people moaning. There was no sun. There was no sky. It was pitch-black. He was trapped by the flame; he couldn't leave. An ugly naked red creature came walking through the flames and joined Namrips.

The creature was twenty feet tall. It had three faces. There was a face in the middle and one face coming out of each side. All three mouths had sharp teeth. It had four arms and hundreds of tentacles. The tentacles came out of its back. It had two muscular legs and a muscular body. Each face had six eyes.

"How do you like your new home in hell?" The creature asked.

"How do I know that this is hell, and I'm not simply dreaming?" Namrips retorted.

The creature didn't care for Namrips' disrespectful tone, so it decided to take care of the matter. It grabbed Namrips by the neck and lifted him off of the ground. "I am fear. You will fear me. If you choose not to fear me, I'll rain down fear upon your head. If you stay in this circle, you will stay safe. If you leave this circle, the powers of hell will devour you. I will crush every bone in your body."

Chapter Twenty-four

Kimberly was terrified. Her legs were trembling. She fell to her knees and began to cry. When she did this, the ants began moving closer to her. They were moving incredibly fast. She felt dizzy. She began breathing heavily as her heart rate accelerated. Her mind was frantic.

Tears were streaming down her face as she cried out, "Please! If there is a God, save me!" Kimberly wasn't religious. She was agnostic. She was indifferent to whether God existed or not. However, in this moment of intense fear, she was grasping for any possibility of being saved.

The ants continued advancing. They covered her body and began stinging her. She screamed in pain as she began rolling around trying to get them off. The ants stung her eyes and blinded her; the pain was so great that she passed out.

As soon as she passed out, the ants dispersed. Small three-foot-tall creatures came out of a cave. They picked up her body and took it back to their cave. Their skin was yellow. They had two arms and two legs. They had seven fingers and seven toes on each hand and foot. Their heads were in the shape of a light bulb, and their eyes were large and purple.

****

The large demon-like creature set Namrips back down. Then, the beast walked away. It walked into the flames and disappeared from sight. Namrips sat down on a large rock. *What else can I do?* He thought.

Namrips began to reflect on his situation. *Am I dead? No. If I die, I will have to confront Jeggolith. I will have the opportunity to get back to my new body with the Nemodians. How can I think? How can I feel? How can I see? My body is physical. Therefore, my existence must be physical. Therefore, I'm not dead. Where am I? How did I get here? I fell into that yellow goo with Kimberly. I don't understand how I got from there to here.*

At the moment that he finished these reflections, he noticed a small hole in the ground. The demon had told him not to leave the circle. However, it hadn't told him that he could not enter a hole in the ground. He would technically still be inside of the circle.

Namrips walked over to the hole. He crouched beside it and looked inside. Going head first made him nervous. Therefore, he decided to enter feet first. The hole was a very small tunnel; it was just big enough for him to crawl inside, and it went down at an inclination.

Namrips advanced down the tunnel feet first little by little. He was inching along by pushing his body off the surface a little with his hands and allowing himself to move down. He continued going down this tunnel as he got deeper and deeper into the planet.

The farther he went down into the hole, the darker it became. He continued to advance until he could no longer see any light at all. Under normal circumstances, he would never have crawled into a dark hole that he had no idea where it would lead. However, this was different; it appeared to be his only possible escape.

After several minutes of inching along in complete darkness, he suddenly felt a sharp pain in his left toe. He couldn't see what it was, but he was sure that some creature was chewing on his foot. He could even hear his bones in his foot breaking as the creature chewed.

Namrips screamed in pain. He tried to back away, but the creature stayed with his foot and continued to eat it. He frantically tried to climb back up the tunnel towards the entrance that he could no longer see. However, no matter how quickly he moved, the creature continued to eat his foot. It was as if the creature was attached to him.

By the time Namrips could see a glimmer of light from the entrance of the tunnel, the creature had eaten his entire left foot all the way to his ankle. The pain was almost unbearable. His screams had become grunts as his vocal chords became worn out.

"Ha ha ha!" A voice bellowed from the entrance of the tunnel. It was the twenty-foot red monster that had threatened him. "You thought you would escape through the tunnel because I'm too big to fit down there, didn't you? Those little shetrins will eat you alive!"

The creature that was eating Namrips left leg, a shetrin, was a round little ball with short insect-like legs to help it move around. It had huge teeth and a jaw that was stronger than any alligator.

Namrips knew that he could not go back up to the entrance. The red creature would destroy him. He had a better chance fighting off the shetrin. So, he began kicking it with his right foot hoping that he could separate it from his left leg.

It seemed to work a little bit. When he put enough force into his kicks, it felt like the shetrin fell backwards momentarily. However, it was able to grab hold of his leg again every time. Therefore, Namrips became desperate for a solution. He began to force his way through the tunnel hoping that he would find an end. He was going deeper and deeper as the shetrin was eating more of his leg.

When the shetrin had eaten all the way up to his left knee, he fell into some water. The water was very deep. However, he noticed that the shetrin was having a hard time maintaining hold of his left leg in the water. It was pitch black. He couldn't even see his hands in front of him.

Suddenly, something else grabbed hold of his right ankle. It was the tentacle of a very large octopus. It pulled him under the water. He hadn't taken a very deep breath before going under, so he was not going to be able to survive for very much longer. However, the octopus continued to drag him deeper and deeper down.

Chapter Twenty-five

Kimberly woke up inside of a cage. However, she didn't know that it was a cage yet because she was blind. Her entire body was swollen, and it was hurting. She moaned.

"Look, the virgin is waking up!" She heard a voice say. It was one of the yellow creatures.

"What does it matter to you if I'm a virgin or not?" She snapped back without even attempting to look in the creature's direction; she wouldn't have been able to see anything even if she had tried to look.

"Oh, is the virgin mad? There is a reason that no man wants you!"

"You don't even know me!" Kimberly screamed.

"Are you sure that I don't know you? I am your worst fears. I am you."

"What is that supposed to mean?"

The creature laughed. "You will know later on."

"Where am I?" She demanded.

"You are nowhere."

"That's impossible!"

"Not if you're already dead." The creature slapped its leg and had another hearty laugh.

"I'm not dead, or I wouldn't be having this conversation."

The creature stopped laughing. "That may be true, but you'll be dead soon."

"Why? Are you planning on killing me?"

"No. You're going to kill yourself."

Even in her pain, Kimberly's body filled with rage at this. "I will never kill myself!" She declared.

"That's what you think." One of the yellow creatures opened the cage. It grabbed Kimberly and carried her out. It tied her arms to a table with her back exposed. Then the creature grabbed a whip. Kimberly began to scream as she felt the whip thrashing her back.

****

There were a few strange things happening that had grabbed Namrips' attention. He should have been bleeding to death because of the shetrin that had eaten his leg all the way to his knee. However, his leg wasn't bleeding at all. Also, he felt like his body wasn't responding properly to the environment that he saw around him. It was hard for him to put his finger on it. It was as if his body was really somewhere else. What he was experiencing seemed more real than a dream, but something within him felt like it was some sort of hallucination.

Suddenly, he saw one of the Merkians swimming with him as the octopus was dragging him deeper into the water. "Breathe," the Merkian communicated telepathically. "The water doesn't really exist. It is an illusion. Stay strong." Then the Merkian disappeared.

Namrips was afraid to try it, but he knew that he was about to pass out if he didn't breathe. So, he began breathing. Oxygen began to pass into his lungs. It was weird seeing water all around himself and be able to breathe like that. This filled his mind with all sorts of questions about what was really happening to him at this moment.

The only thing that Namrips could consider was the yellow goo. That was the last thing that he remembered before finding himself in hell. Perhaps, the goo had some sort of power to make him hallucinate an alternative reality. He wondered how the alternative reality could be broken.

As he considered these things, a very large beast was swimming by. Its mouth was bigger than the octopus. Therefore, the octopus easily fit inside, and it bit down. This caused Namrips to be released. Namrips began to swim up to the surface. It took him a very long time because of how far down the octopus had taken him.

It didn't really matter how long it took since he could breathe normally. When he reached the surface, it was raining heavily. There was a man on a large boat that saw Namrips.

"Hey!" He called out. "There's a man in the water! Pull him on board!" They immediately received Namrips on board.

This brought more reflections to Namrips. He had left the Earth. The Earth had been completely destroyed by Jeggolith. The octopus was a creature from the Earth, and now, he was talking to human beings. It was as if he was back on his home planet. *How was this possible?* This gave credence to the possibility that he was hallucinating. However, if he were inside of the yellow goo, he wouldn't be able to breathe. *How had he gotten out of the yellow goo?* The last thing he remembered was being convinced that he was about to die in the *quicksand*.

"Where am I?" Namrips asked the sailors.

"We are at sea! Ain't it obvious, son?" The captain replied.

"That part is obvious, but where? Are we close to Europe? Are we off the coast of Florida? Are we in Asia?"

"Them be some fancy words, son. I've never heard of 'em."

"Have you heard of America?"

"Nope. Can't say I have."

Namrips scratched his head as he stood there on his two feet. He had forgotten about his left foot that had gotten eaten, and hadn't yet wondered how his foot had reappeared. "What planet are we on?"

"Stop inventing words, son. I ain't never heard of a planet."

"You're making this difficult. Just tell me what part of the sea we are in. Is there dry land somewhere?"

The man laughed at that. "There be dry land! But they be at war."

Chapter Twenty-six

Kimberly's body was swollen from the ant stings and bleeding from the flogging. She was lying in her cage moaning in pain. The yellow creatures were standing there laughing at her. "You will die a virgin," they called out. "No man will ever love you. You are a loathsome creature." They continued to repeat this over and over.

After several hours of this, they opened the cage and took her out again. They chained her to a stone pillar. Then, they put a glass of water at the perfect distance so that she could touch it but not grab it. They had poured a little water on her lips so that she knew that it was water because she was still blind. Then, they led her by the hand so that she could feel where they had placed the water.

Kimberly attempted to grab the water at first, but when she realized what they had done to her, she immediately stopped trying and lay there without moving. The yellow creatures roared with laughter. "The virgin gave up!" They cried out. "She is going to die now!"

Suddenly, a large red creature entered the room. It was seven feet tall. It had ten arms and four legs. It had one eye. Its mouth was full of teeth that literally looked like knives projecting out of its gums. It was naked and had no gender. Its ears were long with points at the ends.

"Make sure you feed her," the creature commanded. "Don't forget that she must kill herself. We will not be responsible for her death."

The yellow creatures immediately took her and led her to an area where the pigs were kept. She was thrown inside with the pigs. They dumped food on top of her head. "If you don't eat, you will die. If you die, we will all be happy. Therefore, do us all a favor and don't eat."

After having heard them so openly declare that they wanted her to kill herself, she became resolved to eat. She wanted to survive. She wanted to show them that they couldn't make her take her own life. Therefore, she began picking the food off of the ground and eating it. She was blind, so she didn't know what the food looked like, but she trusted that it was real food because they had declared that they wanted her to kill herself.

At first, it almost made her vomit, but she got used to it. She didn't know how long she could last in these conditions, but she didn't want to give these creatures the satisfaction of controlling her so easily. Therefore, she continued to strive to keep nutrition in her body to endure the daily floggings.

****

Namrips looked up at the dark clouds. It was starting to rain heavier. The waves were getting larger. The boat was unstable. Namrips was beginning to have a hard time standing in one place; that is when he realized that he had his whole left leg back. *How is it possible for my leg to get eaten and appear again later?* He wondered.

"There be a hurricane, lad!" The captain yelled.

"The way I see it, the hurricane is a punishment from Poseidon," another sailor said.

"That lad got on board, and a hurricane came," said another.

"Don't be stupid!" The captain said. "Poseidon doesn't exist!"

"How dare you say that!" The sailor screamed. "Maybe the hurricane is your fault! I suggest we throw the captain overboard!" All of the sailors began to agree.

"It's mutiny then!" The captain cried out.

"Nooo!" Namrips screamed. "You can't be serious! You can't throw your captain overboard! That is murder."

"What's wrong with murder?" One of the sailors asked.

"You should strive to never take the life of another human being."

"Why human beings? What about chicken?"

"We eat chicken."

"What if I want to eat the captain? Is it okay if I eat him?"

"Where would ya cook me, lad?" The captain asked.

"I could eat you raw."

"No!" Namrips interjected. "He is human. You can't eat humans."

"Why not? I don't understand why I can eat chicken, pigs, and cows but not humans."

"You are sick," Namrips declared. The waves were becoming even larger, and the rain was falling even harder. The boat was being tossed about on the waves. Namrips had to grab hold of the side of the ship to keep from going overboard.

Several sailors attacked the captain. They began to punch him until he was unconscious. Then, one of the sailors did what would seem impossible for a civilized people; he bit the captain's neck and ripped a piece of flesh off of his neck with his teeth. Namrips couldn't believe what he was seeing, but he couldn't do anything about it because of the storm; he was barely able to keep himself from going overboard.

Suddenly, another sailor stabbed the sailor who was eating the captain in the back with a knife. He pulled the knife out and stabbed him again. He continued stabbing him after he fell limp. Another sailor approached and hit the sailor who was stabbing the other with a metal pole.

The boat turned into a blood bath with everyone attacking each other. The scene put fear in Namrips' heart. As his fear increased, the waves of the sea increased in size. The people who were attacking increased in size and turned into zombie monsters with sharp fangs.

N   amrips observed the change and immediately understood it. Something about his level of fear was directly responsible for what he was seeing. He didn't know how or why, but he knew that it was true. The transformation from humans to zombies was unexplainable by any other means.

One of the zombies attacked Namrips. It was twice his size. He ducked and dove face first towards the center of the boat. He slid along the slippery wood to the other side. The monster fell overboard because it couldn't stop. The zombie was swallowed up by the large waves.

Namrips looked up and saw that the boat was completely empty. The hurricane continued to toss the boat back and forth. Waves were crashing down on the it. Suddenly, Poseidon emerged from the water. He was one hundred feet tall.

"I could kill you now," Poseidon declared.

"No, you can't," Namrips said.

"Why not?" Poseidon asked.

"Because you are me," Namrips asserted. Everything immediately disappeared. Namrips woke up. He was lying under the yellow goo in a dark cave. There was a dim light coming from the device that the Merkian had in its hand. It was sitting at a distance.

Namrips looked around. There were six Merkians who were lying as if asleep and Kimberly as well. Kimberly's chest was noticeably moving up and down showing that she was still breathing. However, the six Merkians that were lying down didn't appear to be breathing. There was only one Merkian that was awake.

"What's going on?" Namrips asked the Merkian.

"We had to pass through that trial to get to Queen Death's machine," it replied telepathically.

"So we are on track. What about the others? Why aren't they awake yet?"

"My friends are dead. Only Kimberly is left. Her destiny has not yet been decided."

"How did they die?"

"The yellow goo is under a spell. It causes you to live your worst fears. If you don't overcome them, you stay there, and you die. My friends were overcome by their fears. You overcame your fears. I gave you a little help telepathically, but in the end, you are the one who overcame. We still don't know if Kimberly will overcome or die."

"Can you help her like you did for me?"

"I can connect you to her telepathically. She doesn't trust Merkians yet. She will trust you more because you are human. However, you cannot tell her what is happening. If you do, she will die."

"Why will she die?"

"Because fear of fear is the worst of all. If she knows that fear is causing everything without having arrived at a certain point, she will become obsessed with the fear of fear, and she will never wake up again."

Chapter Twenty-seven
Kimberly lay in the darkness of her mind. She was blind, so she couldn't see the yellow creatures surrounding her and laughing at her. She could hear them laughing constantly. It was as if they never slept. She was inside the cage. She had become so depressed that she was always sleeping. Sometimes, she felt like her nightmares were better than her moments alive. Her cage was filling up with her feces and urine because they never allowed her to leave when she begged to go to the bathroom.

Suddenly, Namrips walked into the room. The yellow creatures stopped laughing and stood back from the cage. He walked up to the cage and kneeled close to Kimberly. "Listen," he said. "I'm going to get you out of here."

"Namrips?" Kimberly's voice trembled with pain.

He smiled. "It's me."

"Don't leave me, here!" She cried.

"Shhh. Don't worry." Namrips stood up and looked at the yellow creatures. "Open the cage," he demanded.

"No one can open the cage," one of the creatures responded.

"If you don't open the cage right now, I'm going to break your neck and kill all of your friends."

"You can't kill me," the creature declared. Namrips didn't waste any time. He wasn't in the mood for being patient. Aside from that, he knew that the creatures were products of Kimberly's imagination. So, he immediately began punching the little creature. The creature fell under the blows of Namrips' fists. Then, he began stomping on its head until it was clearly dead.

He turned to the others and said, "Open the cage now." One of them ran quickly to the cage and began fumbling around with some keys. It was frantically trying to find the right one. Namrips found it fitting that Kimberly's fears would have fears.

When the cage opened, Namrips ran up to the yellow creature and kicked it between the legs as hard as he could. It flew in the air and landed on its back three feet away. Namrips punched the creature that had been beside the one with the key. He went on a rampage and began killing all of the creatures. He didn't leave any of them standing. They were all dead.

After this, Namrips entered the cage. He took Kimberly up into his arms. Kimberly held on to his neck sobbing. He took her out of the cage and laid her down. He looked at her swollen body that had been damaged by the monstrous ants. He observed some of the scars produced by a whip. Her shirt was torn to shreds and was barely still on her body.

"There's nothing to fear," Namrips told her.

"What happened?" She asked still with tears in her eyes. "I remember thinking we were going to die in that yellow goo. The next thing I knew, I was in water, and there was a monster."

"You'll understand later. The most important thing right now is that you understand that you are safe." While Namrips was talking gently with Kimberly in this way, he noticed that her body was healing; the ant stings were disappearing, and the swelling was going down. The scars were also disappearing. Her eyes opened and she could see Namrips.

As soon as she realized that she could see Namrips, she hugged him tightly. "Thank you for saving me!" Namrips held her tight allowing her fear to subside even more.

When they stopped hugging and looked at each other, Kimberly asked, "Do you really think I'm beautiful?"

"Why do you ask?"

"Before we fell into the yellow goo, you told me that I was physically beautiful."

Namrips smiled and brushed his right hand through her hair. It had been sticky just moments before, but as her fear subsided, it looked clean, and his hand was able to easily glide through its strands. "Yes, you are. You are very beautiful. Whoever marries you will be very lucky." Kimberly felt a surge of passion in her heart. It was aching to kiss Namrips. She wanted to be held by him, but she was nervous. She had really just met him.

"You said that your father died when you were only nine years old, and your mother died giving birth. What happened after that? That would mean that you were an orphan. How did you survive?"

Namrips nodded as he looked away. It was a hard topic for him to discuss, but he supposed that conversation would help generate trust and, therefore, alleviate her fear even more. "The day my father died, I was standing there by his side in the hospital. I felt the warmth leave his body. I cried like I'd never cried before. I didn't know the eyes could produce so much water. They let me have my time with him, but you know how it is. They can't stay there forever. The had to pull me away from my father screaming."

Kimberly put her right hand over the top of her breasts. "Oh my god! I'm so sorry! That sounds awful for a nine-year-old."

Namrips looked into her eyes and saw her genuine feelings of sympathy in her eyes. "It was awful at the time, but life moves on, and pain becomes motivation. I died that day, but I was reborn too - like a Phoenix. At any rate, they sent me to a foster home. My father had been disowned by the family for being openly gay after my mother died. They complained that it would hurt me to see a gay father, and they didn't want any part of it. So, when he died, no one from the family wanted to take me. I was angry. I didn't want to be in a foster home. I felt abandoned. So, I ran away three times. They caught me the first two times, but I was sixteen the third time, and it was easier to avoid the police. I got into drugs and alcohol. When I was seventeen, just before my eighteenth birthday, I got caught selling a small amount of crack to an undercover agent. The judge looked at me and my record. So, I guess she felt compassion for this little orphan. She gave me two choices. I could go to prison for a couple years, or I could join the army. I joined the army, and I went to Alcoholics Anonymous meetings to make the judge happy. Then, I went to war and made a life for myself."

    Kimberly had listened to everything very attentively. She peered into Namrips' eyes, and the little flame that she had felt in her heart moments before became a huge bonfire. She couldn't resist another moment. She no longer *wanted* to kiss him; she *needed* to kiss him. She reached her right hand out and stroked his left cheek. Then, she brought her lips in close and kissed him passionately without considering the outcome. She just wanted to continue in that moment and hoped that it would never end.

Namrips kissed her back. Their tongues made contact. Their hearts were on fire. They were enveloped within their passion and within that moment. Then, Kimberly woke up staring up at the yellow goo.

Chapter Twenty-eight

Namrips immediately came back to reality as the Merkian that was connecting them telepathically realized that Kimberly was awake. Namrips ran over to Kimberly and hugged her again.

"Where am I?" She asked.

"We are in some sort of cave below the yellow goo that we had fallen into previously," Namrips answered as he pulled back with his hands holding Kimberly's shoulder's while he looked her in the eyes.

"What happened?" She inquired further.

"There was some sort of spell on the goo. It made us live all of our worst fears. The other Merkians died. This one is the only one that survived. My fear of death and what's beyond death was about to kill me, but he came to me telepathically and helped alleviate my fear enough to save me. Then, he told me that you don't trust Merkians, so only I could help you. He connected me to you telepathically, and somehow my presence helped bring you out of your fear."

Kimberly smiled, but Namrips could see her pain through her smile. "I think I know why." Namrips looked at her with curiosity. "Why?"

"I am afraid of dying without being loved by a man. When you kissed me, I woke up." She was worried that Namrips had only kissed her to save her life. Her mind started circulating with fears of potential abandonment. She had thought that she had finally received genuine love for a man, but what if he only kissed her to make her feel safe and save her life? What if he didn't truly love her? Perhaps, Namrips sensed her fear. Perhaps, there was something revealing about the way she was looking at him. He was still holding her by the shoulders. He pulled her in close and put his right hand around the back of her neck. He drew his lips close to hers and kissed her again. Then, she knew that her fears were for nothing; Namrips had kissed her in the truest way possible, and her fear disappeared.

"I don't want to interrupt such a heartwarming moment," the Merkian declared telepathically, "but we need to get moving."

There was a tunnel there that descended deeper into the planet. There was no light except the light that was coming from the Merkian's handheld device. Therefore, Namrips and Kimberly followed behind the Merkian as they continued on their way. Namrips and Kimberly were holding hands as they walked together. Namrips' AR-15 was strapped to his body.

After walking for about ten minutes in the tunnel, the Merkian suddenly stopped. "Come close to me," it told Namrips and Kimberly. They stood just behind the Merkian. A force field that had a slight blue glow surrounded them. "A creature that lives in the shadows is approaching."

They watched as a shadow moved in the distance. However, it could not touch the blue light, and therefore, it could not touch them. "Is it dangerous?" Namrips asked.

"What kind of question is that?" Kimberly retorted. "It's obviously dangerous, or we wouldn't be inside of this force field."

"I meant to ask how dangerous it is," Namrips claimed.

"If it touches you, you will be slowly shred to pieces," the Merkian explained. The watched as the shadow jumped around back and forth from one side to the other. The felt its presence, and it felt like something sinister like a demon from hell.

Suddenly, the gravity reversed, and they fell up to the ceiling of the tunnel. Their force field reversed directions with them. They all lost their breath for a second, and it took them several minutes to breathe properly. When Namrips finally caught his breath, he said, "The Nemodians have followed me."

Chapter Twenty-nine

Thousands of Nemodian spaceships had surrounded Ademud. They immediately began collecting whatever dead creatures that were falling into space. They collected the water that fell into space. Then, they flew their ships close to the surface and began using their lasers to dig holes in the surface.

They were constructing bases that were similar to the ones that they had put in the Earth. However, this time they were interrupted by the presence of someone else. Queen Death had brought her army of orange men. They began to fly around and destroy Nemodian ships.

It took a moment for the Nemodians to realize what was happening and adjust. They began firing lasers at the orange men. Therefore, from a distance, a person would have seen Nemodian spaceships exploding, and orange men being obliterated by lasers. When the lasers hit the orange men, their blood would spray in every direction. Their body parts and blood would fall up towards space. Fireballs were also flying out into space;

these fireballs were the pieces of Nemodian ships that had been destroyed.

Inside one of the Nemodian spaceships, Fiki was standing as he watched a screen. He was surrounded by many Nemodian officers. "Fiki, what is happening on Ademud?" A voice asked him over the radio.

"There is a large resistance on Ademud," Fiki responded. "It seems that they have a strange form of technology that gives their people unusual powers."

"How many casualties have there been so far?"

"They have destroyed hundreds of ships. So, I would estimate that our death toll is several thousand."

"What do you suggest?"

"I suggest we call for reinforcements and land on their planet. We should turn off the antigravity ray so that gravity can return to normal. We need to land on the surface of the planet and attack whatever ground force they have with CRCs."

"No. We have the advantage when the gravity is reversed. The gravity should never be allowed to be returned to normal until the planet is under our control."

"Sir, that isn't the case this time. They have the advantage against us with no gravity. Their people can fly, and they don't need spaceships to do it. Just one of them can completely destroy one of our ships as if it were a piece of paper. In this case, having normal gravity would give us a better chance at winning because we can use other aspects of our superior technology. I could prepare another army of dead with the dead animator. I could send out another batch of CRCs."

"Ah yes. That worked out really well against the Theadlians, didn't it? Have you done a report on that yet? Which one was more effective, the clones or the dead? We could invest all of our resources into the one that is more effective."

"I think that they are both equally effective as they both have advantages and disadvantages. Neither of them feels pain. They both have to be completely destroyed. The clones are stronger and kill more, but the dead are cheaper to create, so we can create a much larger army of them. Would I rather face ten clones or one million dead? Either way, I would be annihilated. I think we should continue to use both strategically."

"Collect the dead that flew out into space. Then, turn off the antigravity ray and proceed with the clones and the dead animator."

"You won't be disappointed." The transmission ended. Fiki didn't know that this was the planet that Namrips had gone to for refuge. He didn't know that the Retagians had found him. Namrips thought that they had followed him, but in reality, it was a coincidence that was leading toward their fate. Namrips would eventually have to face Fiki.

Chapter Thirty

Namrips stood up. He grabbed Kimberly by the hand and helped her stand up as well. Then, he walked over to the Merkian and helped it up. Inside the tunnel, it was impossible to perceive that they were upside down.

The shadow creature moved quickly around them looking for a point of entrance. They could see the shadow, but they could not see what was causing the shadow. They continued to walk forwards close to each other inside the force field produced by the handheld device that the Merkian carried.

Suddenly, they could see a multitude of little creatures lined up in the tunnel. They were two feet high and three feet long. Their teeth were razor-sharp. They were growling like a dog. They had ten legs. Each paw had sharp claws.

"If I use my device to eliminate the ten-legged creatures, the shadow creature will get to us," the Merkian explained. "If I don't eliminate the ten-legged creatures, they will eat us. If I move us outside of this dimension to change our locations, we can't re-enter. The yellow goo is the only entrance."

"So, what are we going to do?" Namrips asked.

"I'm going to give you my device. Use your mind to make it do whatever you want it to do. It receives telepathic commands. It can be used as a light. It can be used as a force field. It can be used as a force field that emits light. It can be used as a weapon. It can send creatures to other dimensions. It can shoot lasers. You think about what you want it to do, and if it can do it, it will do it."

Namrips scratched his head. "Why can't the force field keep both the shadow creature and the ten-leggers out at the same time?"

The Merkian smiled. "This force field works on the shadow creature because of the light it emits. It does not work on physical entities. If I create a force field for physical entities, it won't work on the shadow creature."

"Why are you going to give the device to me?" As soon as Namrips asked this question the ten-legged creatures began running towards them.

"No time to explain," the Merkian said. "Just do what I told you." The Merkian allowed the force field to turn off, and the ten-legged creatures immediately disappeared (the Merkian had sent them to another dimension). The Merkian immediately threw its device into the air towards

Namrips as it jumped towards the shadow creature, which had already entered their area.

Namrips caught the device and immediately thought about the same force field. As the force field came back, the Merkian's blood began to spurt everywhere. The Merkian was carried away screaming in pain. It had sacrificed its life to save Namrips and Kimberly.

"It looks like we are alone now," Namrips said looking at Kimberly. Her face was completely white. She sat down.

"I can't go on," she whispered.

Namrips sat down next to her. "Yes, you can," he whispered into her ear.

"No, it's not that I'm afraid to go on. I physically can't do it. I feel dizzy."

"I have an oxygen tank. You can take some breaths if you need it." Namrips turned his oxygen tank on, and both of them began taking turns breathing. When the gravity had reversed, the oxygen had begun to fall away from the surface of Ademud. It was starting to feel like they were trying to achieve an impossible goal. They would almost certainly run out of oxygen long before they had finished their mission.

Chapter Thirty-one

Namrips and Kimberly didn't have to wait very long for the gravity to return to normal. They fell to the ground as soon as it happened, and Namrips was in shock. Kimberly didn't know what to expect, but Namrips knew the Nemodians personally. It was hard to understand why the Nemodians would reverse the gravity and, then, let it go back to normal. Namrips couldn't wrap his mind around it. They sat there for about another ten minutes trying to catch their breath.

"Let's get moving," Namrips whispered. Kimberly followed him down the tunnel. As they traveled, they saw a purple light in the distance. It was a portal that extended into another dimension. The portal was placed at the end of the tunnel, so they had no other choice but to go through it.

When Kimberly and Namrips crossed over into the next dimension, their nostrils were filled with an amazing aroma. They were in what appeared to be the lobby of an expensive hotel. Just the smell alone almost brought them to ecstasy. There was a mahogany spiral staircase that seemed to go up infinitely; they could not see a ceiling. The floor was a soft pink color. Everything else was either red or purple. There was a very beautiful woman standing behind a red counter that was looking straight at them. "How may I be of service to you?" she asked.

Namrips looked at Kimberly. Kimberly raised her right eyebrow. Namrips turned to the woman and said, "We aren't really sure why we're here or where here is."

"This is the pleasure realm," she responded. "You must know where you are to get here. It isn't easy to open up a portal to get here."

"That's just the thing. We didn't open up the portal. Someone else did it and sent us here. How can we get back?"

"You can't get back. No one ever leaves our realm. My suggestion is to relax and enjoy your stay here."

"There must be a way out."

"Yes, but, first of all, you have to be the one who opened the portal to open it again. Secondly, no one has ever wanted to leave our realm after having spent even one hour with us. Allow my assistant to show you to your rooms so you can relax a little." Another woman appeared and began walking up the stairs indicating with her hand that they should follow her.

Namrips and Kimberly walked slowly toward the stairs. Namrips put his lips against Kimberly's ear and whispered, "I didn't want her to know what we are looking for or how we really got here. I am sure that there is another portal somewhere that can lead us to our destination; we just got to find it. If all else fails, I have this thing from the Merkians that can get us out of here." They followed the assistant up to the third floor into a hallway. The hallway did not seem to have an end; doors seemed to continue for infinity. The numbers started at 3000A and then went up, 3001A, 3002A, 3003A. At 3999A, the next door said 3000B. After 3000Z, it eventually becomes 3000AA.

After walking for ten minutes, they stopped in front of a door. The number on the door was 3333A. The door opened on its own, and a sudden invisible force shoved Namrips into the room. Kimberly tried to follow him, but the door was closed before she could get inside.

"Namrips!" She cried out. "Where did he go?"

"This is his room," the assistant replied. "Your room is at 3333B. Don't worry, you will see each other later."

"I demand to be in the same room!" Kimberly screamed.

"There will be no screaming here," the woman said with a soft voice. Kimberly was lifted up by an invisible force and carried all the way to 3333B. The door opened, and she was placed inside gently. Then, the door shut and locked itself.

Chapter Thirty-two

Inside 3333A, Namrips stood on his feet. He looked around. It was a place full of strange paradoxes for sure! It was humungous. He was inside what appeared to be a mall. Thousands of women were shopping in the stores. He did not see a single man anywhere; he was the only one.

Where are all the men? He thought to himself.

There were women getting manicures, pedicures, haircuts, shampoos, and shopping for clothes everywhere. He walked along looking into the various stores. Then an idea occurred to him. *It has been such a long time since I've had a good bath*, he thought. *It really wouldn't hurt to get my hair washed.*

Namrips walked into the hair salon. It was called *Eternally Beautiful Hair, Nails, and Body*. "How much would it cost me to get my hair shampooed?" Namrips asked one of the ladies who worked there.

"It doesn't cost anything," she replied. "It looks like you're new here. We have an honor system. If everyone does their jobs, we don't need money to make our society work. If you receive services, you just have to promise to do some job for our society."

"What kind of job?" Namripsn inquired.

"That depends on you and how much you want from us. It could be something simple like take out the trash and clean the floor, but if you decide to stay long term, you might want to consider something more enjoyable."

"So you're telling me that if I take out your trash and clean your floor, you will wash my hair?"

The woman smiled radiantly. "Oh heavens no! I'll wash your hair just because you asked me to. However, at some point after staying here for a few days, someone will ask you to do a job. Do you just want to wash your hair? Are you sure I can't do anything else for you? Maybe a manicure and pedicure too?"

"Let's just start with washing my hair."

"This way."

****

Kimberly tried to open the door. When she saw that it was locked she began banging on the door with tears in her eyes. "You can't do this to me! I'm not your prisoner! Open up!"

A lady tapped Kimberly on the shoulder. "Miss, I see that you are new here," she said. "This is definitely not a prison."

Kimberly spun around and realized that she was in a massive city of gold. Literally everything her eyes could see was made of gold. The streets were gold. The buildings were gold. Houses were gold. The streets were full of men and women walking around dressed elegantly. Some were wearing dresses, others were wearing skirts, and others had skin tight jeans and designer shirts. It didn't matter what they were wearing; everyone looked stunningly beautiful. "Is this heaven?" Kimberly asked.

The woman smiled and said, "Allow me to show you around and introduce you to people." Kimberly followed her along the street and admired the tall golden skyscrapers. They were on the sidewalk as shiny cars came whizzing past them. Kimberly almost felt dizzy with all the turning her head was doing. At every turn, something wonderful caught her eyes.

There were three parts to this kingdom of gold. There was a modern area with modern clothes and buildings with all the luxuries she could desire. Then, in the distance, there was a gold castle, and it was guarded by people who were wearing medieval armor of gold. Then, along the highway of gold even farther away, there was a stunning red palace that was the only thing not made of gold.

"There is a castle in the distance," Kimberly observed.

"The castle was built in wait of the fulfillment of the prophecy of the long awaited queen who will rule over our kingdom. Some people love the long distant past that was full of magic and dragons. Those people live in the castle. However, some people prefer the luxury of technology and modern life. Those people live here. We are a kingdom that truly embraces all desire."

"And the red palace? It is the only thing I have seen not made of gold."

The woman smiled at Kimberly. "That is the place of wizards and enchantment. No one is allowed to go there."

Chapter Thirty-three

As Namrips was getting his hair soaped up, he asked, "I haven't seen any men in this place. Is there a reason for that? It just feels a little strange being the only guy here."

"There is a reason for it, but I am honestly not sure what the reason is. Once in a blue moon, I see a man come in like yourself. After a little while, I never see him again. I don't know why."

Namrips glanced at her quickly and returned his head to its position. "Really?"

She shrugged. "Yeah. It's kind of strange, you know. I think the last man I saw was about one hundred years ago. After one week, I never saw him again."

"Does someone kill the men? Or do they kick the men out?"

"Oh, God, no! We are a peaceful loving society. No one ever kills anyone. If someone tries to kill, a protective force field shields the victim. The person who attempted murder is taken to the psychiatrists where rehabilitation can occur. We are also a very inclusive society. We don't have any rules against the presence of any type of person, and that includes men. So, there is no way men are being kicked out for being men."

Namrips fell silent trying to understand what was happening to the men there. *If they aren't being killed or kicked out, where are they going?* He wondered to himself.

His thoughts were interrupted as his hair was finished being rinsed. He looked at himself in the mirror and saw that his hair was extremely bright and shiny. He had never seen his hair look so good before. Not only was his hair beautiful and brilliant, but it seemed to be a little thicker and longer. Namrips' eyes widened. "Wow! What did you do to my hair?"

"Do you like it?"

Namrips caressed his chin with his right hand as he studied himself in the mirror. "Oddly enough, yes. I don't know what it is or why. It's hard to put my finger on it."

"I can shave your beard and brighten your skin too."

"Sure. Why not? I have some time to kill."

****

The person had brought Kimberly to a nearby spa. Her dirty clothes were replaced with a golden robe. She bathed, got a manicure, a pedicure, her makeup done, and a shampoo. She looked at herself in the mirror and couldn't believe her eyes. "Wow! I've never seen myself look so beautiful!"

The woman clapped her hands with excitement. "Do you want to go look at clothes?"

A gentle smile came over Kimberly's face. She couldn't remember the last time she had really smiled. "Yes! That sounds wonderful." They left the spa and went directly to a large clothing store. It felt weird just wearing a robe out in public, but she didn't want to put those dirty clothes back on her clean body.

They looked at short dresses, long dresses, tight dresses, loose dresses, jeans, business attire for women, turtlenecks, long skirts, short skirts, and anything else could come to mind. When they finished shopping, Kimberly was wearing a black skirt that went down to her knees, high heels, a pink button-up blouse with sleeves that went below the elbow but exposed the upper forearms, and she had a small pink purse. She was carrying two large bags full of clothes that she wanted to keep, and they left together.

She was brought to a large house made of gold. Well, it was not pure gold but rather lined with gold. Even the bed sheets were sparkling with gold. All of the furniture, the TV, the tables, the chairs, and even the windows all shined with gold. "This will be your home," she was told. "You can leave your bags here. Would you like to get something to eat?"

"Oh, yes! I'm starving!" She followed her new friend down the street from her new home to a restaurant. They sat down at a golden table with golden chairs and ordered from the golden menus. The waitresses brought their food on golden plates, and they served their drinks in golden cups. Kimberly was living in a dream, and a part of her didn't want it to end - ever.

Chapter Thirty-four

After Namrips' face was completely shaved, the lady applied different creams to his face. Namrips could feel a slight burn, but it wasn't too bad, so he sat there patiently until the lady washed it off. He looked at himself in the mirror, and he was absolutely shocked at what he saw. His rugged masculine appearance was gone; his face had soft shiny skin. He couldn't put his finger on why he liked it, but he did. It complemented his hair perfectly. He had never seen his face look so feminine before, but for some odd reason, he kind of liked it – no, he loved it. He felt a strange sensation inside that he had never felt before.

"Oh, dear! Look at those nails! That will never do!" The lady exclaimed. "I'm going to have to give you a manicure."

Namrips smiled and sighed. "Okay. Let's do it."

After some time sitting there, he looked at the finished product. She had done much more than a manicure! His nails seemed a bit longer and pink!

She had painted them too, but how did she make them grow?

Namrips looked at his face in the mirror again. Suddenly, he realized what was happening to all the men. They had not been killed or kicked out. The lady was absolutely right about that. Everyone who spent some time in this place eventually became a woman!

Namrips' face was now extremely feminine. In fact, he felt like he was looking directly into the eyes of a woman. His eyebrows were a little higher and arched. His lips were a little bigger with a nice shape and noticeable Cupid's bow. His eyelashes were longer and curled up. His head had more of an oval shape. He looked down and noticed that his breast had grown considerably larger.

The worst part about it was that he was enjoying it! He liked it. He was enamored with his face. It was so beautiful. Something within him told himself that he should fight against it, or he was going to be stuck in this place forever, but he had already forgotten about the technological stick he had received from the Merkian. It had disappeared from sight.

He couldn't recall what his face had looked like before with enough strength to resist what he saw now. All of his memories from before were fading away. He couldn't remember how great it had felt to fight and bend someone else's will to his own. He couldn't remember what satisfaction he got in a little bit of ruggedness. The only thing that he could see was his feminine face.

His heart felt a strange warmth within. It felt so natural to be a woman. It felt so right. He enjoyed being beautiful. He sat there staring for at least twenty minutes, but it felt like an eternity. The lady simply stood there and allowed Namrips to admire her work.

Namrips would have continued to stare at himself for longer, but it was interrupted by the fact that he was no longer a he, but a she, and this was testified to by the fact that Namrips could feel blood running down her leg. She didn't know it was the beginning of her first period, but she was soon to find out.

"This is what happens to men here," Namrips said. She was jolted by how her voice was not deep, but soft like a woman's voice might be. "They become women."

"Wow! I guess you do look like a woman now! I didn't even think about it until you mentioned it. I had forgotten that you were a man before. Do you want me to do your makeup?"

"Oddly enough, I actually would like you to do my makeup. But I have something running down my leg. It feels wet. I think I need to go to the bathroom to check it out."

"Oh, I see it. It's seeping through your pants. If it isn't pee, then it could be your period. You've never had a period before have you?"

"You mean it could be blood?" Namrips looked utterly shocked.

She looked at Namrips thoughtfully. "Listen, I have some maxi pads and some extra clothes in the back. I'll show you how to use the maxi pads, and then I'll do your makeup."

****

How long did Namrips and Kimberly spend in this place? It is hard to say, for one hundred years there is like one day on Ademud. At least a few days had passed on Ademud. There was a battle raging between Queen Death's forces and the Nemodians. Erif was staying with the Filoses to protect them, so as long as Queen Death could hold the Nemodians at bay, Erif and the Filoses were out of sight and out of mind.

Chapter Thirty-five

Kimberly was walking around looking at the kingdom and the beautiful scenery. She looked again upon the palace in the distance that appeared to be made of glass and was a deep red color. There was a golden highway that led from the kingdom to the palace. On the right and left sides of the road were fields full of flowers and roses. *I wonder why that palace is the only thing that isn't gold!* Kimberly thought to herself. *In a place where everything is gold, to see something of that sort is intriguing.*

At that moment, a large group of soldiers being led by a tall muscular commander approached her marching down one of the golden roads that led to the castle of the kingdom. They were all wearing gold armor with steel shields that were lined with gold, and they had steel swords with gold handles. As they approached, it was the first time that Kimberly noticed that the sun never moved. It was literally always in the same position.

"We were notified of your arrival," the leader said to Kimberly. "We need you to come with us."

"Have I done something wrong?" Kimberly asked puzzled.

"Not at all. On the contrary, we are to declare you queen of our kingdom today."

Kimberly gasped. "What? Why me? I literally just arrived here."

"The wizard has seen your coming in a vision and prophesied that you would bring our kingdom great success for all of eternity. As long as you are our queen, we will have eternal life."

Kimberly screwed up her face in disbelief. "That is weird, but I guess it won't hurt to go with you. Who is this wizard?"

"He lives in that red palace in the distance, and he holds this place together. We live in a dimension that isn't touched by the decay of the outside dimensions, so we don't have to die. But for death to cease among us, we have to have the right leader to keep us in peace who will always make the wisest decisions. He prophesied of your coming. Once you are queen, death will cease to take us. We will live forever."

Kimberly rolled her eyes. "Is that why the sun never sets?"

"I'm not sure I understand your question."

"That big light in the sky never moves. How do you sleep? Is it ever night time?"

The man laughed. "That light is there for thirty-three hours and disappears for seven hours. This completes a forty-hour day. Then, the cycle repeats again. We sleep for seven hours while the light is gone."

Kimberly followed the soldiers to the castle. There they conducted an elaborate ceremony declaring her the queen of their kingdom. As the ceremony came to a completion, her subjects cried out in unison, "All hail the queen!" She felt so good and so satisfied. She had never been gifted with such power. She felt like she could live here for all of eternity. She stood there in awe of the crowd that was before her. She knew that she would probably never leave this place.

Just like he had explained to Kimberly, the "sun" turned off after a certain time. Since Kimberly was officially the queen of this kingdom, she ordered her servants to prepare her bed. Her bed was the largest and most comfortable bed that she had ever touched in her entire life. It made her wonder if she would even be able to wake up in the morning. She felt like she would probably sleep for several days.

****

As was already mentioned, Namrips had completely turned into a woman, and she loved everything about it. Her first period wasn't exactly exciting, but she began realizing that there were so many wonderful things about being a woman that it outweighed the pain. Headaches and cramps were bad, but they had so many doctors and medicines designed for this occasion (considering the fact that everyone there was a woman, it made it top priority) that it was relatively easy to mitigate these symptoms and go on with her life. Then, she had the three weeks of bliss.

She was spending day after day here in this new home of hers going to the beauty salon. One day, she would get her hair done. The following day, she would get a manicure and pedicure. The next day, she would go shopping for clothes. There was always something to do. Besides, she began making lots of friends, and they would talk about everything going on in town. Life was beautiful, and the state of the Earth started becoming some distant memory that was like a dream that never happened. What was happening here was reality, and this was the only thing that mattered. She felt like she could live here forever.

****

As Kimberly slept, she could see Namrips with clarity. She could see that Namrips had become a woman! One thing that Kimberly took special notice of was that it seemed that several weeks had passed for Namrips whereas only one day had passed for herself. However, all of this was relatively unimportant to Kimberly. She could also see that the women surrounding Namrips were plotting to kill her. She loved Namrips. She didn't know why or how she had fallen in love with this person, but she knew that beyond any doubt she loved her. She had to find a way to rescue Namrips.

The entire place is probably a death trap! She thought. She got out of bed. She might have been asleep for just three or four hours, so it was still dark outside. She put on some jeans and a white blouse (short-sleeve V-neck). She grabbed a sword on the rack inside, and she walked out to the horse stable. She mounted a horse and began riding on the highway towards the palace with the wizard. Her idea was that if he held the place together, he should be able to free her so that she could save Namrips.

As she rode towards the palace, a legion of horses appeared in front of her standing there waiting. She slowed her horse to a walk and approached them slowly. When she arrived up as close as she wanted to come, she said, "Why are you in my way? I demand that you remove yourself from the highway so that I may pass."

"You cannot go there," the leader said. "We know your intentions. No one may escape our city."

"I am the queen. Y'all have declared me so. Therefore, you must obey me."

"Don't be silly. We declared you queen to make you want to stay, but if you decide to leave, you will be forced to stay in the dungeon. You aren't the queen in reality - only in your mind."

Kimberly glared down at them with anger. "I will pass even if I must fight my way through."

The man laughed. "You will die."

"Then, so be it." Kimberly didn't really know where this sense of new-found courage was coming from. Perhaps, it was always within her. She knew that she loved Namrips and that she preferred to die than to give up because Namrips was going to die if she didn't try. It seemed quite clear that she had no way of winning this battle. Fighting wasn't about winning at all. It was about not giving up. It was about dying with honor rather than being a coward. Knowing that death was waiting for her made no difference at all. The only person she had ever loved was in danger, and she was willing to die trying to get to her (Namrips).

Kimberly charged forwards on horseback with her sword drawn. She was able to cut one person down before someone else had cut off the horse's front left leg. Kimberly flew off the horse onto the ground surrounded by soldiers. She quickly stood up and went to strike one of the soldiers, but a soldier behind her cut off her right arm that was holding the sword. So, she fell down with blood gushing out of her right stub, and her sword lay on the ground too far for her to grab with her left hand. She knew that this was about to be the end of her life, but that same spirit that knew she had to at least try to fight to save Namrips blazed within her heart. Thinking about her own death made her think about the helpless Namrips. That fire grew exponentially in her heart. She focused all her mental energy within herself. She knew that she was in a different dimension that didn't play by the same rules as the dimension with Earth. So, she tried something in her desperation. She imagined her arm being fully regenerated.

    This all happened in the blink of an eye. There was a soldier preparing to cut her head off as she sat there just after having her right arm taken. But in the quantum realm, things can happen at the speed of light. She suddenly had a new arm. It was huge. It was the arm that belonged to a 6'6" man and was extremely muscular. As the soldier swung his sword to take off her head. She ducked in time for it to miss. She rolled close to her sword and picked it up and began taking people's legs off, then heads, then arms. She killed maybe ten soldiers when her left arm was taken off along with both of her legs. She again imagined her body regenerating. Suddenly, she had muscular legs for a 6'6" man and two muscular arms. Kimberly was previously 5'3", so her torso and head looked ridiculous with these arms and legs, but it did the job. She again was able to kill several more of them. As this happened, she decided to be proactive and create the perfect body for herself. Suddenly, she had rock solid abs, bulky muscular shoulders, and an attractive masculine face to fit her new 6'6" body that looked so artificial, it made Arnold Schwarzenegger from his body building days look weak. On top of that, she was able to move one hundred times faster than a normal human being. Kimberly, in all visible respects, had become a he. So, he continued to fight and demolished the soldiers before him. Whereas Namrips had become a woman, Kimberly had become a man.

Kimberly walked down the golden highway until he arrived at the red palace. He went inside. It wasn't guarded at all. This made him a little nervous. He had his sword drawn and ready for anything.

"Why have you come here?" A voice inquired of Kimberly.

"I want to be freed from this realm and this dimension," Kimberly answered, "but I want to save my friend Namrips who is being held captive by a multitude of murderous women as well. I was told that you hold this place together. So you must have the power to free us."

"You haven't understood anything yet?"

"What do you mean?"

"You alone have the power to hold yourself captive here or to free yourself. You are here because you want to be. Your friend is where she wants to be. I am not a real wizard. I am a piece of technology that reads your desires' manifestation at the quantum realm, and I manifest what you want. You broke free of what you truly wanted because you care more about your friend than yourself. This place only holds power over the selfish. Love is the only thing that can free you, but that love must be pure. If your friend loves you in the same way that you love her, she can break her own bonds. There are no murderous women who want her dead. It is a manifestation from her heart. If she can't free herself from her selfish desires, her own ego will kill her. It will simply manifest itself as her friends."

Kimberly sighed profoundly. "Then, how do I get out of this kingdom and get to her so I can talk to her?"

"How did you grow new arms? Everything here happens as an action of the will. I will tell you no more. You have already freed yourself from my grip since you desire nothing here."

"Technically, if what you are telling me is true, then I'm having a conversation with myself, and you are a manifestation of my heart. You need say no more." After this, Kimberly sat down in that spot, and he began meditating. He began looking as deeply as possible within himself so that he could see Namrips' location and try to manifest himself there.

****

Namrips was walking down the street going to get her nails done when Kimberly appeared before her. Namrips looked at him stunned. "Who are you? It isn't often that we see men here."

"I know you don't recognize me like this," Kimberly explained, "but it's me, Kimberly. You turned into a woman, and I turned into a man. So, it shouldn't be so far beyond your ability to believe me."

"If this is true, tell me something that only the two of us would know."

Kimberly nodded. "You told me you loved me and saved my life when we passed through the yellow goo. My fear was to die unloved, and your love made my fear subside enough to bring me out of it alive. Now, I feel that you are in danger and that we need to continue our mission to save the planet. We have to defeat the Nemodians."

Namrips took a deep breath. "Okay, that was a mouthful, but why can't we just stay here? You can stay here with me. We don't need to kill the Nemodians. The Earth has already been destroyed and so there is nothing else to go back to."

At that moment, a multitude of women began surrounding that area. They came from every direction. Kimberly immediately knew what was happening. Since this place was a manifestation of their desires, Namrips' desire to stay was manifesting in the women to come to protect her from leaving. Everything that was manifested in this place came from their own hearts. Once Kimberly broke free, there was nothing to restrain him. His love in his heart and lack of desire created a conversation with his subconscious that manifested as the wizard with wisdom. It had all come from within. Now, he was looking at Namrips and her manifestations. Therefore, he understood that he could not manipulate this reality has he had done his own - only Namrips could do that.

"We can't stay here because it is a lie, and it isn't real. It is a manifestation of our own desires. I wanted to be stronger and braver, and I manifested a reality and became that. I wanted to be in charge and worshipped. I got that as well. But I saw you stuck here, and it made me sad, and my love for you brought me out of the delusion. I think you desired to not always have to be the one who was rescuing others and fighting since you had your fair share. You desired to be beautiful, and you became beautiful. You found a peaceful place where there is no more war and no fighting. Unfortunately, it isn't real. Our world is threatened, and we need to help it. I love you. Take my hand, and let's go together. Let's go home."

Namrips reached her hand out ready to take Kimberly's hand. She remembered when she was still a man and kissed Kimberly. Man or woman, she loved this person. As their hands got closer, Kimberly was lifted off the ground into the air. "All so touching," said a woman nearby, "But Namrips isn't going anywhere. She must stay here forever. Don't you love being here, Namrips?"

"Yes, I love being here, but I love Kimberly too," she responded.

"Well, Kimberly," said the woman, "It looks like you have to die now so that Namrips can live in peace." When she said this, Kimberly stopped being able to breathe. He put his hands around his neck in the way a person who is choking does. He starting getting frantic with pleading eyes looking at Namrips. His face turned red. He began mouthing the words, "I love you," knowing that Namrips would be able to read his lips since no sound could come out. He started to feel light headed and the lack of oxygen was ready to cause him to pass out.

Then, it happened. Namrips loved Kimberly more than that place. The conflict caused her to look deep within herself until she emitted a light that surrounded them, and they disappeared from there and appeared back on Ademud in front of the device that they had sought. If they destroyed this device, Queen Death would lose her powers, but it was Queen Death that was holding the Nemodians at bay. So the real war was just about to begin.

Chapter Thirty-six

Namrips and Kimberly woke up laying on the ground in a dark cave. There was no way in and no way out. It was completely sealed from any outside light source, but there was a dim light on the other side of the cave from them. It was the object they sought – the source of Queen Death's power.

Namrips was still a 5'4" woman, and Kimberly was still a 6'6" man. Whatever had happened inside that other dimension seemed to have permanent effects on their physical bodies. They walked over to the machine and stared at it for a moment.

"Once we destroy this, we have no way to get back up to the surface of Ademud," Namrips said. "We will destroy Queen Death's hold, but we will die here, and the Nemodians will not be affected."

"What do you want to do?" Kimberly asked. "There might be a way to harness this device's power to allow us to get back to the surface."

At that moment a portal opened and a yellow creature stepped through. The creature was an extraterrestrial race known as Julivers, and this Juliver's name was Keejam.

****

On the surface of Ademud, Queen Death's army was still engaged in a battle with the Nemodians. The army of dead was actually being easily defeated by the orange men because of their particular powers of flight and their superior speed to the dead. It was a little slow and tedious since they had to rip them all up into little pieces. This distraction is, perhaps, what made the CRCs even more effective when they were released. The CRCs could not fly, but they were much faster than the orange men. The CRCs came out while the orange men ripped the zombies to shreds and attacked them mercilessly.

Queen Death tried freezing the zombies, and it worked for a time so that they were able to kill a large number of them. However, because of the scale of the battle, Queen Death did not have the means to maintain that level of energy output. She sacrificed every animal that she could, but she needed her people in battle as orange men and couldn't afford sacrifices of any sentient beings. So her magical powers became more and more ineffective until it was just a raw battle between the two forces.

****

"My name is Keejam," the yellow Juliver said to Namrips and Kimberly.

"Wait a minute," Namrips interjected. "I remember something about you. You are the one that invented the helmet of infinite knowledge, right?"

Keejam smiled. "Yes. That's me. No one can arrive to this place without going through the trials you have gone through, but I was able to use quantum entanglement so that my atoms were entangled with yours. When you passed through the trials, it was as if I had passed with you. So, I was able to create this portal to get here. Everything hinges on what we do here. If we don't destroy this machine, there are two possibilities: Nemodians win and kill Queen Death anyway, then afterwards us, or Queen Death wins and then kills us afterwards. I have seen these two outcomes in my helmet and what causes them. On the other hand, if we destroy this machine right now, the Nemodians definitely win because Queen Death is what is holding Nemodians at bay right now, and Erif isn't powerful enough to defeat the Nemodians on his own. If the Nemodians win they will also destroy the life on my planet. So winning here is not just about Ademud, it's about life across many galaxies. The Nemodians are a threat to life as we know it in the observable universe."

"But I just heard a bunch of scenarios where we die," Kimberly observed. "Is there one where we don't die – or at least win even if we die?"

"If we do everything perfectly in the right timing, we might be able to stop the Nemodians. Instead of destroying this device, I'm going to try to hack the system. Queen Death will get killed as I do this because she is going to lose her powers. Then, I must quickly make it so that we can use the device for ourselves. If we are not quick enough, Erif will be dead before we arrive. We cannot win this battle without Erif."

"But you've seen all the possible futures," Namrips said. "So, you know exactly what has to be done to win."

"There wasn't a single future where we won. I had to ask the helmet how we could win to see this possibility. I have tried to commit the steps to memory, but once I start, there has to be a perfect flow non-stop from beginning to end. Meaning, if I get interrupted even once, there might not be enough time to save Erif."

Chapter Thirty-seven

As Keejam began making preparations for tinkering with Queen Death's machine, he had encouraged Namrips and Kimberly to use his helmet. He hoped to accomplish two things by doing this: it would be less likely for them to interrupt him as he worked and, more importantly, if they had any questions, the helmet could satisfy their desire for knowledge.

Namrips' desire to know where the Nemodians came from was still plaguing her mind. To make matters worse, not even Nogar, the most honest human-like and emotional Nemodian she had ever met, was willing to answer her question. So she put the helmet on and asked about the origin of the Nemodians.

The first thing she saw was a UFO crash in the USA. Because of how things began to evolve, she recognized that it was the well-known crash close to Roswell. It was commonly believed that the UFO crashed in Roswell, but this particular version had it in a place slightly outside Roswell but reasonably close to it.

This was captivating for Namrips because she had heard all of the theories including the government's version of events. So she was comparing what she saw with all of the things she had heard. None of them really captured the events correctly. For example, there had been speculation from conspiracy theorists that the government had captured one of the extraterrestrials alive. This did not happen. They had only picked up dead bodies of extraterrestrials.

What seemed to be the case from what Namrips could see is that a group of extraterrestrials that she now recognized as Merkians were making scientific observations of the Earth and its inhabitants when a malfunction caused them to crash, killing everyone on board. The USA began attempting to recreate the technology by reverse engineering it. Most of the technology was incomprehensible to them and, therefore, very little progress was made.

So, sometime in the 1960's, a group of scientists were secretly employed to see what they could create. This group of scientists worked diligently for a few years and disappeared from the face of the Earth. However, Namrips was able to watch what happened to them since this helmet accessed the quantum memory of the universe.

Namrips watched them successfully create a ship that was identical to the UFO that was capable of interstellar travel. When she saw that they were about to leave Earth on this ship in exploration, she began to deduce what would probably happen next. Humans were about to make contact with Nemodians, and she would finally know what planet they came from. This would simultaneously connect and explain how Nemodians knew about humans and our planet. This was definitely starting to make sense for Namrips now. She continued to watch as they left Earth opening worm holes to go faster than the speed of light.

However, what Namrips had imagined as a probable outcome didn't happen; the humans did not immediately come into contact with the Nemodians as she thought. When humans flew outside the galaxy, their lack of knowledge of space and what was out there caused them to make some fundamental mistakes, and they went into a white-hole, which is the opposite of a black-hole. Whereas in a black-hole, time slows down relative to whatever is outside of it, in a white-hole, time moves much faster than whatever is outside. So, while Earth experienced ten years, this group of scientist experienced one thousand years. In eighty years, they would experience eight thousand years.

So, Namrips knew that they were going to meet the Nemodians after they came out of the white-hole, and he was going to see the evolution of humans over thousands of years first. Or maybe, as humans were evolving, the Nemodians would meet them inside the white-hole.

Namrips watched fascinated as the events of evolution unfolded before her eyes. The scientists were a mixture of men and women. So, she got to see the babies that they produced and the lack of bone density and other physiological changes one would expect from living in space. They were growing food in a garden that was on the ship, and they were able to get any extra nutrients that they needed from these genetically modified plants.

As they flew through space for hundreds of years, they began modifying the plants more and more and perfected this science. This was important to give them proper nutrients that they would have gotten from meat. Then, they began modifying their children.

They had lost considerable size due to traveling in space, so they found a way to modify their genetics so that future generations were growing seven feet tall and with a lot more muscle. Then, they increased brain power in future generations. This particular modification caused their blood to turn black since it was their blood cells that needed to bring more oxygen to the brain tissue.

Then, someone choked on their food and died. There was such outrage that a race as advanced as they were would have a young person die in this way. So, they modified their genetics so that there were two different tubes. There was a trachea and an esophagus that was completely separated. This caused this generation of seven-foot humans to have two mouths – one for eating and one for breathing. The nose was no longer necessary and atrophied. Over the years, Namrips watched their skin turn blue, two eyes become seven, two ears become four, and cloning replace child bearing.

    When they started cloning and stopped having children, they sterilized the rest of their race so that no more natural children could be born from the males and females in existence. The clones no longer had a gender, and so only approved cloning could increase their numbers based on the needs of the government.

    Perhaps, it was the blue skin or the black blood. Perhaps, it was the six arms or the seven eyes or even the two mouths. However, whatever it was and whenever it happened, Namrips had to face the fact that Nemodians were humans in the future. So, when the Nemodians began their destructive reign throughout the universe, she saw that it was future humans who were bringing this chaos.

Chapter Thirty-eight

The CRC's were killing Queen Death's army of orange men in droves. There was one interesting development to the battle against the CRC's. Even though the Tiskolas did not die at the reversal of gravity, they were able to capture one for cloning. So, they were able to employ several hundred flying monstrous CRC's that came from Tiskolas. This is not all, they used the Tiskolas' DNA to give all other types of CRC's the power of flight except those that came from Funglians. This was an important turn of events in the battle because the orange men were getting their advantage from the power of flight, but they no longer had this advantage if the CRC's could fly.

The battle raged in this way for a long time, and it was clear that the Nemodians were going to defeat Queen Death's army. As their numbers dwindled down, Keejam was taking apart the Queen Death's machine. As soon as he removed certain key elements, the orange men fell from the sky into the hordes of zombies; they had done well to destroy many zombies, but it was impossible to get them all due to the multitudes of dead that the Nemodians had collected.

They were Delikies, Primees, and Seregines again for just one moment; then, they were torn to shreds and eaten alive. Just as humanity was almost extinct save Namrips and Kimberly, Erif was the last of his kind on Ademud. Even Queen Death wasn't spared. Now that she had lost her power, the Nemodians killed her easily. She had fled the battle just before losing her power because she saw that there was no way to win. A ship had followed her from a distance and fired lasers at her, but the lasers were blocked at first. However, when she lost her power, they fired again, and she exploded leaving her blood and guts on the nearby trees.

Keejam was presently working hard trying to reconnect the parts he had removed from the device so that he could officially hack into it for their own use. He knew that they would come after Erif as soon as they had defeated Queen Death, and he didn't know if he could make it in time to save him. His sweat dripped off his forehead, and his hands moved nimbly. He picked up a wrench, used it, and set it down. He connected a wire and wiped sweat from his face.

Meanwhile, the Nemodians began spreading across the entire planet searching for any life to make sure they had complete control over it. A certain group of Nemodians came across the waterfall where Erif and the Filoses were staying.

They detected the life inside of the cave, even though they didn't know if it was intelligent life or not.

Erif always kept a good watch on the area. He only stopped observing momentarily for eating and sleeping. Otherwise, he was always watching. Therefore, he knew of the Nemodians presence in the area. He left the cave from a back entrance after having blocked the front entrance with a large stone. Then, he also blocked the back entrance so that only oxygen and small bugs could enter through a small crack. Next, he flew over to the Nemodians and began killing them one at a time from behind as they searched the area.

There were five of them in front of the waterfall. He moved at his superior speed and had them all dead in the blink of an eye. Those who were searching the surrounding forest also began dying one by one literally disappearing from sight.

After having killed a multitude of Nemodians, it was bound to come to Fiki's attention. Fiki asked for a report from a certain ship, and there was no answer. So, he sent another ship and lost contact at the same location where those that didn't respond were located. Therefore, Fiki knew that something was either killing or trapping their people. An entire brigade of ships arrived at that location where fire shot out of Erif's hands and devoured one of the Nemodian ships.

Erif was strong with immense power, but he was technically still young and didn't consider battle strategies. He didn't consider that he was giving up his position by destroying a ship like this. He was simply fighting and protecting that which he loved. Unfortunately, now that Fiki saw who was causing the problem and what he was capable of doing, Nemodian strategy was bound to outwit the brave soldier.

Erif shot flames at another ship, but the flames simply turned around and went back towards Erif, which he reabsorbed with no damage. Erif didn't know what a space-time bender was, but he could see that he would no longer be able to destroy ships in this way. So, he flew over to a ship ready to smash it with his hands. However, in some weird paradox, he found himself flying in the opposite direction. He turned around to face the ship that somehow was behind him when, just a moment before, he had been going in that direction.

Suddenly, he felt something closing around him, and he was having a hard time breathing. He couldn't move his arms either. He was still hovering in the air, but he felt like his arms were bound by an invisible rope to his sides. The amount of pressure put on his body would have already crushed the bones of a normal man, but Erif was not a normal man by any stretch of the imagination. His breathing was shallow and restricted, but he was getting enough oxygen to survive.

Then, the Nemodians aimed a laser cannon at Erif. Could Erif withstand the strongest laser in the universe? He was soon to find out. It wasn't like the Nemodians had any reason to stall this execution. They wanted a being as strong as Erif to be dead as quickly as possible. Erif truly struck terror in their hearts. The Nemodians were mainly emotionless beings because they had worked hard to eliminate emotion in their process of genetic engineering during cloning. They saw emotions as something that would only get in their way and would weaken their species. However, extreme situations were able to spark some emotions that they hadn't completely eliminated, and Erif was one of those extreme situations. They had never encountered a single being capable of what he was capable of doing. If they survived this encounter, you could bet that they would try to find genetic modifications that would give their race the same powers. So, they wasted absolutely no time at all; they immediately aimed their laser cannon and fired.

This became something even more impressive to the Nemodians. The laser didn't seem to be doing any damage to Erif. Erif, being able to move so much faster than the normal man, could also see and interpret what was happening as if it were in slow motion. When he saw the laser was firing at him, and that he couldn't move, he emitted a fire from his entire body that generated enough force to keep the laser from destroying him immediately. The laser passed around the flames as the Nemodians continued concentrating the beam.

Therefore, the Nemodians decided to fire a missile at Erif to see what would happen. They continued to fire the laser as they fired the missile. The logic was that if Erif was using his flames to protect himself from the laser, he would not be able to shoot his flames and destroy the missile while at a distance. If they stopped the laser and shot the missile, he could shoot the flames and destroy the missile while it was still close to the ship.

Thus, they fired the missile hoping that it would blow Erif into oblivion. However, just as the missile was shot, a bright light was emitted from below, and the missile stopped in midair. The bright light was low to the ground, and Keejam walked out with Namrips and Kimberly, and the light disappeared. The missile had stopped one inch in front of Erif. Even though the light had shone right as it was fired, one has to know just how fast a missile travels and reaches its destination. If Keejam had arrived even a fraction of a second later, Erif would have been obliterated. The missile deactivated and fell into little pieces as it fell to the surface of Ademud.

Erif was then released from the invisible force that was holding him in place as a new battle was about to rage. Four insignificant beings were poised for battle against a legion of the universe's most technologically advanced and ruthless race, the

Nemodians. Erif flew down and stood next to Namrips, Kimberly, and Keejam.

Chapter Thirty-nine

Erif didn't try to destroy any Nemodian ships and permitted them to land because he knew that they would just cause him to spin out the opposite direction. So, a multitude of Nemodian ships landed there surrounding these four warriors. After the ships landed, the four of them stood there watching, and they became surrounded by the army of dead.

This sea of dead came forwards. Erif shot fire out of his hands and consumed a great number of them burning them down to ashes. In the opposite direction, Kimberly ran with his sword and superior speed, and it was here that they knew beyond any doubt that all the changes they experienced in that other dimension were permanent since even the strength and speed of Kimberly as a 6'6" muscular man were the same as when he was on the other side. Something about that dimension had made changes to their atoms and genetics even down to a subatomic level.

When Kimberly arrived at the sea of monsters, he began cutting them into little pieces with lightening speed. However, the zombies outnumbered Kimberly by such an extent, there would have been no possibility of him escaping harm. Nevertheless, every time one of the dead attempted to harm Kimberly, the attack bounced off as if there was something magical protecting him. Indeed, this was one of the things that Keejam was doing. Keejam had used the machine to provide invisible protective shields for everyone. So every dead spider that bit Kimberly broke its fangs. Every zombie insect that grabbed hold of Kimberly in its jaws had its head ripped off as Kimberly just continued moving as if nothing was holding him. Every giant scorpion broke its stinger in two as it attempted to come down upon Kimberly. Every zombie was unsuccessful against him in every way so that the superior numbers were unimportant as Kimberly continued to thrash around destroying the dead army one by one with his lightening speed.

With Erif burning up everything into ashes on one side, and Kimberly cutting up everything on the other side, there were still two sides that were unprotected where the zombies were advancing. However, Keejam having used the helmet to know all before the battle had seen that Namrips was gifted a single psychic power that didn't require any machine because of what had happened to her in the other dimension. That power was to move objects with her mind. So Keejam had told Namrips before the battle to attempt to use this power whenever she sensed it was necessary to help out. So, when

Namrips saw that two sides of zombies were closing in on them, she stood there and pointed her hands in both directions and imagined a force pushing outwards from each hand. Immediately, the zombies went flying backwards because of an invisible force. This battle continued in this way for five minutes while Fiki observed from a distance.

There were a couple of ideas that Fiki had as to how to defeat these four warriors who stood in their way. One consideration was that the number of zombies would eventually wear them down. They were very close to killing off all the giant bugs. However, there were plenty of other dead entities that they had, and the four of them would need to stop to sleep and eat. So, Fiki knew that if he waited patiently in this way, they would eventually run down and get killed. But he might not need to wait that long if he sent out the CRCs. If, somehow, they survived all that, they would be sleep deprived malnourished people that his own soldiers and technology could overcome. So, as far as Fiki was concerned, he was guaranteed victory. Therefore, he decided to release the CRCs to help speed up the process of victory.

At that moment, they saw monstrous extra-large tiskolas fill up the sky. They saw monstrous flying Theadlians, flying ten-arm Nemodians, and all of the various CRCs who now had the power of flight. They had wings of a gargoyle that were carrying them through the sky swiftly. As they closed in for the attack, they all froze in the sky and so did the zombies. Then, what appeared to be a force-field surrounded them preventing anything from coming in, so if for some reason Nemodians had decided to shoot any lasers or missiles, they would have been protected. Then, Erif shot fire out from his hands destroying everything that was within a ten mile radius in the blink of an eye. This didn't include destroying the Nemodian ships that were using protective shields of their own, and the fire simply went around them.

When Fiki saw this, he realized that he misjudged them. They were simply using just enough power to deal with the situation. Erif had just destroyed every zombie and all the CRCs in less than one second. Fiki was wrong. Erif by himself could kill everything he threw at him. It was time to become brutal and use technology to kill these four warriors once and for all.

"We are going to implement the crusher," Fiki told his captain. "Don't release any more dead."

Suddenly, time and space became paradoxical from our four heroes' perspective. It seemed like gravity was getting stronger and stronger. Namrips fell under her own weight as she felt like she went from one hundred fifteen pounds to three hundred pounds. She couldn't breathe hardly at all. She lay there gasping for breath. Keejam kneeled down feeling his weight increase and tried to clear his mind in meditation knowing that he needed his wits if they were going to survive this. Kimberly was standing up just fine, but he definitely felt the weight change. His muscles were so strong that it hadn't taken him down yet, but he knew that Namrips would likely suffer broken bones if it continued. Everything looked warped from within their circle as time seemed to slow down relative to the Nemodians. But Erif was not affected so much at all as he was capable of flight. From Erif's perspective he saw things bending out of shape and becoming distorted sizes.

"Erif, only you can stop the Nemodians," a voice came to him. "We are with you." He didn't know that the voice was telepathic communication from the Funglians, but he interpreted it to be The Great Dweller from the Other Realm. In his mind, the "we" was because his ancestors were there. So, this voice gave him such strength, and Keejam was trying to do everything in his power to keep from passing out before it happened. Keejam had seen it and knew it was the only possible future that meant their survival. But if Keejam didn't stay conscious, it wouldn't work because he needed to use the machine one last time to strengthen Erif for what Erif would try to do.

Erif's flames could not penetrate the Nemodian force-fields. But here were all the Nemodian ships in one place. If there was one blast that could go through their force-fields, they could kill off the attacking force. They would still have to fight the Nemodians in other parts of the galaxy to protect the universe from the threat, but it would be a beginning. They had not told Erif, Kimberly or Namrips about this. If Erif had known, he wouldn't have done it. It had to come to him in the moment as a selfless sacrifice for the good of all those around him.

      Erif flew up into the sky. Keejam put a force-field around Kimberly, Namrips, and himself. Then, he put one around the Filoses inside of the cave. Erif released all his power from within his heart and became a ball of light. The force-field that was created by Keejam was different because it was a psychic creation and was maintained by the Funglians. The force-field of the Nemodians was technological and only worked against so much power. So, when Keejam connected Erif to the power of the Funglians' psychic power, his blast from within his heart increased more than one million times more powerful. All of the Nemodian ships melted there at that spot, but the planet Ademud became unstable and exploded as well.

Chapter Forty

"Try not to use too much oxygen too quickly," Keejam said. "I don't know how long it will take for the Funglians to arrive." Namrips, Kimberly, and Keejam were floating in a transparent bubble that was flying through space. They could see another bigger bubble that contained thousands of Filoses in the distance as they were all flying away from the exploded planet at roughly the same velocity.

"Where's Erif?" Kimberly asked.

"I would assume that he didn't survive," Keejam answered. "The blast that destroyed Ademud came from him."

"But it's far from over," Namrips interjected. "I know the Nemodians. The majority of those who died here will be reborn in a laboratory on a distant ship - including General Fiki."

"It is definitely far from over," Keejam agreed. "You are definitely right about that. There is still a battle raging at my home planet, and the Theadlians aren't just going to let the Nemodians wipe them out so easily. They control multiple planets."

"   Speaking of planets," Kimberly began, "wasn't the idea to save Ademud so that we could make a new home here? Earth has been destroyed and now Ademud. Where will humanity start over now?"

"It's hard to say." Keejam scratched his head. "Maybe, the Mogians will allow you to reside on their planet. We have to find allies to help us fight against the Nemodians, and I'm thinking that the Funglians will go to the Mogians' planet first."

"What are the Mogians like?" Namrips inquired.

"They aren't too different from humans. They have the typical humanoid shape - two arms, two legs, five fingers, and such. The main difference is that they have greater diversity in their skin colors. The Moldrekians left Moldrekia when their star was ready to supernova. The Moldrekians had every skin color for the rainbow. Well, I suppose that Mogians are the most similar to those distant ancestors. They are missing a few colors. No one has gray skin or white skin anymore. I think skin colors closer to yellow, orange and red have also been eliminated. However, they have people there with blue skin, green skin, purple skin, pink skin, and such, but their hair colors are still equally as diverse as their ancestors, the Moldrekians."

"So, what you're telling us is that they are basically people with more skin colors," Kimberly stated. He looked down and flexed his muscles. "I don't understand why I still look like a huge man when I was a woman before."

Keejam laughed. "You entered a very magical dimension. All the changes there are permanent."

"I don't mind being a woman," Namrips said as she looked toward the *bubble* with the Filoses. "What is weird is that we still have our powers. I can move objects with my mind, and Kimberly can move faster than lightning. Kimberly..."

"Yes?"

"It is so weird saying your name, Kimberly. You are huge. Kimberly just doesn't feel like a man's name."

Kimberly laughed. "Do you want to call me something else?"

Namrips scratched her head. "Maybe if I just called you Kim... Or Kam?"

"I should call you Eve," Kimberly responded. "You don't look like Namrips anymore, and it would be symbolic of a new beginning."

Namrips chuckled. "Like Adam and Eve. You would be Adam, and I would be Eve. I should call you Adam."

At that moment, the Funglians arrived in massive spaceships coming through portals. The three of them watched as a door opened at the bottom of one of their ships. A blue light came out and absorbed them into it, and they were pulled onto the vessel.

Upon entering the ship, their bubble disappeared, and the three of them walked together and came into a large room filled with blob-like creatures full of eyes. One of them took the form of Kimberly. Some took Namrips' form, and others transformed into the shape of Keejam. They studied the three beings before them.

"Welcome aboard our ship," one of their leaders communicated telepathically. "There is still much work to be done to save the galaxy from the Nemodian threat. We will go to Mog and ask for an alliance. They won't want to do it, but we will convince them by agreeing to the treaty that they will propose. They will want to create an intergalactic council where each planet has a voice."

"That sounds reasonable," Namrips said.

"Let them speak, Eve," Kim said to Namrips winking at her.

The one speaking had taken the shape of Keejam. Now, he took Namrips' shape. "It sounds reasonable, but the Mogians will want to be in charge of this proposed council. That would effectively give them an empire that controls the entire local group of galaxies."

"The enemy of my enemy is my friend," Kimberly quoted.

"They are not enemies," the Funglian responded promptly. "That might be truer of the Theadlians who we will have to help in battle to get their aid in the war, but the Mogians are like any other living organism. They are just like humans who seek power and their own selfish benefit. If that is left unchecked, they will destroy themselves and everyone around them. Namrips and Kimberly... or should I say Adam and Eve... You of all people should know this truth. You have had the battle up close and personal. The greatest war that one will ever fight is the war that rages within their own heart."

****

Erif found himself falling into what he thought was a bottomless pit. He could still fly, but to where? He couldn't see anything. Therefore, he preferred to allow himself to fall wondering when and where he would land. Suddenly, he could see something. He could see trees. There was a forest. He fell into the forest, and when he landed, his body created a large crater from the force of his fall.

There was a castle nearby, and those who dwelled there came running. Soldiers mounted their horses wearing bronze armor, and they rode out on horseback to see what had fallen. The villagers and the soldiers looked into the crater and saw Erif whose eyes were still closed. The fall had knocked him out.

One of the soldiers entered the crater with sword in hand and approached Erif. Erif's eyes began to open, and he saw the man coming closer. He stood up slowly as pain went through his body like waves of electricity. "A god has fallen from the sky," someone murmured above. "He came to save us!" Another said. Soon the whole crowed was singing and dancing except the soldiers who stood there looking upon Erif. The man who stood in front of Erif sheathed his sword and bowed his head. "I hope you've come to rescue us my lord!" he cried out.

Erif was wide-eyed and scratched his head. He had no idea where he was or how he could get back home.

Made in the USA
Las Vegas, NV
04 February 2025

8012686e-2061-4ad3-8b0e-5189a5250ad4R01